JOY STREET JAIL MURDER
IN A
NUTSHELL

JOY STREET JAIL MURDER IN A NUTSHELL

A Nutshell Murder Mystery

Frances McNamara

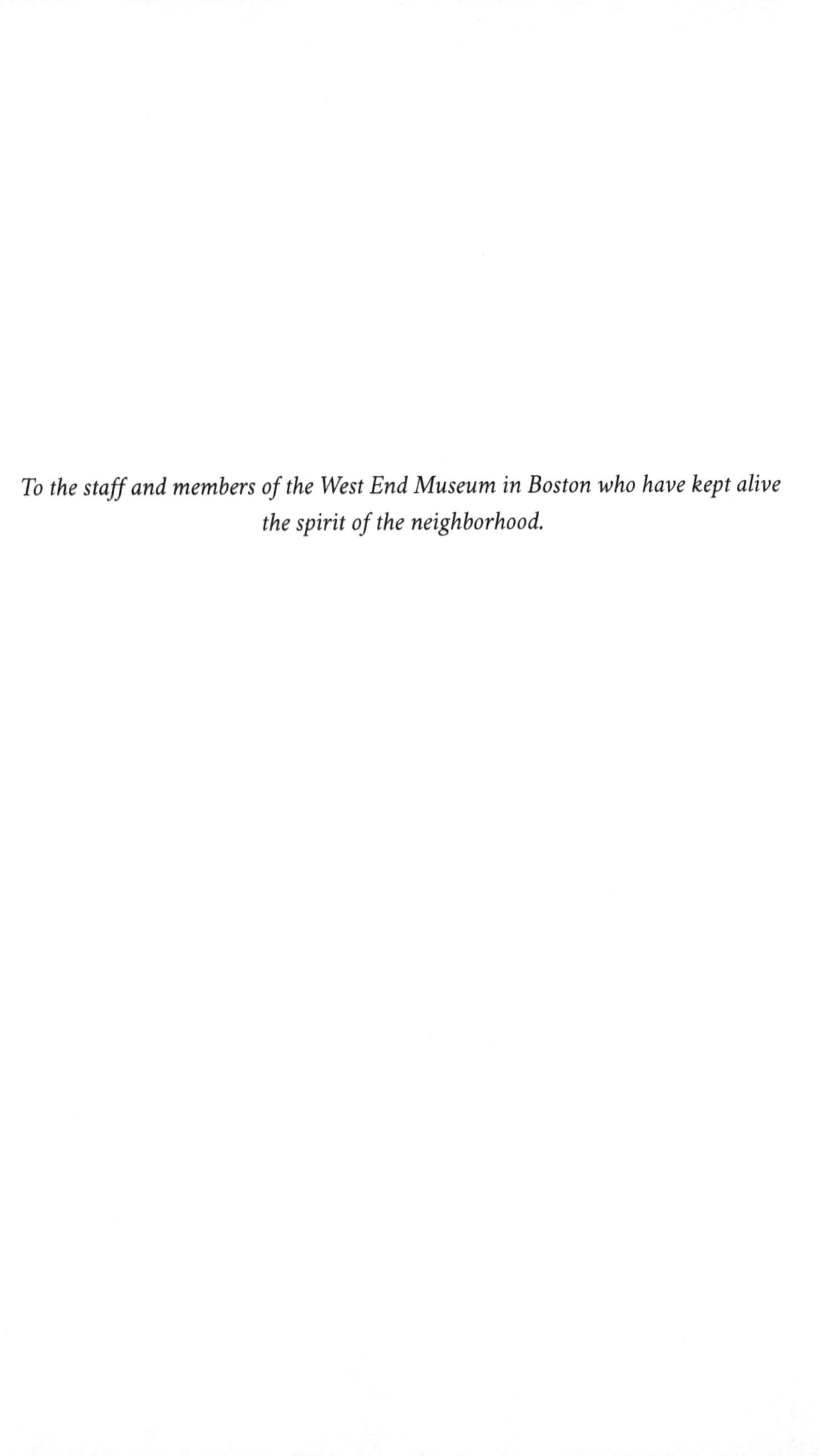

To the staff and members of the West End Museum in Boston who have kept alive the spirit of the neighborhood.

Praise for The Nutshell Murder Mysteries

"What a treat to watch Frances Glessner Lee again bring her keen eye and talent for creating miniature crime scenes to bear in discerning a dead man's truth. McNamara brings 1920 Boston to life with the details of her storytelling; readers won't want to miss this third Nutshell Murder Mystery."—Edith Maxwell, Agatha Award-winning author of A Case for the Ladies and the Quaker Midwife Mysteries.

Praise for Molasses Murder in a Nutshell

"One of the challenges of anyone writing historical fiction is to tell a compelling story while getting the setting and the time period 'right.' Frances McNamara masterfully accomplishes both with *Molasses Murder in a Nutshell*—a riveting read that occurs amidst the sights and sounds of the early 20th century. What more can lovers of historical fiction ask for?"—Stephen Puleo, author of *Dark Tide: The Great Boston Molasses Flood of 1919*

"Overall, *Molasses* is a real treat. Settings and back stories about the time period run smoothly. Particularly delicious is the unexpected denouement. This reader, for one, looks forward to the next Nutshell mystery."—*Historical Novel Society*

"Once again, Frances McNamara brings together the 'dynamic duo' of Frances Glessner Lee and Dr. George Magrath, who use the evolving field of forensic science to lead the reader through their methodical journey of investigation. Magrath's decades of experience and Lee's inquisitive mind that 'work(ed) with the accurate precision of a railroad watch,' according to

Perry Mason novelist Erle Stanley Gardner, chart a course that keeps the reader on the edge of their seat, until the clues sprinkled throughout the story come together for an exciting conclusion."—William Tyre, Executive Director and Curator Glessner House

"This book is a delight for fans of stories set in the early days of forensic science. It presents characters determined enough to test authority and patient enough to test theory against practice. It also offers details about time and place, political and social situations, and major historical figures. In this case: the days before Prohibition, the Brahmins vs. the workers, and former Boston mayor "Honey Fitz" Fitzgerald. Suitably twisty-turny and yet surprising; plot resolution centers not only on the usual forensic suspects—bullets, fingerprints—but also on a piece of delicate handiwork."—Historical Novel Society

Chapter One

June 2, 1920

Mortuary North Grove Street, Boston

Michael James McNally was pleased with himself. He straightened the bottle of ink, two pens and lined notebook on the small high desk he'd been assigned. Perched on a stool, he looked over the big room with four surgical tables, empty of dead bodies this morning. "Investigator" was Mack's title these days. It might not come with a gold star, but the pay was satisfactory, and his work was appreciated by Dr. Magrath, Suffolk County Medical Examiner. Not bad for a poor mick from East Boston who'd been blackballed from the police after the strike.

Mack could hear Edwin clinking glass in the laboratory next door. That lad was always gluing an eye to a microscope. When he wasn't reading his big heavy books or attending classes at Harvard Medical School a few blocks away, Edwin scurried around trying out every new instrument or procedure to catch a criminal. Matching fingerprints or bullets, testing blood, flashing photographs with the big camera he'd gotten, and developing prints, Edwin was a busy bee. Sometimes, Mack wanted to tell him to slow down. He knew the veteran had returned from the war with burn scars down one side of his face and body. He tried to hide his scars. But they didn't prevent him from walking out with a pretty widow. Mack envied him that.

Edwin had recently found Mack a room in the West End. Mack loved his sister and brothers over in East Boston, but he'd had enough of the struggle to get to the morgue every day. He'd had to wait for the crowded streetcar that ran through a tunnel under the harbor or wait for the crowded ferry to sail across the water. Mack was not a patient man. He'd finally moved across to the rooming house where Edwin stayed, just a few blocks from work. Mack didn't see why Edwin didn't just marry his widow and move in with her, but who was he to advise the lad on a love life when he'd none of his own.

The shrill ring of the doorbell pierced the air. Dr. Magrath was due in, but he had a key. Perhaps he'd forgotten it. Or it might be Mrs. Lee, the doctor's old friend, who had an unwomanly interest in everything criminal. Still, she was a good soul, and did great drawings of crime scenes. She'd even built little miniatures of crime rooms in a couple of difficult cases. She had a mind for remembering every tiny detail in a way that surprised Mack.

He hopped down from his stool and happily dashed to open the door.

It was Peter Attwood. Poor Pete had recently lost his gold star and been demoted to patrol officer. Mack had disguised his glee when he heard. After all, Pete was a Harvard student who'd taken one of the jobs of blacklisted policemen like Mack. Still, he didn't envy the kid having to work for Bill McKenna. The guy was a drunk and a bully who'd gotten himself promoted after betraying fellow officers during the strike. Peter reported to him.

Peter looked flustered. He wore the pointy helmet and encompassing blue coat with pewter buttons of the patrolman. He was out of breath.

"Mack," he said. "Is Magrath here? He's got to come. The guy in the jail cell won't wake up. He's dead. I brought him in last night to sleep off a bender, but now he's dead. I didn't do anything to him, Mack, I swear. McKenna's going to kill me."

Chapter Two

Frances Glessner Lee got a telephone call from medical examiner Jake Magrath while at breakfast. "Fanny, we've got a problem at the Joy Street Station. It's young Peter Attwood. He's in trouble. I need you to bring your sketchpad. There's a man dead in a jail cell."

She agreed. As she packed up her materials, she felt a pang of guilt. Her daughter expected her in New Hampshire for the summer the following week. If she got caught up in another investigation, she'd be late. So be it.

Since the investigation of a murder during the molasses flood in the winter of 1919, Fanny had been drawn to the study of "legal medicine," as it was called. It was a new field pioneered by Magrath that used science to help explain unexplained death. It fascinated her. When she'd turned forty-two in March, she'd realized she was happier than she'd been in a long time. It was because she felt useful. At last.

* * *

Fanny was staying with her friend Cornelia Thornwell on Louisburg Square. Wealthy Bostonians like Cornelia had family homes on the side of Beacon Hill that faced the Boston Common and were topped by the golden dome of the state house. She walked up to Joy Street and turned down the north side, away from the Common.

The back of the Hill was considered part of the West End. It was packed with rooming houses and tenements that spread down to Cambridge Street. Fanny knew the area had been a hotbed of abolitionists and freedmen before the Civil War, and now it teamed with recent immigrants.

Fanny walked down the steep brick sidewalk of Joy Street to the police station. At the bottom, Cambridge Street was full of motor cars and horse-drawn traffic. The West End continued across the main street towards the banks of the Charles River and the North End. The police station was a brick building with stone facings to the doors and windows. Iron railings surrounded the front. An attached garage held police vehicles. She climbed the four stone steps to the front door.

Inside, a group of men stood around. She recognized Jake, Mack, and Edwin carrying a bag, photographic equipment, and a tripod.

"Mrs. Lee, thank you for coming." Peter Attwood was at her side. He wore the helmet and great coat of a patrolman. She knew he'd suffered a demotion recently. He was the grandson of her hostess, Cornelia.

"Peter, what's going on?" she asked.

Jake was discussing arrangements with a sergeant manning a tall desk. As usual, the well-known medical examiner was treated with respect.

Peter pulled off his helmet. It was a warm June morning, and Fanny could see he was sweating. "I found a man on the street last night. He was passed out; I'm sure he was drunk. I could smell whiskey. I called for the paddy wagon and brought him here. We put him in a cell to sleep it off, but when I checked at the end of my shift, he was dead. I can't believe it."

Fanny felt sorry for the young man, but at that moment, Jake motioned for them all to follow another policeman down the hall lined with jail cells. At the very end, he turned to them. "We put them in here when they're drunk. He's all yours."

It was a dismal place. Cold cement with chipped green paint covered the floor, walls, and ceiling. The doors to the cells were barred doors. Fanny glimpsed a cement bed on the right and a narrow place to stand on the left. Lights were only strung in the corridor, so the back of each cell was dark.

The policeman unlocked the cell with a large key, opened the door, and left them. Jake leaned on the door as he looked inside.

A man lay on his face on the cold floor. He wore a plaid cap, a rough wool jacket, and brown pants. Fanny couldn't see the man's face. Jake bent over the body, lifted the head, and felt the bones. Then he stepped away. "All right, let's get some pictures before we move him."

Fanny, Mack, and Jake waited while Edwin set up his big camera on its tripod. He focused the lens, then unpacked the T-shaped flash lamp and carefully sprinkled it with powder. He beckoned Mack to assist. With a sigh, the big Irishman took the lamp and the lighter. While Edwin looked through the lens, Mack waited. At the signal, Mack lit the lamp, squeezing his eyes shut as the blinding light flashed, and Edwin clicked the camera shutter.

Fanny and Jake waited as the men repeated the process several times to get different angles. Fanny began her sketch as they were working. The photographs would be used for the record, but they found Fanny's sketches useful when reconstructing a scene later. When Edwin finished photographing, they made way for her to get several more sketches. As she stepped inside, skirting the body, she saw something. She plopped down on the cement bed and bent forward. "Jake, come look at this." Letters were scrawled in black ash. On the ground below, she saw a pipe lying beside the body and noticed one finger of the right hand was blackened.

Jake squashed in beside her, forcing her to inch further into the darkness of the cell. He squatted on the bed, bent forward, and squinted through his glasses. He pulled off his hat, the better to see. "I can't make it out. Looks like 'N' 'I' 'K' something." He stood and shook himself with frustration. "Can't see. After we move the body, Edwin can get in here and get a photograph of it." He stepped over the dead man's head. "Fanny, come out. The men are here with the stretcher. Mack, help them get him out of there."

Fanny finished her reproduction of the graffiti in her sketch and slid over to the door, where Mack reached in a hand to help her out. She and Jake moved down the corridor to get out of the way of the men with the stretcher. Jake always called on men from the hospital next door to the morgue to get stretcher-bearers and an ambulance for a body.

Leaving Jake and Edwin to finish up, Fanny climbed into Jake's tricked-out old Ford Model T to drive back to the morgue just a few blocks down Cambridge Street and to the right. Jake had fitted the jalopy with bells, whistles, and lights. He'd even named it "Suffolk Sue" after Suffolk County, where he was the official medical examiner. His jurisdiction extended beyond the city of Boston to some outlying towns. The vehicle made a horrible noise as he started it up with his new automatic starter and put it into first gear. Fanny held on to her seat.

Jake was shaking his head. "No blood," he muttered above the roar. "No signs of a beating. Something wrong there."

Chapter Three

At the morgue, Jake directed the hospital men to put the body on one of the tables in the big autopsy room.

"Come here, Fanny," he said when the men left. "Can you do a portrait of his face? I checked his pockets and there's nothing to say who he is. First thing we'll have to do is identify him."

Fanny brought her sketch pad and a stool over to the table. Laid out on the steel table, the man seemed small. He looked to be in his fifties or sixties, with a lined face, salt and pepper hair worn a bit long, and a well-trimmed beard and moustache. Jake had removed the plaid cap and laid it aside. The man wore a ratty-looking jacket, but under it, he wore a well-pressed linen shirt, a neat tie, and suspenders. His brown pants were made of fine wool, and Fanny thought they should have been the bottom of a business suit. The police had obviously thought the man was a drunken bum from the street, but Fanny could see he was well cared for and clean. His boots were of a worn but good leather quality. The closer examination only raised more questions about who this man could be.

Edwin, Mack, and Peter trooped in. Edwin began removing the clothing from the body. Jake sat himself down on a rolling stool and beckoned Peter over. Fanny could sense that her old friend Jake was worried.

"So, tell me. Exactly what happened to this man?" he asked.

Peter moved from foot to foot, like a schoolboy called before the principal. He held his helmet in his hands. "Last night, I was on patrol. On Charles Street, by the Peabody House." Peter turned to Fanny to explain politely. "That's the settlement house; it's a seven-story building near the river."

He turned back to Jake. "Across the street, there's a block of shops with apartments above them."

Fanny knew the West End was crowded with tenements. The settlement house provided classes, sports, entertainment, baths, and all sorts of activities for the immigrants who lived in the area.

"That's around the block from us. Me and Edwin," Mack called out from his seat at his high desk in a corner. Fanny could see he was proud of his newfound knowledge of the neighborhood where he'd moved.

"That's right," Peter said. He was sweating. "So, there's a candy and cigar shop there, and beside it is—was a bar. Pat's Place. It's shut down now, of course, with prohibition, but the signs are still up. They plan to turn it into a shoe shop but haven't done it yet."

"I know it," Mack said. "There's a speakeasy in the basement."

Peter sighed. "Yeah. Basement of the candy shop. They've been raided. It's supposed to be gone now." He shrugged. "These places keep popping up all over. At the station, they don't want to hear about it. Most of them make a contribution to the policeman's fund or something. Anyhow, usually, there's no trouble, but this man was lying on the ground. I stopped and prodded him with my stick. Tried to wake him up, get him moving to go home. I could smell liquor on him. But he didn't wake up, so I went to the nearest box and called the station to bring the paddy wagon. We got him into the cell and laid him down on the bed there. He was fine. He stank of booze, was breathing heavy but he was breathing. At the end of my shift, this morning, I went to check on him before I went home." Peter gulped. "He was on the floor, like you found him. I tried to wake him by yelling but when I touched him, I could feel he was cold and stiff. I couldn't believe it! Did he hit his head or something? In his condition he could have fallen. Maybe back at the sidewalk. He was in the cell all by himself. Could he have fallen there?"

Poor Peter was distraught. He rubbed a hand to his forehead. He looked ready to cry but Fanny saw him swallow hard.

"Sure you didn't give him a hit to knock him out when you put him in the cell?" Mack asked.

"NO. No, I didn't. I wouldn't do that."

Fanny knew Mack asked because there were many cops who would knock around a prisoner, but she was confident young Peter hadn't learned those bad habits yet. He'd been a plain clothes detective until recently. Fanny knew it was a great disappointment to Jake that the young man he'd been training to investigate was struck back down into the ranks. She feared Jake's frustration with the city was reaching a boiling point.

Meanwhile, Jake was gently examining the dead man's head, moving it from side to side and using a magnifying glass to examine the skull while Edwin continued to remove the clothes from the body.

"I don't see any signs of contusions. We'll know more when we cut him open, but it doesn't look like he'd hit his head before you found him and then bled out. That would be possible with the cap jammed on his head. No signs of that. But see how his lips are blue." He pointed to the edges of the neat moustache. Fanny and Mack rose to come over and see what Jake mentioned. To Fanny, it looked like the dead man's eyes had rolled up so you could see the whites, as well. "That could tell a different story, eh, Edwin?"

"Poison, are you thinking?" Edwin asked.

"Not cyanide or arsenic, there would have been more contortions of the body. But something, perhaps. We'll have to test some of the body fluids."

Edwin provided a glass tube and gently brushed in a bit of saliva from the mouth.

The man's body lay naked on the table now. Fanny wondered who was looking for him. Surely, someone had missed him when he didn't come home the night before. A wife or daughter or even mother was feeling butterflies in her stomach today wondering what had kept him out all night. He looked too well cared for to be alone in the world. She was certain of that.

Chapter Four

It was late afternoon by the time the autopsy was finished. Jake Magrath was not happy with the results. Here was a well-fed, well-dressed man who had died in a cell at the Joy Street Station. Young Peter was the one who'd brought him in, so young Peter would be the one to shoulder the blame. There seemed no reason for the death.

The organs were those of an aging man, but none had enough wear and tear to cause the death. They'd been removed, weighed, and preserved. Fanny could be trusted to have taken down all the measurements. She'd become adept at transcribing the notes from his autopsies. Especially now that Edwin was busy with his studies.

Jake would miss her when she went up to New Hampshire for the summer. He'd been suspicious of her enthusiasm when she first began to help him. She had no medical training and no secretarial training. But she was precise and logical. She retained information that she heard or read better than many of the Harvard medical students when he taught pathology and anatomy. He recognized that her work with him had given her some peace. When she'd first appeared in Boston after all those years, she'd confided in him that she resented being thought "a rich woman with not enough to do." Feminine pursuits like needlework or social engagements were never enough for her. She was a fine needlewoman but preferred to exercise her talent in creating meticulous miniature reproductions of crime scenes than in decorating napkins or baby clothes. He had to admit he enjoyed her company when working out some of his more complicated investigations into unexplained deaths. And she obviously enjoyed it just as much as he did.

When they were young, and her brother was his fellow student at Harvard, she could have gone to Radcliffe College. She'd chosen marriage and children instead. He couldn't help thinking she was making up for that choice now that her marriage was over and her children grown. Jake rejected regret as an interpretation of the past. He had no regrets himself. He was a confirmed old bachelor with a vigorous schedule between his job and other interests. He had no patience with people who wallowed in regrets. He applauded the way Fanny was throwing herself into an area of study so completely foreign to her. He knew his own enthusiasm for his subject inspired her. Good for her!

But this case was puzzling. Despite the very thorough autopsy, they still had no idea who this man was or why he'd died. Edwin would be performing tests to see what was swirling around in the body fluids. Jake had found a small puncture in the left forearm. Had the man seen a doctor? Or what else could have caused the prick? Jake had seen such marks on addicts of heroin or morphine, but those bodies were wasted by the time they got to his table. This man couldn't be one of the growing numbers of lost souls who gave up their lives to the dreams the drugs gave them. Who was this man? Not one of the drug users, surely. Could someone else have injected poison into him? Why would he allow it? There were no defensive wounds.

Jake pulled off his apron and stuffed it in a dirty linen bin. "Fanny, let me see that portrait you did."

She was finishing her notes. She opened her drawing pad and pulled off the picture. Jake thought it was a good likeness. "Where did you find this man?" he asked Peter.

The disconsolate patrolman sat astride a hard chair with his head propped on his forearms on the chairback. His coat and helmet were on the floor. "Over on Charles Street."

"Near the Peabody House," Mack piped up from his desk. He'd done some tramping about and was in and out of the room during the autopsy, but now he sat up straight like a hunter waiting for a command.

Jake was happy with his decision to take on the blacklisted former police detective as an investigator. Impatient with the lack of action by the police,

Jake used the big Irishman to help identify bodies so their loved ones could bury them. He'd gone out and asked questions Jake wanted answered before he set his name to a death certificate when there was any doubt about the death. So often, the police didn't ask the right questions. It frustrated Jake in his role as medical examiner. He was, after all, the final advocate for the dead. He demanded the circumstances of the death of any person that came into his morgue be clarified. Mack was especially good at interviewing people to find out what had happened. It was a task Jake lacked patience for himself.

Mack appeared to find something amusing about the fact that Peter had been near the settlement house. Jake wondered at that. Mack lived nearby. Perhaps he'd seen the patrolman on his beat. There was an understandable rivalry between the ex-policeman and the former Harvard student. But Jake thought Mack sympathized when young Peter was demoted. He hoped he'd help clear the novice of the suspicion that something Peter had done had caused the man's death. But first, they needed to know who he was.

"Well, someone has got to know this man." Jake waved the drawing. "I say we go over there while Edwin does his tests." He looked at Fanny with frustration in his eyes. "I cannot say what caused this man's death. But if we can find out who he was, I may be able to get to the bottom of it. Let's go!"

Chapter Five

Fanny packed up her drawing materials and followed Jake, Mack, and a weary Peter out the door. The morgue was on North Grove Street, only a few blocks from where Peter had found the dead man. Peter led the way.

It was a warm spring afternoon. While dogwood, magnolia, and cherry blossoms were in full bloom up on Beacon Hill, Fanny breathed in the scents of cooking and rotting garbage as she followed the men down Charles Street. Brick tenements had storefronts at the street level, and fire escapes climbing to the apartments above. Laundry swung from lines in the warm breeze. They had to dodge carts of street peddlers as they walked single file through crowds speaking foreign languages. Soon, they'd almost reached the Charles River. At a corner stood a seven-story brick building.

Peter stopped, a bit dazed from lack of sleep, she thought. He looked up at the building. "Peabody House," he said, then turned on one foot to face in the opposite direction. He pointed across the street. "That's where I found him."

Mack and Jake trooped across to stand, staring at the storefronts. "Here?" Mack asked.

"That's right." Peter walked across.

Fanny stayed where she was and got out her drawing pad. She perched on a low stone wall to draw. Peter stopped in front of a store with big windows labelled "Candy/Cigars." Fanny began sketching. The window display included baseball gloves and bats, roller skates, lollipops, stacks of comics and magazines. Two boys ran out the open door with bags of candy in their hands.

To the right was another door with a stained-glass transom beside big glass windows labelled "ALE" and "BEER." Bottles were painted on the bottom part of the glass. A sign hung in the middle announcing "Harvard has what it takes." All of the decorations dated from before the implementation of prohibition in January. Fanny could hear Mack holding forth on the sidewalk as she drew her pictures.

"Yeah, this was Pat's Place. Belongs to Pat Ryan. Brother-in-law to the widow Edwin's walking out with. He had a pub in Southie, then he opened this one, but now, of course, it's all down the drain with the ban on liquor." He knocked on the door, and it opened. "Hi there, just showing the law here," he slapped Peter on the back, "that you're making it a shoe store. That's right, isn't it?"

Fanny heard murmuring from inside, and eventually, the door closed.

Jake stood in his wide-brimmed hat with his hands on his hips. He was asking Peter exactly where he'd found the dead man. Peter waved his arms to demonstrate his actions and where the man had been. Finally, he threw off his big coat, handing it to Mack and he laid down on the sidewalk in front of the shoe store that was a former bar.

Fanny quickly sketched in the body. She noticed a metal lunchbox and a banana peel nearby and dutifully added them. She was so concentrated on her task she jumped when a shadow fell across the page. A young woman had come up behind her. "Mrs. Lee, what are you doing?" she asked.

Fanny looked up. Holly Attwood, Peter's sister, and Cornelia's grand-daughter. Dark-haired with a short bob for a haircut. She wore a neat striped blouse of sturdy cotton, with a pretty blue bow at her throat and a dark, narrow skirt. Her dark eyes were sharp, but she seemed amused by the sight of Fanny's drawing. Her eyebrows rose as she glanced across at the men where Peter still lay on the ground. Fanny hoped he wasn't falling asleep.

Behind her stood a pale but earnest-looking girl in a silk dress that was both rich-looking and modest. She was a blonde with golden curls pinned back on her head.

"We saw you from a window and came to find out what you're doing here." Holly Attwood had a merry disposition, and Fanny was always glad to see her. Now, she looked across at the men. "Oh, no, is that Peter on the ground? What's wrong with him?" She didn't appear to be overly concerned about her brother, but the blonde inhaled a breath.

"He's quite all right," Fanny reassured them. "They're just reenacting a scene. Peter found a man drunk on the sidewalk during his patrol last night. He took him in to the station, but the poor man died. We're trying to find out who he was. What are you doing here, Holly?"

"Oh, I help teach a class in woodworking at Peabody House. This is Mildred Greene. She works at Peabody House. I doubt it could run without her and her brother Teddy. Mildred this is Mrs. Lee, a dear friend of my grandmother."

Across the way, Fanny saw Peter notice the girls and suddenly rise from the ground, brushing himself off and grabbing his coat from Mack. Peter blushed. Mack grinned as he looked back and forth between the young policeman and the girls. Fanny suspected something was going on.

"You must know a lot of the people around here, Miss Greene. Perhaps you can help us identify the poor man." Fanny led them across to the men and introduced them.

"Good," Jake said. "You can help us. Where's that drawing of Fanny's? Have you got it, Mack?"

The big Irishman brought out the drawing and unfolded it. He handed it to Miss Greene.

"It looks like Mr. Kessler, Rachel's father," Mildred said.

Chapter Six

"Rachel Kessler teaches woodworking with me. She and I are both apprenticed to Mrs. Shurcliff this summer." Holly was no longer merry. Her face was white. "I think she's still at Peabody House. I'll get her."

When Holly hurried away, Mildred Greene looked grim. "I hope I'm wrong, but I'm afraid I may be right. Mr. Kessler is a jeweler with offices on Causeway Street. I don't know why he'd be here. I can't believe he'd be drunk." She stared at the candy store. "We've complained about the speakeasy over here, but the police do nothing."

Fanny saw Peter's face redden. She was about to suggest they find somewhere in Peabody House to talk to Miss Kessler when Holly returned with a tall, thin young woman with dark hair in a bun at the base of her neck. Mildred Greene showed her the drawing.

"Yes. It looks like my father. What is this about?"

Everyone looked at Peter. Fanny noticed that he glanced up at Mildred Greene before answering. "I was on patrol last night. When I got here, I found a man on the ground. He seemed fine; he was out cold. Sleeping, I thought." Peter clutched the heavy coat that he had in his hands in front of him. "He smelled of liquor."

"This cannot be. You said the man was drunk. My father doesn't drink. Never. What happened?" she demanded. She was very pale but appeared determined.

Peter was sweating. "I'm sorry. He must have been sick or something. I called the paddy wagon, and we got him to the station. He seemed all right.

We left him in a cell to sleep it off. He really seemed fine. I'm so sorry. In the morning, he was cold, and he wasn't breathing."

Rachel was outraged. "No, it's not possible. It can't be my father. My father is not a drunk."

She grabbed the sketch out of Mildred's hands. "No, no, no," she murmured.

Mildred put an arm around her shoulders. "Oh, Rachel, I'm so sorry. Let us take you home. Do you want me to find your brother for you?"

The girl was shaking with sobs she tried to suppress. She wiped her hands across her eyes to rid herself of tears. "No. I must see for myself. Please, you must take me to him. Only if I see him, can I be sure."

Fanny knew Jake would have many questions, but she admired the way, he put an arm around the young woman and ordered Mack to find a taxicab. He took Rachel with him. Fanny offered to go, but he waved her off, choosing Holly to accompany Rachel to the morgue.

Fanny knew Jake approved of Peter's sister. He thought she was a sensible girl. Jake was sensitive to the grief of relatives of the dead he handled, but he would appreciate the lack of drama Holly would bring to the viewing of the body. He had only too much experience with identifying the dead, and Fanny was confident Jake would make it as painless as possible for Rachel. He gave Mack instructions in a whisper and took Rachel and Holly off in the cab.

Fanny stood awkwardly with Mildred and Peter. Mack came back to them and slapped Peter on the back. "Wake up. We need to find out as much as we can about Mr. Kessler. You," he turned to Mildred Greene, "who are you again?"

Peter frowned at Mack's manner. He straightened up. "This is Miss Greene from Peabody House." He gestured to the tall brick building across the street. Fanny could see that Peter took some pride in announcing this. She thought he must know Miss Greene fairly well.

"Well, good," Mack said. "Now, what can you tell us about this Mr. Kessler, eh?"

Mildred Greene was petite, but she stood to her full height and looked

Mack in the eye. "I will tell you what I know, but first, I must get my brother to find Bernard Kessler. He has to know about his father's death, and Rachel will need his support—if the dead man really is Mr. Kessler." She pointed across the street. "I need to go back and find my brother, Teddy. Please, come with me."

Fanny followed as Mildred led them into Peabody House. The building had high ceilings with linoleum floors. Activity bustled everywhere in the big foyer and the corridors and staircases leading to other parts of the building. Young boys and girls hurried along, talking in loud voices. Young men in basketball shorts and tops carried bags. A troop of boys with baseball bats and gloves dashed out the doors as Mildred led them in. Sounds echoed as if they were in a canyon and there was a smell Fanny couldn't identify in the humid air.

Mildred grabbed one boy and sent him to find her brother, Teddy, then led Fanny and the others to a big office off the foyer. There were two desks and a number of chairs and filing cabinets. Mildred motioned them to find seats while she stood in the doorway, peering out, looking for her brother. Peter remained standing behind her, looking helpless. Soon, a short young man with blonde hair in a neat shirt and tie hurried over.

"This is my brother, Theodore Greene," Mildred told them. She turned back to the smiling young man and Fanny saw the resemblance between the siblings. The brother had a pile of golden curls on his head and blue eyes like his sister. "Teddy, you must find Bernie Kessler and take him to the morgue on Grove Street. Ask for Dr. Magrath. Hurry." She grabbed his shirt sleeve and whispered in his ear. His eyes opened wide, and he rushed away.

Mildred closed the door and came in to sit behind the desk. Peter fumbled with a chair. Finally hanging his coat on the back, he sat down.

Fanny had taken an armchair at a corner of the desk, and Mack had pulled up a chair directly opposite Mildred. He glanced at Peter, shrugged, and took out a small notebook. Fanny thought the ex-detective had no confidence in Peter's ability to investigate. It was true. Peter was still very new to the process, although Fanny thought he'd learned a lot in the past year. But this death had thrown the young former Harvard student off balance. First, he'd been demoted to patrol, then he'd taken in a man he assumed was drunk and found him dead in the cell, and then he'd discovered the dead man was the father of a friend of his sister and of Mildred. Fanny suspected there was something between the young people. Peter seemed flustered in front of the girls

Completely unflustered, Mack questioned Mildred. She explained that she and her brother worked at Peabody House. Fanny could see Mack was familiar with the settlement house and its work in the West End. She thought he seemed just a bit critical of their activities. He made a sarcastic comment about how the settlement workers influenced immigrants they were helping out of the goodness of their Yankee hearts. Mildred had a response.

She looked directly at Mack. "You're Roman Catholic, I expect?" she asked.

With raised eyebrows, Mack said. "Yes."

"We're aware that Cardinal O'Connell does not approve of settlement work. He fears some kind of Protestant contamination. But we do not teach religious values here, we help people to adapt to American society and American values. We teach English to those who come here speaking German, Lithuanian, Italian, Gaelic and even Hebrew. We provide healthy outlets for the young, with sports and bathing facilities. We have a large swimming pool on this floor." Fanny realized that explained the echo and the smell of chlorine in the foyer.

Milly stood and pointed to the door. "We are the first in the nation to provide homogenized milk as well as medical care for new mothers." She sat down again. "We also provide cultural activities like theater and literature, and discussion groups for those who want to talk about politics or history. Despite what the cardinal says, we have a friendly rivalry with the sports groups from St. Joseph's, and we cooperate with other groups in the area, including the West End House that Mr. Storrow supports."

"Mack, Milly, and her brother work hard to help the people of the West End. All of them. They'd be lost without all the things Peabody House gives them," Peter said.

Fanny noticed he called the young woman "Milly", and she was sure the slip was not lost on Mack. The ex-detective, now morgue investigator, continued. "What can you tell us about the Kessler family?" he asked.

"Rachel Kessler helps to teach a woodworking class here. She and Officer Attwood's sister, Holly, have been trained by Mrs. Shurcliff to do woodworking. Mrs. Shurcliff has a woodworking studio in her house on Mount Vernon Street. It's a woman-owned business that produces pieces in the style of early American carpenters."

Fanny recognized the name of Mrs. Shurcliff. Before her marriage, she had been Margaret Nichols, sister to Rose Nichols, a social activist who lived on Beacon Hill. Rose was also a professional landscaper and a friend of Cornelia and Fanny herself. Margaret, Rose's younger sister, was married to a well-known professional landscaper, Arthur Shurcliff, and was also a suffragist and political activist. She wasn't surprised that Peter's sister Holly had been drawn into the circle of the Nicols sisters.

Mildred continued. "Rachel's family are orthodox Jews from Russia. Her father is a jeweler. He has offices in the Shapiro building on Causeway Street. He's a very respectable businessman in the community and very strict with his children. I know he was arranging a marriage for Rachel within their orthodox family. He'd never be found drunk on the ground." She sounded shocked. "He must have been ill." She glared at Peter.

"I swear to you, he smelled of whiskey. Honestly, Milly, he didn't seem sick at all. He seemed just sleepy like you get when you've drunk too much."

Fanny felt bad for the young man. He obviously wanted to impress Mildred Greene.

Mildred sighed. "I know you were doing your duty, Officer Attwood. It's just a terrible tragedy, that's all."

Mack coughed. "What else can you tell me about the Kesslers?"

"Not much. Mrs. Kessler died in the flu epidemic. Bernard Kessler is Rachel's younger brother. He's at Harvard. His father wants him to take over the jewelry business, but I believe Bernard is resisting that. I suppose he'll have to take it over now if Mr. Kessler is really gone. Poor Rachel. Rachel works in a garment factory as well as doing the woodworking. In the summer, Bernard works at a print shop in the same building as his father's business. This will be very, very hard for both of them."

"Do you know of anyone who might harm Mr. Kessler? Any enemies? Business rivals?"

"I wouldn't know." She thought for a minute. "I do know there was a robbery in Mr. Kessler's building last week. I don't know what was stolen. I heard they broke into several offices and ruined some safes. I'm not sure if Mr. Kessler lost anything."

"I see," Mack said. He rose. "Thank you for your assistance. If you think of anything else, please let us know. You can reach us at the mortuary on Grove Street."

As Fanny gathered her things, she noticed Peter looked dejected. He was having a truly bad day, and he'd had no sleep for more than twenty-four hours. She was glad to see Mildred weaken her strictly official stance enough to pat the young patrolman on the arm as she pushed him out the door. Fanny wondered what Jake had found out at the morgue. Poor Rachel and Bernard Kessler.

Chapter Seven

Jake escorted Rachel and Holly to his office and left them sitting opposite his cluttered desk while he went to find Edwin and prepare the body for identification. He found Edwin in his laboratory off the main room.

"It was morphine," Edwin told him. "Just as you suspected. See, here's the test. I checked for heroin, too, but it was morphine." He held up a beaker.

Jake shook his head. Recently, he'd seen a number of deaths from drug overdoses. "This will be uncomfortable. He's a businessman, and his daughter is here to identify the body. She vehemently denied he drank. I can't imagine what she'll think when we tell her it was morphine. Come help me get the body."

As they moved the corpse from refrigeration and wheeled the body into the main dissection room, Jake found himself preoccupied with doubts. If Mr. Kessler was as upright and sober as his daughter believed, how had he gotten enough morphine into his system to kill him? Jake knew people who succumbed to morphine, heroin, and other drugs were often ashamed and went to great lengths to hide their addiction. Had this middle-aged man hidden an awful secret from his family? Jake had seen more and more families shocked by a drug-induced death. The West End, in particular, suffered from an influx of these dangerous drugs.

Jake escorted Rachel and Holly to the examination table that held Mr. Kessler and Edwin gently folded back the sheet to show the man's face.

Rachel gasped. Holly stepped forward to help her, but Rachel brushed her off and grasped the edge of the examination table to stare at the lined face, empty of any spirit. "Papa," she whispered. "Oh, Papa." She shook with restrained sobs, still waving off Holly. Taking a big breath, she bent down to kiss the dead man's forehead. She straightened and turned away with heavy steps, walking back to Jake's office and collapsing in a chair. Holly hurried after her.

Jake indicated for Edwin to remove the body and joined the women in his office.

"I'm so sorry," he told Rachel. "Do you have any idea how your father came to be on that sidewalk?"

Rachel sniffed into the handkerchief Holly thrust into her hands. She curled forward as if her stomach ached. "No," she said, pulling herself together. Her eyes were bleary with pain. "He went out last night. I didn't see him return. I assumed he had left for work this morning before I was up. He often went in early. But he wasn't a drunk."

Jake could see that the assumption her father had collapsed from drinking pierced through her sorrow. She saw it as a vicious insult to the dead man. She was hypersensitive to the slight. Jake cleared his throat. "No, he wasn't drunk. Tests on his remains show that he died from an overdose of morphine. Did your father take that drug, as far as you know?"

Rachel's head popped up. "No, never. What are you saying? Was he sick? Was it an accident? Morphine? Why would he have morphine?"

Jake could see the young woman had no knowledge of the cause of her father's death. "Have you ever seen your father inject himself with a hypodermic needle?" Jake searched among the papers on his desk. He knew he'd taken out a hypodermic after the autopsy to compare the needle to the mark on the dead man's arm. He held it up. "Like this."

"What are you talking about? Of course not," Rachel snapped.

Holly looked on with concern, but Jake was glad to see that she kept her thoughts to herself.

"Was your father under the care of a doctor? Had he been ill lately?"

Rachel's face reddened. "No. He was fine. He walked to work every day. He was fine. You can't think he took morphine. He didn't do this to himself. Is that what you're saying you found?"

"No, no. I'm not suggesting any such thing," Jake protested. He hated to burden the grieving woman with doubts, but he needed an explanation of the needle mark and the morphine in the body. "It's possible he was injected by accident, but do you know of any reason someone would wish your father harm? Did he have enemies?"

Rachel nearly rose from her seat. "Enemies? Enemies? What are you saying, that someone killed my father?"

Jake rose and came to her side. She tensed, ready for conflict. Holly stood and reached out a hand to Rachel's arm. Jake spoke. "Miss Kessler, please, don't upset yourself. I only ask these questions to help me to find out the cause and manner of your father's death. It's my duty as medical examiner to clarify what happened to him. I only want to help you." He nodded to Holly. "We all want to help you. Miss Attwood and I are terribly sorry for your loss."

At the kind words, Rachel broke into sobs, and Holly helped her back into her chair.

Edwin stood in the doorway. Behind him, Jake saw a slight young man. "Miss Kessler's brother, Bernard Kessler, is here."

Jake stepped out to the main room and introduced himself. Bernard Kessler was thin and dark. There were shadows around his eyes. He was in shock, his face a pasty white.

When Jake asked if Bernard also wanted to see his father's body, the young man looked sick and refused. He glanced in the office at his sister, and Jake stepped aside to let him go in to comfort her. Rachel rose and embraced her brother. They spoke in Yiddish, weeping as they clung to each other. Jake heard the word "morphine," but the brother flushed red and had to sit down. Holly edged out of the office to allow the siblings to sit and talk.

Outside the door, Holly spoke to Jake. "Dr. Magrath, what does this have to do with my brother, Peter?"

"Peter found Mr. Kessler unconscious on the ground. He took him to jail, thinking he could sleep it off, but he was dead in the morning. He wasn't drunk; he died from morphine poisoning." He could see Holly contemplating the situation and what it meant for her brother. "There's been a rash of deaths from morphine in the West End," he told her. "Do you know why Mr. Kessler would have been in that area last night?"

"No, they have an apartment up on the north side of Beacon Hill, and he has an office on Causeway." She glanced at the siblings in Jake's office and moved a few steps away. "Bernie goes to Peabody House for classes, I think. He's usually in woodworking, but he wasn't there today." She bit her lip. "Bernie's father wanted him to work in his jewelry business, but he sent him to Harvard. Bernie has more of an artistic tenement. He resisted his father. Rachel absolutely defied him when she started working with me at Mrs. Shurcliff's. Mr. Kessler was very old-fashioned. I can't believe he used drugs. Unless he was sick."

"His daughter says he wasn't sick. What about Mrs. Kessler?" Jake asked.

"She died of the flu," Holly said.

The young people would have to cope on their own, rely on each other.

Rachel appeared at the open doorway. Her face was pale and grim. "We must prepare my father for burial," she said.

Jake knew that Orthodox Jews buried their dead as soon as possible after death. In deference to the religious customs, he would release the body even though he hadn't concluded his report on cause and manner of death. He nodded.

"My brother will stay here, with the body. I'll go and make the arrangements," Rachel said.

"You belong to a burial society?" Jake asked. Most Jews were members of a "landsmanschaft," a sort of fraternal organization that provided the essential ritual death preparations for its members.

"We belong to Vilna Shul," Rachel said. "My father was so proud of the new shul building he helped to build." Tears flooded her eyes, but she swallowed and quietly left. He was glad the Kessler children would get the support of their shul.

Jake thought Rachel was the rock foundation for the Kessler family. Perhaps she'd stepped into her mother's position. She would pull herself back from the brink of despair to organize the funeral rites. There was always someone in every grieving family who had to take on that burden. He could see that Rachel was determined her father would receive the dignified burial rites that he believed in. Jake would help her as much as he could.

26

Chapter Eight

The next day was bright and sunny as Mack led Peter and Holly Attwood to the Jewish cemetery in East Boston. They rode the trolley that ran through a tunnel under the harbor to get there. Mack, who'd lived in East Boston all his life, guided them to the cemetery. It seemed to Mack much too cheerful a day for a funeral.

Rachel, Bernard, and a crowd of mourners were already at the open grave. Mack was shocked at how quickly the funeral had come together and the bare pine casket that held the remains. The body must not have been embalmed. A few prayers were chanted, the drab casket lowered, and then clumps of dirt dropped in the grave, then people left. Mack was outraged. Did they just plunk a man in the ground and forget about him?

"A poor way to bury a man," he grumbled.

Holly was bemused. "They're Jewish. It must be a different tradition," she said. Both she and Peter looked like they didn't know what to do next. The Kesslers had been escorted to a motorcar and whisked away.

"Wait, I see someone who can help." Holly stepped away briskly to stop a young woman dressed in a black walking suit and small beret. She led the woman over to Mack and Peter. Holly introduced them to Miss Goldstein. "She's the first Jewish woman to be appointed head of a branch of the Boston Public Library," Holly said. "She's a friend of Rachel and Milly's." She turned to the neat young woman. "Can you help us? We came to show our sympathy to Rachel and her brother, but we didn't even get to talk to them. Is there some way we can show our support? Should we send flowers or something?"

Miss Goldstein smiled. "You just don't understand the Jewish traditions," she said.

Mack couldn't restrain himself. "Why'd they dump him in the ground so quickly? Is it because of how he died?" Mack was beginning to think there was something fishy about how the dead man was treated.

"Mack," Peter snapped. Obviously, he was embarrassed by Mack's outburst. Mack glared at him. With his Protestant Brahmin background, he had no more idea of what was happening than Mack did.

Miss Goldstein waved a gloved hand. "It's all right. Let me explain. In Jewish tradition, a person is buried as quickly as possible. The body is not embalmed. It's washed and dressed in white burial shrouds and prayer shawl. Only the simplest of caskets is used, so as not to distinguish between rich and poor in death."

"But they just drop the poor sod in the cemetery and forget him?" Mack asked.

"Ma-a-ck," Peter moaned. Mack ignored him. It was important to him that a man be treated decently in death. He didn't understand this at all. Didn't these people have any respect? He noticed Holly smile a little and it made him self-conscious. Was he being a brute to ask?

Miss Goldstein was unperturbed by the questions, in fact she seemed to sympathize with Mack. "Oh, no. He's not forgotten. Mr. Kessler was buried quickly, but now his family, Rachel, and Bernard will sit Shiva. That is a custom by which the family stays at home for seven days mourning their dead relative."

"Is there anything we can do to show our sympathy?" Holly asked. "Should we send flowers?"

Miss Goldstein shook her head. "Not flowers, but it's a custom to visit the family while they are grieving."

Mack was relieved. "Oh, they have a wake after the burial?" It seemed strange to him, but at least it was something. Peter grimaced at him. Mack would have liked to kick the stuck-up Yankee.

"Not like an Irish wake," Miss Goldstein said. "The family members tear their garments and cover any mirrors during the period. Friends make short visits of condolence and bring food, not flowers. That's so the mourners don't worry about cooking or cleaning or how they look for the seven days of mourning. During this time, they share memories of the dead person, so, in that way, it might be like an Irish wake."

"Thanks so much, Miss Goldstein," Holly said. "We'll visit the Kesslers and bring food. I just want Rachel to know she's in our thoughts and prayers. I was embarrassed not to know what to do."

Miss Goldstein nodded. "I'm glad to help. One of the things I'd like to do at the library is to put out displays about the different groups of people in the West End. At Christmas, we had tables with information about Christian celebrations and Jewish Hanukkah celebrations. Around Easter we showed traditions for Passover as well as Easter, and Roman Catholic as well as Eastern Orthodox and various Protestant customs."

As Holly continued to talk to the librarian, the four of them walked towards the exit. Mack was impressed by Peter's sister. Unlike the uppity Harvard boy, she didn't put him down. Both she and Miss Goldstein were different from other young women he knew. They weren't married, at least not yet, and they seemed very forward in their beliefs. It surprised him that they'd found other occupations that seemed more important to them than raising a brood of children and bossing around a working husband, like his sister did. It was all part of a strange new world he'd entered since he'd been expelled from the police. Never before had he hung around with so many Yankees, Jews, and Italians. Working for Jake Magrath was turning out to be an eye-opening experience. But Mack felt he was ready for it. Ready for anything! He wondered if Holly Attwood was being courted by one of Peter's Harvard friends.

When Mack returned to the mortuary, he found that Dr. Magrath was looking for him.

"Glad you're back," Jake said after Mack explained how he'd gone to the burial. "We've been summoned to Hendricks Club."

Chapter Nine

Mack straightened his tie before he followed Dr. Magrath out the door of the mortuary. As they walked to Green Street, the medical examiner asked him if he knew Martin Lomasney, the political boss of Ward Eight.

"Not personally, no," Mack told him. He figured Magrath brought him along because of his Irish roots. Magrath was an old Yankee, graduated from Harvard. Mack was a typical Irish Bostonian, and Lomasney was an old Irish ward boss. Magrath assumed Mack would know him. But the ex-policeman grew up in East Boston where Honey Fitz was the most conspicuous politician. He'd heard of Lomasney. He'd never met him. In fact, Fitzgerald and Lomasney were sometimes at odds in the rough and tumble of Boston politics.

Magrath pocketed his pipe as he walked along. "He doesn't like being called 'boss' or 'czar.' Some newspaperman labelled him 'mahatma,' and when he looked it up, he thought it fitted. More of a spiritual leader," Magrath chuckled. "He says a boss gives orders. He claims he doesn't tell voters how to vote, he suggests. His suggestions are well received. He's never lost an election in his ward. Quite the canny politician. I'm surprised you haven't been approached by a Hendricks Club member."

Mack didn't comment. He was thinking that Lomasney must have a lot of political pull if the medical examiner hopped to it as soon as he called. Magrath wasn't one to kowtow. Mack figured he'd keep quiet. With his height and big shoulders, acting as the quiet strongman suited him. He knew it was when he opened his big mouth that he sometimes got himself in trouble.

At the four-story brick building, a chubby man let them in. The first floor was a big open space. "Used to be a Baptist meeting house, held revival meetings," he said as he led them up to the second floor.

They entered a room with a long table. On the right, Mack recognized McKenna and Peter Attwood. Mack growled to himself. Chief of Detectives McKenna was a scab as far as Mack was concerned. He'd kept his place in the department after the police strike because he'd pretended to be with the men who wanted a union but had reported back to police brass. He was a drunk who kept rooms in a brothel. Mack despised him. McKenna sat with Peter on the right side of the table. Peter had his helmet on the table in front of him and looked dejected.

Opposite were five men in dark suits. All had beards and sideburns. Despite being indoors, they wore hats, black with wide brims. Mack fingered his own clean-shaven face. Looking at those beards on this warm day made him feel itchy. He was glad he'd found a barbershop run by some Italian guy near his rooming house.

"Dr. Magrath, welcome. Come on in," Lomasney, at the head of the table, rose to shake Magrath's hand. The doctor introduced Mack. He could see the politician sizing him up. Lomasney had broad shoulders and a receding hairline with a brush-like moustache. He must have been in his sixties with a pot belly. He looked ready for work. His suit jacket was hanging from his chair, his tie and collar were pulled off and lay on the table. His sleeves were rolled to his elbows. He waved them to chairs beside Peter and remained standing.

"Now, I hope we can come to an agreement. There's been a terrible death in our ward. Terrible. And these upstanding citizens here," he pointed at the men in black suits, "have come to me for my help, and I've promised to look into it. We all appreciate the hard work of our police force, so when citizens come to me with complaints, I want to get to the bottom of the problem immediately. Mr. Abrams, would you like to explain."

Mack frowned. Surely, Lomasney already knew about the man found dead in the jail cell. He was a wily politician to pretend ignorance. He wouldn't want to be seen as anti-police. Suddenly, Mack remembered what he'd heard about the West End ward boss. In some ongoing dispute with other Irish politicians, Lomasney had supported the Republican for mayor. It was a Republican Police Commissioner's wrath that caused the police strike. The strike that cost over a thousand policemen their jobs, including Mack. He clenched his jaw. Now was no time to accuse Lomasney of treachery. But Mack would remember.

Meanwhile, a young man stood without removing his hat. His face was pale under all that hair. Mack thought he'd seen the man at the gravesite. "Mr. Isaac Kessler was found dead while in the custody of the police in the Joy Street Station. Instead of finding out how a perfectly healthy man dies in a jail cell, the authorities are blackening the dead man's name by claiming he took drugs that killed him. We protest. If Mr. Kessler were not a Jew, these horrible accusations would never have been made. We want justice for Mr. Kessler. He was in a police cell when he died. Why aren't the police found responsible?"

A gray-haired man beside Abrams spoke to him in Yiddish. No wonder the younger man was spokesman. "Our people escaped the pogroms of Russia to come to America where we could be treated fairly," Abrams translated. "But now it seems the police are allowed to slaughter us. This isn't what we came to America for."

Lomasney had sat listening but now he jumped up. "No, no. We won't allow that to happen. Chief McKenna, is this true? Did Mr. Kessler die at the hands of the police? We can't have that." He struck the table with a fist.

McKenna hunkered down in his seat. His brow looked like a storm cloud. Mack clenched his jaw again. Things were not looking good for young Peter Attwood. McKenna had already found an excuse to demote the former Harvard student to patrolman when he'd come in as a detective. Now, he'd throw the boy to the wolves for sure.

Dr. Magrath spoke up before McKenna could answer. "Mr. Lomasney. I've done the autopsy on Mr. Kessler. It's true his dead body was found in the cells of Joy Street, but he didn't die at the hands of the police. He died of morphine poisoning. That's clear from my examination. Officer Attwood found Mr. Kessler lying on the ground and assumed he was drunk. He took him in to let him sleep it off. The police do this all the time. Unfortunately, this time, Mr. Kessler was ill and died before anyone realized it. The police did not beat, or harm Mr. Kessler. Officer Attwood didn't know Mr. Kessler was Jewish, Irish, or anything else, I assure you."

Abrams turned to the older men and translated Magrath's speech for them. They talked among themselves.

Lomasney crossed his arms on his chest. He was still standing. "Are you implying that Mr. Kessler was a dope fiend?" he asked angrily.

Abrams turned to him with wide eyes. "That's a lie. Mr. Kessler was my boss. I worked with him every day. I'm engaged to his daughter. He never even drank or smoked. He was an honest man, an important man in our community. How dare you imply he used dope?" He translated for the older men who began to rise. They were angry.

Dr. Magrath tried to calm them down. "I'm not saying any such thing," he said loudly.

Chief McKenna stood. "Don't worry. I'll take care of this right now," he proclaimed. Mack could see he was mainly concerned with Lomasney's anger. Ignoring the black-suited men on the other side of the table, he turned to Peter Attwood. "Attwood, you're suspended as of now. I'll be doing a full investigation of Kessler's death, and if you're found responsible, you'll face criminal charges."

Much as he disdained Peter Attwood's wealthy Brahmin background, Mack felt sorry for him today. There was no sense staying in the room to be accused of murdering Kessler. The big Irishman stood and grabbed Peter by the shoulder, pulling him up. With a big paw, he scooped up the helmet and pushed Peter out the door and down the stairs. Outside, they waited for Dr. Magrath.

The medical examiner joined them in a few minutes. He was angry. "I tried to make them listen, but they're all excited. They think Kessler was mistreated because he's a Jew. They must be an important voting block for Lomasney. He's certainly trying to placate them." He looked at Peter. Mack could see the young officer was still gazing with shell shocked eyes.

"I never hurt Mr. Kessler," he said. "I wouldn't do that."

Mack huffed. "Yeah, but McKenna would've. There's nothing he'd like better than to get you convicted of killing the man. Two birds with one stone. He solves the Kessler murder and gets rid of you permanently."

Peter looked at him in disbelief. "He can't do that."

"Wanna bet?" Mack said.

"Not if I have anything to say about it," Magrath said. "Come on. Back to the office. We need to find out what really happened to Mr. Kessler."

Mack shook his head and followed Magrath and Peter. It didn't look good. But Mack thought there was a bright side. He'd relish showing up McKenna, traitor that he was. Magrath wouldn't let it go. Mack was sure of it. They'd have to battle the official police, but Mack looked forward to that, even if it did get poor little Peter back on the force.

Chapter Ten

Back at the morgue, Dr. Magrath stomped into his cluttered office. Exchanging a look with Magrath's assistant, Edwin, Mack pushed Peter onto a stool and followed the medical examiner. Something was up with Magrath. It wasn't like him to vent his anger by stomping around.

"This is ridiculous," Magrath fumed. "How many times do I have to tell them the man died of morphine poisoning? Facts mean nothing to them. They blame Attwood in spite of the facts. Where does McKenna think Attwood got morphine to inject in Kessler? He doesn't care. I've had enough of these incompetents. I've had enough of political interference. I've a mind to put in my resignation over this. Enough." He threw up his hands.

Mack's stomach turned over. Magrath couldn't resign. Where would he be then? This job as investigator for the medical examiner's office was his lifeline. He felt it slacken, as if someone had let go of the rope. "We'll prove them wrong," he said. "You'll see. We can do it."

Edwin stuck his head in to tell Magrath there were two new bodies to be autopsied. There'd been a motor accident. Magrath growled, then pushed past Mack to the door.

As Edwin helped the medical examiner prepare the bodies, Mack took a lost-looking Peter by the shoulders and pushed him out the door. Magrath stopped to watch and exchanged a look with Mack. He nodded. He understood that Mack needed to pump the suspended policeman for more information about the night Kessler died. Mack believed Magrath would continue the investigation into Kessler's death. For once, he wished Mrs.

Lee would visit Magrath. She had big plans to help the medical examiner train detectives in scientific methods. Mack sometimes found her earnest enthusiasm annoying, but he hoped she could cure Magrath's exasperation with the authorities.

It was all due to the failures of Peter Attwood. Mack grumbled to himself as he dragged the young man down a few streets until they were back to where the body had been found. Peter looked across at the Peabody House and tried to pull away. "I can't be here," he said.

Mack wasn't letting go. "Oh, no, you don't. I've got some questions for you. Come on." He thought Peter didn't want to be seen by the woman from the Peabody House, what was her name? Greene. Mildred Greene. Mack didn't care about that, but he pushed Peter into the candy shop.

Inside were glass counters displaying lots of candies. Comic books and illustrated magazines were set out on some shelves. In one corner were bats, gloves, balls, and some wooden toys. Two small round tables with marble tops and metal wire chairs stood in the back.

Mack nodded to the woman behind the counter and headed to a door in the corner. It opened on steep stairs.

Peter squirmed. "What're you doing? This place got shut down."

"Yeah, right," Mack said, giving him another shove. "For one day. Go on, go down."

They descended into a small speakeasy. The man behind the makeshift bar glared at Peter's police coat. Mack pushed Peter towards a bench in the back and waved the helmet at the barman. "It's OKAY, Pat. He's not really on the job, just playacting."

He pulled Peter's heavy coat from him and grunted in disgust before shoving the young man onto the bench. Unlike when Mack was on the force, the city paid for police uniforms now. Mack threw the coat and helmet after Peter, then he pulled up a chair and sat opposite. A rough table stood between them. It was dark in the dank cellar. The only light was from lamps hanging over the bar.

"Whiskey with a beer chaser for both of us," Mack called to the bartender. "And none of that bathtub stuff. Jameson's."

Peter was staring around.

"They don't close ones like these down for good, you know," Mack told him. "Even the cops need a drink. Pat here is friends with your fellow officers at Joy Street." The bartender brought the shot glasses of whiskey and foaming mugs of beer over on a tray. Mack turned to him. "Pat, two nights ago. Was there an older man, cap, and jacket, drinkin' here? He was kinda small and had a beard. Attwood here found him outside the front door smelling of whiskey, so he says."

After unloading the tray, Pat stood up. "He didn't drink here. We were closed. There'd been a raid around the corner, and we were playing it careful. We heard about how they found a man on the sidewalk, and he died in the jail. We didn't open back up till today because of it."

Mack grabbed his arm. "You're not lying to me now, are you?"

Pat pulled away. "No. You can check with Mary upstairs. We were closed, I'm tellin' you." He went back to the bar. A couple of men had entered.

Peter sat up. "He smelled of whiskey, Mack. I swear it." He picked up the shot glass and sniffed. "Whiskey, like this. I had no idea he was sick from morphine." He watched as Mack quickly swallowed his shot of liquor and followed his example, coughing at the heat of the whiskey.

Mack quenched the heat with a sip of the beer. "What in the name of God were you doing around here anyhow? Why weren't you down on Causeway Street or Cambridge?

Peter put his face in his hands. Mack couldn't understand what was eating the boy. Didn't he realize he could be arrested for Kessler's death even if he didn't do it? Surely, he'd seen enough of McKenna to fear the man's viciousness.

Mack pulled Peter's hands away from his face. "Wake up. Answer the question. What were you doing down here?"

Peter swallowed and looked down at the table. "I was on a break. I was having a sandwich."

"In the candy shop?"

Peter gulped a mouthful of beer, then said, "at Peabody House."

Mack sat back with a frown. "Peabody House? Oh, I get it. You were visiting the charming Miss Greene. Is that it?" He snorted.

Peter's face reddened. "Yes. I was. I've known Milly since we were children. She went to school with my sister. She was at Wellesley College with Holly, but last year, her father's business went under. He was ruined. He hung himself. Her mother died years ago, so it was just her and her brother. He's still at Harvard. But she got a job at Peabody House, and she has rooms there. Milly never complains. She always says no matter what her family lost, they're still better off than the immigrants down here, and she does everything she can to help them. She's not like the other girls I grew up with. She did the coming out parties with Holly and the others, but she's always been interested in working with the poor."

So, Peter's girlfriend was one of these Brahmin do-gooders who liked to come down to the tenements and civilize the ignorant immigrants. Mack knew the type. They meant well. He could see Peter's eyes shine as he recited praises of Miss Greene. The boy was smitten, all right.

"So, what's the deal? You were over courting Miss Greene, and when you finally came out, you found Kessler?"

"I wasn't courting her," Peter protested. "I'd met her when I started patrolling down here. McKenna tricked me, made me look bad to the higher ups and got me put on the night beat here. Trying to get me to quit the force." Mack could believe that. The slimy McKenna wouldn't want someone as naïve and stalwart as Peter Attwood around. The fact that Peter was a scion of a wealthy banking family would stick in McKenna's craw. He'd be afraid the young Harvard man would tell tales to the brass.

"I met Milly one of the first nights I was down here. She knows all the local families. She helped me make peace on one of the street corners my first night." He took another sip of beer. Mack huffed. Peter ignored him. "We got to meeting when I'd do my rounds. She suggested I take a break at Peabody House. I started doing that and we'd talk. She helped me to see that my demotion wasn't the end of the world."

Peter was much more interested in telling Mack about his girlfriend than in keeping to the topic of how he found the dead man. "Right. So, you were there the night you found Kessler?"

"Yes. I stopped at Peabody House. I had the right to take a break before the end of the night. I left it till late, so I could see her."

"So, when you went into Peabody House, Kessler wasn't lying on the sidewalk across the street. You would have noticed."

Peter looked blank. "No, he wasn't there." He paused, then admitted, "I was a bit preoccupied, though."

Preoccupied? Mack snorted at that one, too. This nincompoop didn't seem to realize the danger he was in. "What time was that?"

Peter was still staring into space. "Time? Must have been ten o'clock. Yes, ten. I knew I could see Milly then, and I had something important to say to her." He shook his head sadly.

Mack plunged on. "How long were you in there?"

"I'm not sure. I met Milly in the big office on the first floor. She went out to make me a cup of tea. It seemed like a long time, but that's probably because I was nervous."

"Nervous? Why?"

Peter's face reddened. "I had something important to say, and I was preparing myself for it. Anyway, she finally came back. She was standing in the doorway, the light shining behind her like a halo."

"Right. Did you have your say then? When did you leave?"

Peter collapsed like a balloon. "No, I didn't get to talk to her. A little newsboy ran in and said someone was dead across the street. Of course, he wasn't dead, just drunk. I ran out and found Mr. Kessler. He smelled of whiskey, I swear it. I never got to ask Milly."

"Ask her what?" Mack was exasperated.

"I was going to ask her to marry me."

Chapter Eleven

After the funeral, Holly Attwood was at a loss. She wished she could do something to support Rachel Kessler, but she felt shut out by the foreign customs of Rachel's community. She took the ferry back with the formidable Miss Goldstein and visited the West End branch of the library with her. Holly had research to do for her woodworking, so she often spent time at the library. The building had been a church with high ceilings and portraits of Protestant ministers still hanging on the walls. It kept the hushed quiet and white walls of a church.

When Holly sat down at one of the wide wooden tables, Miss Goldstein kindly brought her a pamphlet about Jewish mourning customs. Holly was a bit afraid of the librarian. Although she was probably only about thirty years old, she had the aplomb of a much older woman. Holly thought even her father would be impressed. She was a friend to Rachel Kessler, although Holly had never met her before

Holly was ashamed at how little she knew about her Jewish colleague, Rachel. They were both apprenticed to the carpenter, Margaret Nichols Shurcliff. Holly's grandmother was a great friend of Rose Nichols, Mrs. Shurcliff's older sister. Miss Nichols was a Beacon Hill activist who also had a business as a landscape architect. Holly was excited to meet women of her own background who managed to establish professional careers.

She didn't know how Rachel had met Mrs. Shurcliff, but the energetic woodworking master was also active in political matters and taught immigrants the practical skills of carpentry in the North and West Ends. Perhaps that was how Rachel had met the entrepreneur, who was also a wife and mother. Holly rued the fact that she didn't know. She hadn't cared enough to find out.

She'd only cared for Rachel's enthusiasm and skills in woodworking. Together, they'd worked on carving and finishing tables, chairs and boxes in the Early American style that was so popular at the moment. They'd researched the work of early cabinetmakers and imitated their decorations.

Setting aside the pamphlet on Jewish customs, Holly retrieved some of the illustrated manuals and continued the research she'd begun with Rachel. She soon lost herself in the charts and illustrations of earlier master carpenters. Miss Goldstein had to tap her on the shoulder at closing time.

Exiting into the waning sunshine and soft breezes of the June afternoon, Holly climbed the back of Beacon Hill on Joy Street. She passed the police station and jail where Mr. Kessler had died. She wondered if Peter was there, but she hurried on. Poor Peter. If only he'd seen that Mr. Kessler was ill, perhaps Rachel's father might have been saved.

She walked up the steep street, crowded with tenements and crowds speaking Yiddish or Italian on alternating corners. At the top, the noise and smells retreated, and she entered the rarified air of the Brahmin side of Beacon Hill. Behind the statehouse, she turned down Mount Vernon, where proud single-family townhouses had tiny gardens with flowering trees. She walked by several standalone mansions and turned into Louisburg Square, where her father's townhouse faced her grandmother's across a small green park with flowering dogwood and lilac bushes. She'd crossed over into a world away from the grime of the West End.

Up the steep gray stone steps, she stepped into the foyer. The door to her father's study on the right was closed, but she winced at her father's loud, angry voice.

"...if you think I'm going to put up with your arrogant refusal to heed my advice, you are sorely mistaken. I told you this fantasy of yours to wear a badge and a gun is below you. You should have finished your degree at Harvard. Your brother has. Why can't you? Your brother prospers in the banking business that has been in our family for half a century. While you're a disgrace to the family name."

Holly heard a murmur. Peter. It had to be Peter, facing off with her father yet again. She had an impulse to throw the door open and rush in to come between them. Peter was so easily cowed by their father. She wanted to show Peter how to stand up to him when he was in his Rupert Attwood III tyrant mode. But she stopped herself. She'd only make it worse. When *she* defied her father's demands, he was nonplussed. He didn't know what to do simply because she was a woman. In dealing with her, she knew that he felt at a loss without his wife. It irked him that her grandmother encouraged defiance. Holly's attempts to defend Peter were never successful. When her father got frustrated in dealing with her, he came down even harder on Peter. So, she crept up the stairs and sat on the top, waiting for the outcome.

Whatever mild protests Peter came up with didn't make an impression. She heard her father again, "You admit now not only did you join the police force against my express wishes, but now you've been demoted and expelled. Do you see what a disgrace you are? You make me a laughingstock at my clubs. My son the failed policeman. Policeman! Never has anyone in our family stooped so low, and you can't even do that menial job competently. You're a stain on my honor. I won't have it. You'll resign immediately, and I'll see if I can get a place for you at Harvard. You'll finish your studies and take whatever position I can find for you. Those are my terms. Obey me in this or get out of my house!"

Holly half rose, thinking to interrupt the argument before Peter did something irreversible. She was too late. Peter slammed open the door. Looking back at his father, he said, "I'm suspended, not expelled. This isn't academia. I've been accused of something, and with or without you, I'll prove my innocence. I'm a grown man. You don't get to tell me what to do. Don't you understand? I don't need you. You want to keep me on a leash. I'm your son, not your dog."

He glanced up as he headed for the front door. When he saw Holly, he shrugged, but he didn't stop. He threw open the shiny black door and jumped down the stone steps as it slammed behind him.

Chapter Twelve

The next morning, Fanny greeted Holly Attwood and Milly Greene at Cornelia Thornwell's house on Beacon Hill, where Fanny was staying. In addition to being Fanny's dear friend, Cornelia was the grandmother of Peter and Holly.

The women planned to visit the Kessler family. Holly told them Peter was suspended from the police force and had stomped out of the family home. Fanny knew her friend, Cornelia, would welcome her grandson if he needed to get away from his father. She'd make sure Cornelia knew of the problem when she returned. Holly was worried about her brother.

"I hope Rachel doesn't believe Peter hurt her father. My brother would never do that, but I think that's why he was suspended. Maybe I shouldn't go today," Holly said.

"I'm sure Rachel won't blame you for your brother's actions," Milly said. Fanny wondered if the petite blonde believed Peter was guilty.

Holly looked appalled. "But he didn't do anything," she protested.

"I think Miss Kessler will understand that you only want to pay respect to her dead father," Fanny said.

Holly carried a hamper of food. "Miss Goldstein suggested what to bring," Holly explained. "The Kesslers live on Phillips Street. It's not far."

They walked up a block, then turned down the north slope of the hill. Fanny noticed the change in atmosphere as they walked the two blocks to Phillips Street. The Kessler's had the second floor of a well-maintained brownstone. Opposite were storefronts for a kosher meat market, a barber, and a haberdashery. Tenements loomed over the streets that descended the back of the hill, with laundry strung on the fire escapes. Children swarmed in the streets. It was a warm June day.

On the second floor, a door was propped open. Inside, it was dark, with only a few lights on. Rachel and her brother, Bernard, sat on a sofa with their backs to the door. Around them sat other women weeping softly. A large candle glowed on a low table. Miss Goldstein peeked out from the kitchen in the rear and beckoned. They followed her into the small room. "Thank you for coming. Here, let me take that." She relieved Holly of the basket, unpacking the goods.

Fanny was completely unsure of the etiquette for this occasion. "Should we go in and speak to Miss Kessler and her brother?" She stood in the doorway where she could look into the parlor.

Miss Goldstein came over to her. "Yes. In a moment. You don't need to stay long." She turned back to the women huddled in the kitchen, speaking softly. "You'll see that Rachel and Bernie wear torn clothes. That's traditional. As is the candle in front of them. Your being here will be a comfort to Rachel. Don't worry."

At that moment, a young man joined them. He wore a beard and sideburns. Fanny noticed that Miss Goldstein's eyebrows rose at the interruption. She introduced him as Leonard Abrams, who worked with Rachel's dead father. Fanny thought he was a bit officious.

"I'm engaged to Miss Kessler," he told them. Miss Goldstein turned away to stow the unpacked goods from Holly's basket, as if to ignore him. Holly looked surprised. "May I ask who you are," he said.

Milly introduced them and told him that Holly worked with Rachel at the woodworking class at Peabody House. He nodded as if to reassure them that he was familiar with every part of Rachel's life. "So good of you to come."

Another young man appeared in the doorway behind Abrams. "Excuse me, can I leave this?" He was of medium height with dark curling hair cut short. He wore a crisp white shirt and a dark tie. Compared to Abrams, he was quite handsome. And very quiet. Fanny noticed both he and Leonard Abrams wore black silk skull caps.

Miss Goldstein greeted him warmly, taking the bag of bread and introducing him as Mr. Ari Zellman. Fanny noticed Leonard Abrams stiffen. They weren't friends, it seemed.

"Mr. Zellman works at the West End House," Miss Goldstein said. "He's a friend of Rachel's brother. West End House is another settlement like Peabody House."

Milly Greene obviously knew Zellman. They nodded to each other, but Fanny thought the atmosphere was a bit chilly. It was getting crowded, so Fanny suggested they give Rachel their condolences.

In the parlor, Holly, Milly, and Fanny each quietly expressed their sorrow at Mr. Kessler's death. Rachel didn't rise from the sofa. She and her brother wore jackets that had been torn in big slits. Rachel's eyes were full of tears. Bernard ignored the women. He seemed entranced by the flame of the candle on the low table in front of them. He was a thin young man with straight black hair hanging down into his face.

As Rachel reached out to thank each of the women with a handshake, Fanny noticed the blanket strung across what she guessed was a large gilt-framed mirror on the opposite walls. The room was cloaked in sadness, but she thought the glow of support from neighbors and friends like Miss Goldstein was also present in the room.

On the street, Holly's eyes were brimming with tears. "Rachel, poor Rachel. What will I do if Peter is found guilty of her father's death?"

Milly took her friend's hands. "Rachel won't blame you." She bit her lip. "Please tell Peter I'm sorry for his troubles. You must get him to make up with your father. I know how proud Peter was of his job in the police. But we have to help him reconcile himself if that career is gone for him." Fanny thought she truly felt bad for Peter.

"He would never harm Mr. Kessler. You know that, Milly, don't you?" Holly said.

"Of course, I know. You know how fond I am of your brother." Fanny saw tears sparkling in the girl's eyes. "I don't think it's right for him to be cut off from his family at a time like this. Please help him to make peace with your father. I can't bear to think of him as alone." She wiped her eyes with the back of a hand. "I have to get to Peabody House now. I'll see you later."

As Milly walked away through the busy streets where peddlers hawked fish and pots, and children ran in and out of doorways. Holly took Fanny's arm. "She's thinking of her own father," she told Fanny. "He hung himself when he went bankrupt. It was terrible for Milly and her brother. I think she's afraid to care for Peter. It's a shame. He's made such a mess of things."

"I'm sure Dr. Magrath will be able to get to the truth of Mr. Kessler's death," Fanny told her. She didn't believe her old friend would abandon Peter, and she was sure he was innocent of the death of Rachel's father. She knew Kessler had died of morphine, not from a beating, but she didn't think it was right to share that information with Holly. She'd have to ask Jake. She changed the subject. "You said you're working with Mrs. Shurcliff on woodworking? I know her older sister, Rose Nichols."

Holly let go of Fanny's elbow and looked up. She seemed happier. "That's right. In fact, I'm heading to the workshop. Want to see it?"

Chapter Thirteen

When Mack arrived at the Grove Street Mortuary that morning, he found Peter asleep on one of the metal tables, curled up under his big policeman's coat. He could hear Edwin clinking glassware in his little laboratory next door. When he asked, Edwin said the body on the table had been there when he arrived that morning. Seeing that it was still warm, he hadn't prepped it for autopsy. Dr. Magrath was due at any moment.

Gallows humor, Mack thought. He perched at his own desk and wrote up his notes from the day before, ignoring snores from the sleeping Brahmin. A door slam at Dr. Magrath's entry woke the suspended policeman, who sat up with a bleary look around the room. Shivering, he hunched down, pulling his coat around him. "What are you doing here, Attwood?" Dr. Magrath asked.

Peter bowed his head. "I'm sorry. You gave me a key last fall when we were working on that investigation in East Boston. I had a fight with my father last night. I couldn't go back there."

Mack thought the medical examiner and his friend Mrs. Lee treated Peter too gently. If the young man was going to make it on the streets of Boston, he needed to be toughened up. It was high time Peter got out of the Beacon Hill house, where he was pampered. Mack wondered if Peter's wealthy banker father was going to use influence to get him reinstated. "Your dad going to have to call someone for you? Get you back on the force?"

Peter bristled. "No. He hates that I joined the police. He demanded I go back to Harvard. I told him I was going to fight the suspension. He laughed."

Peter gulped. "He's expecting me to take the coward's way out. I told him I could be charged with killing the man, and he said I should resign, go back to Harvard, and he'd fix it so I wasn't prosecuted. The nerve of him. I told him I didn't do anything to that man. He didn't care. I told him I had to clear my name. He told me if I didn't do as he said, I should get out of his house. I left." After this impassioned tirade, Peter slumped. "I didn't have anywhere to go, so I came here. Sorry."

Dr. Magrath frowned, pulling off his overcoat. "Well, you can't *stay* here. We only offer overnight accommodations to the dead." It worried Mack that Magrath was still angry about the case. He had hoped the medical examiner would be in a better frame of mind after a sound sleep. It seemed not. Magrath stomped off into his office, where he hung his coat and hat on a coat rack. He came back into the room, pulling a rolling chair with him. Sitting down, he called out, "Edwin!"

Edwin joined them, and Magrath led them through a review of the case. Kessler's body was gone, but the medical examiner hadn't completed his report.

"It's a strange way for a man like Kessler to die," Dr. Magrath said. "Where did he get the morphine? Was it an accident?"

Edwin was willing to speculate. "Perhaps someone who used the drug got into an argument with him and stuck him with the needle by mistake. Although I don't think the needle would go through a wool jacket like that. So, he must have put on the jacket after he got the injection."

Mack tried to imagine how someone could stick a needle into a man by mistake. Seemed unlikely. Maybe if Kessler was trying to stop someone from sticking himself? Magrath was worried about something else.

"Where was he that he removed his jacket then?" Dr. Magrath asked.

"Not the speakeasy. I checked, and it was closed, like the bartender told us," Mack said. "Would he be able to put on his coat and walk away if he had morphine in him?" Mack asked.

"It would start to make him drowsy in five to ten minutes," Dr. Magrath said. "But if he struggled with someone, and they injected him, why would they let him go?"

"Maybe it was an accident, like Edwin said," Mack contributed.

"He stunk of whiskey," Peter insisted, shaking his uncombed head. "I swear to you." He was pigheaded in his belief the man was drunk.

"I know, I know," Dr. Magrath said. "Edwin smelled it too. But it was soaked into the jacket, not in the man's stomach."

"Maybe he was with a drunk," Mack suggested.

"There were bruises on his arms and neck," Dr. Magrath said

Mack saw Peter stand up; he was defensive at the suggestion that he'd roughed up Kessler. Edwin piped up. "Not from a beating, nothing like that."

"He was drunk," Peter said then sunk back down on a stool. The suspended policeman was a stubborn cuss. Bleary from lack of sleep, Mack doubted the kid was paying close attention to the argument. He was just intent on defending himself. Righteous idiot.

Ignoring the grouchy kid, Mack told Dr. Magrath and Edwin that he'd been unable to find any other source of the liquor. Other speakeasies in the area were also closed down that night. Dr. Magrath was more anxious to know where the morphine came from. Was there a doctor involved? Or was it an illegal dose? Mack said he'd check around the neighborhood for a supply.

"Someone must have seen Kessler that night before he died," Mack said. "I'll visit his office, see what they say. And I'll check with people around the corner where he was found. Don't know about the family. They stay home for a week to mourn from what the librarian told us."

Edwin had classes to attend. Dr. Magrath agreed that Mack was the best one to question people in the neighborhood. "You might talk to Miss Greene at the Peabody House as well."

When Mack heard a snore from a dozing Peter, he turned his back to the sleepyhead and quietly told them about how Peter had planned to propose marriage to Mildred Greene that night.

"No wonder he was distracted the night Kessler died," Dr. Magrath said.

Edwin moved close to speak softly. "Maybe he didn't see Mr. Kessler on the ground when he went into the building."

Mack shook his head, and Dr. Magrath looked doubtful. Edwin's face reddened where his skin was clear around his burn scars. "I only say that because I know how I felt—when I proposed to Mrs. Ryan."

Mack slapped him on the back. "About time you did. You've been seeing the widow Ryan for the longest time. Never thought you'd get up the nerve. Good work, man!"

Mack's congratulations woke Peter up. "What?"

Mack turned towards him with a wicked grin. He didn't mind needling the dope. "Edwin popped the question. He asked Theresa Ryan to marry him, and she said…" He gestured to Edwin.

"She said yes," he admitted.

Peter's face fell. He stared. "Congratulations," he finally mumbled.

Mack thought he was a real spoilsport. "Come on," he said loudly. Peter winced. "You're no use to anyone like this. You can come back to my room and get some shuteye." Mack looked at Edwin. "Mrs. O'Reilly won't mind, will she?" Mack was grateful to Edwin for getting him a room. He didn't want to upset his landlady just when he was getting settled.

"I don't think so," Edwin said.

"Get up." Mack grabbed Peter by the shoulder. "Get your boots on. Time to move."

Chapter Fourteen

anny struggled to keep up with the long-legged Holly Attwood as they climbed the back of Beacon Hill. They were heading to the woodworking shop of Holly's mentor, Mrs. Margaret Shurcliff. After escaping the heavy sorrow of the Kessler apartment, Fanny was glad to feel the soft spring air. She had never attended a Jewish home in mourning before. Her parents had Jewish friends, especially among the musicians they knew, but they kept their religious practice private. She'd found the grieving in the Kessler home moved her to the brink of tears, with a stone weight on her breast. In the mild air, she felt she could breathe again.

Fanny wanted to cheer up Holly. The young woman was pained by her friend Rachel's loss and worried about her brother Peter. Amazing how concentration on a task like woodworking for Holly or death investigation for Fanny could relieve you of the anxieties of life. Fanny knew that being able to act, to do something positive was the best way to counteract the feeling that you were being shoved around by powers over which you had no control. There was nothing Holly could do about the death of Rachel's father or Peter's suspension from the police force.

Fanny followed Holly to a brick townhouse with dark green trim on Mount Vernon Street. It sat halfway up the hill, not far from the Attwood home on Louisburg Square. They rang the bell, and a young woman opened the door. Holly introduced her to Fanny as one of Margaret Shurcliff's daughters. Despite her friendship with Rose Nichols, Fanny had not met the youngest of the Nichols sisters. She knew Margaret had six children in addition to her thriving business and her political activities.

"Mother's upstairs," the girl said. "Come on." She started up the steep staircase.

"The workroom is in the attic," Holly said. "Margaret and two other women have a company called the 'Pegleggers.' Rachel and I are apprentices. We make reproductions of American Colonial style furniture." Holly was proud of her connection to the firm.

"Colonial style is popular in the antiques business, too," Fanny said. "My daughter and I have started a shop in New Hampshire. We motor around finding old pieces of furniture to buy and sell to people who like the style." Fanny's daughter was enthusiastic about the antiques business, like Holly was about her woodworking. Fanny was glad this younger generation of women were seeking out ways to live their lives with a purpose that went beyond being a wife and mother. That had never been enough for Fanny herself. It made her wonder about Rachel Kessler. She seemed to want to pursue a profession like Margaret Shurcliff, yet her father apparently had engaged her to a young man from their Orthodox community. Fanny wondered how Rachel planned to reconcile the constraints of her culture with the profession she wanted to follow. It would be a difficult road.

They stopped on the first floor, where several trunks lay open around the parlor. Margaret Shurcliff, a tall, rangy woman, was wiping a stray lock of hair from her eyes as she spoke to the young boy before her. "Well, you'll have to choose. You can take some of your books, but you must fit in your bathing costume and plenty of shirts and pants. We'll be in Ipswich all summer, and I'm not sending back for more clothes. It's your choice." She saw Fanny and Holly in the doorway. "Holly, I'm glad you're here. I have some things to go over with you."

Holly introduced Fanny.

"Sorry for the mess. We're packing for the move to our summer home on the north shore. But come upstairs, and we'll show you the workshop." She looked at her son as if to say, "your choice." From her own experience moving her three children from Chicago to New Hampshire every summer, Fanny understood the effort it took. She shivered at the thought of twice as many offspring to transport.

Margaret led them up three more flights. At the top of the house was a woodworking shop with tools hung neatly on the wall and stacks of wood in various sizes. The wide room smelled of pine and varnish. A solid bench sat in one corner, varnish drying. Margaret pointed at it, talking to Holly. "Movers will come next week for that piece. The Warners of Pinckney Street ordered it, and we promised to have it delivered before summer."

Holly grinned. "I can be here if you give me the details." She picked up a card from the desk at the top of the stairs and turned to Fanny. "We get commissions from all over the city, but mostly on Beacon Hill where Colonial American style is all the fashion these days." Fanny could see that Holly took a proprietary interest in the firm. Not many women ran their own businesses. Mr. Shurcliff must be a big supporter of the enterprise since it took up a whole floor of their family home.

She looked at the business card. It read "'PEGLEGGERS' Makers of BENCHES AND TRESTLE TABLES OF PINE, Carpentry Shop at 66 Mount Vernon Street Boston." It named the three women owners and gave a telephone number.

While Holly consulted with her employer, Fanny looked around. It was an impressive space with another table in progress and plans for more spread out on the desk. A couple of hard chairs were set against the walls. There was a skylight partly open on this warm day and dormer windows at regular intervals. Fanny couldn't help thinking the workshop would be a perfect place to build the type of miniatures she'd created in the past. She'd started with a miniature orchestra as a present for her parents, but she'd recently used miniatures to recreate crime scenes. She wondered if Holly would be interested in working on that kind of reconstruction.

"The invoices are on the desk," Margaret told Holly. "You're welcome to come in and do some work on your projects while we're away. I'll be back every couple of weeks to check on things. And thank you so much for watering the plants downstairs, otherwise they'd go thirsty. I'd ask my sisters, but Rose is travelling, and Marion is planning to run a political campaign. Would you believe it? Women will actually get to vote this year. We're just waiting for final ratification. It should come by the end of August, and my sister plans to run as an Independent for Ward 8! We'll be back in time for that in the fall."

"It's no problem," Holly assured her.

"There's one more thing." Margaret looked distracted. "I heard the awful news about Mr. Kessler. I plan to visit the family tomorrow and bring some food, as I know that's the custom in Jewish houses. But there's something else. Over here." She led the way to a back corner and opened a closet door. Inside were two carpet bags and a few frocks and coats on hangers. Margaret bit her lip. "Rachel asked me if she could leave some things here. Of course, I said she could. I think she was smuggling things out of her home, bit by bit. I imagine she was trying to hide the fact." Margaret's brow was furrowed as she looked at Holly, who also seemed disturbed. "I think Rachel was planning to run away," Margaret said.

Chapter Fifteen

Mack hustled Peter along a crowded Blossom Street. They had to push their way around a peddler's cart. Crowds of boys at each corner scattered at Mack's hulk. When any young tough dared to stare him in the eye, Mack stared right back and put out a big paw to move the body out of his way.

There was a pharmacy on the ground floor of the building where Mack and Edwin had rooms. In a doorway set back into the wall, a thin Negro with some gray in his curly hair stood watching. Mack knew he worked as a night janitor. He wore overalls and a sleeveless undershirt. Mack thought he must be chilly in the shadows of this otherwise warm afternoon. There was a breeze from the river when you were out of the sun. Usually, Mr. Johnson wore a brown jacket and a plaid cap. He wasn't chewing on the curved pipe that habitually hung from his mouth, either.

"Nice day," Mack nodded. He grabbed Peter by the collar. "Got a stray here in need of a bed. I'm thinkin' Mrs. O'Reilly won't mind if I take him in for a night or two." Mack wasn't sure about that. One reason he stopped to talk to Johnson was that he knew the older man kept an eye on the comings and goings in the building. It was a mix of people, with Johnson's family of six children in the attic, a Polish couple with two sons and a grandmother below, with Irish Mrs. O'Reilly and an Italian lady on the second floor. Mack often heard the Italian lady yell down to call children home at dinner time. He'd also noticed that Johnson was quiet but never missed a thing going on in the building.

"Reckon she'll mother him," Johnson said.

"You stopped smoking?" Mack was curious.

"Pipe got lost. Haven't replaced it yet."

Mack felt a pang of sympathy. Poor guy was wanting a quiet smoke before trudging off to work for the night. Must be hankering for the tobacco, though Mack didn't know how he could lose the pipe he was so fond of. Yet, looking around at the hubbub of the streets, anything could happen. He took a cigar from an inner pocket and offered it to Johnson. With a look of surprise, Johnson took it.

As Mack pushed Peter up the stairs to his room on the second floor, he reflected that his Negro neighbor was a good man to cultivate. He obviously knew a lot of what went on in the area He'd be a good source for gossip.

Edwin had a room in the second-floor apartment, and he'd gotten his landlady to rent Mack the second bedroom. Mack figured he could stash the exhausted patrolman there for the time being. He tossed Peter on his narrow bed, pulling off the kid's boots to protect Mrs. O'Reilly's quilt. He warned Peter he'd get the floor when Mack came back for the night. Peter just groaned and rolled over.

Mack shut the door and hurried back downstairs. He joined Johnson, pulling out a cigar for himself, biting off the end, and spitting it to the ground. Johnson made room for him to lean against the wall side by side.

"Something I wanted to ask you," Mack said. "You ever hear of anybody using morphine around here?" Mack knew morphine and heroine could be found in some of the Negro dives in the South End. He didn't know about the West End.

Johnson puffed out a cloud of smoke. "Bad stuff. Awful stuff. Somebody's putting it about. Sellin' it to people for next to nothing to get them started, then raising the price." He shook his head. "Really nasty. I know a guy lost his wife, his job, everything, chasing the demon."

"Where's it coming from?"

Johnson huffed. "They sellin' to Negroes in the clubs. But it ain't Negroes makin' money off it."

"Who then?"

Johnson puffed his cigar and turned to look Mack up and down. "You police?"

Mack grimaced. "Not since the strike. The bastards cut me off. I work for the medical examiner, Magrath."

"Hmm." Johnson looked away. "You heard of King Solomon?"

"Charles Solomon. Yeah. Gangster. You saying he's the one selling the stuff?" Mack knew Solomon ran a Jewish gang on a par with the Italians in the North End and the Gustin Gang in South Boston. It made sense he'd be a power in the West End, where so many Jewish immigrants had moved in.

Johnson grunted. "Distributing. He's got others on the hook who sell for him."

"Any idea where I could find him these days?" Mack asked.

Johnson raised his eyebrows. "You want to find him? Not lookin' to buy some, are you? Go lookin' for gangsters you can end up dead, you know."

"Not me," Mack said. "Don't worry. I ain't crazy."

Johnson shook his head again. "Hear he hangs out at the speakeasy on Causeway. Big fancy place. One fifty-three. You can't miss it."

Mack stubbed out his cigar on the brick wall. "Thanks."

"You take care now," Johnson said.

Chapter Sixteen

Mack went to the Shapiro Building on Causeway. He needed to check out Kessler's office before the end of the working day. After reading the board in the foyer, he took the elevator to the fifth floor and followed signs to the jewelers. The glass door, with "Kessler Jewelers" in gold script, was open. Inside, a young man in shirtsleeves and a black fedora was bent over a counter.

"Are you Mr. Kessler?" Mack asked as he strolled in. He was thinking this must be the son, Bernard Kessler.

The young man stood up. Mack recognized him from the meeting with Lomasney. He was the interpreter for the group of Jewish men who had complained. He had a full beard, long sideburns, dark hair, and eyes. He was slight, a foot shorter than the big Irishman. "Mr. Kessler has sadly passed away. I'm his associate, Leonard Abrams." He squinted. "Have we met before?"

Mack hadn't spoken at the meeting. "I was at the Hendricks Club."

"Yes. I remember. You were with Dr. Magrath. He promised the man responsible would be punished. Mr. Kessler is a great loss."

Mack looked around. "Are you taking over the business, then? Isn't there a son?"

Abrams flushed. He looked quite young, barely twenty. "Bernard is in mourning. He won't leave his house for a week. It's our custom. In any case, Bernard was not employed in the business. I was working with Mr. Kessler, and I am engaged to his daughter, Rachel."

He said it as if he could hardly believe it himself. Having seen Miss Rachel

Kessler, Mack was of the opinion she far outclassed the weak young man before him. But that was none of his business.

"Lennie, dear, this room is full of dust. You must get a cleaner in. Right away." A woman bustled through an open door on the left. She was older, wearing a taffeta dress that made a swishing noise with every move. Her square, lined face was surrounded by unnaturally black curls and on her head sat a black hat with a sharp feather. She wore what looked like dead foxes biting each other over her shoulders. Mack knew it was a fashion, but seeing little black eyes on the fur wrap made him want to shiver. "Who are you?" she demanded. "The shop is not open. Mr. Kessler has died."

Mack introduced himself as an investigator for the medical examiner. Before Abrams could speak, the woman expressed her outrage. "Investigator! And what is it you investigate? Is it not enough the poor man is dragged to a cell and left to die? Do you wish to blacken his name? My son will not put up with it. He will marry into the family, as poor dead Isaac would have wished. He will defend the name. Morphine! I heard the accusations. You should be ashamed of yourself."

"This is my mother," Abrams said unnecessarily.

"We want to find out what caused Mr. Kessler's death," Mack explained. He recognized the storm of feminine wrath. His sister would have acted out the same way if one of his brothers had died as Kessler had. Mack took a chance and turned to the young man. "Mr. Abrams, when did you last see Mr. Kessler? Was he at work the day he died?"

"Yes, he was," Abrams rushed to answer before his mother could interrupt. He waved gently at her. She frowned but shut her mouth. "He was here until four o'clock. Then he said he had business to attend to. He was upset about something." Abrams pursed his lips as if trying to picture Kessler on that last day. "He didn't say what it was about or where he was going." He looked away.

Mack sensed the young man wasn't telling him everything. He wondered if the presence of his mother was the reason. "Had anything happened that day, or recently, that was a problem or out of the ordinary?"

Abrams was about to murmur "no" when Mrs. Abrams piped up. "He was robbed! The police did nothing! The robbers took money. They tried to get into the safe, but they just dented it. Look here." She backed up and pointed to a large iron safe against the wall. It had a big dent. Mack imagined some huge hammer must have been banged against it. That would make a loud noise. Must have been frustrating for the robber. Probably got mad and tried to clobber the thing.

Abrams jumped back from the counter, as if to block Mack from seeing the safe. He was sweating. "That was a week ago. They tried the offices next door and downstairs, too. The diamonds were in the safe, though. We lost some cash but not much. It's not as if someone was trying to do something to Mr. Kessler, everybody in the building was robbed. Well, not everybody. The police were coming for a fight on the street, the thieves heard the sirens and ran off. They almost got caught. It can't have anything to do with Mr. Kessler's death."

"Nonsense," his mother said. Mack could see the young man was used to being contradicted by his mother. Mack sensed she couldn't help herself. Whatever he said, she'd refute just on principle. He felt sorry for Abrams. "He could have figured out who it was. How did they know when to come, how to get in? It must be someone who knows the place." She raised a hand and shook a finger in Mack's direction. "Mr. Kessler was a very smart man. He could have figured it out."

Abrams sighed. "It happened at night. Anybody would know the office would be empty."

She shook her head. "Mr. Kessler figured it out."

Mack held up a hand. He'd be here all day if he let them continue. "Mr. Abrams," he spoke loudly. "Did anything else happen that day? And did Mr. Kessler have any enemies?"

"Enemies!" Mrs. Abrams shouted. "He was a fine man, a fine upstanding man. Where do you get these enemies? Of course not. He kept the sabbath, went to the Vilna Shul. He was a good man."

"Mother, please! No. Mr. Kessler had no enemies." He frowned. "There was one thing happened that day." Abrams glanced at his mother. "Mr. Kessler—he agreed that his daughter Rachel and I could be married next month. He told me that day."

"YES!" His mother jumped toward him and gave him a hug. "Finally. You see? I told you. He was a good man, Mr. Kessler, a very good man." She gave Abrams a kiss on the cheek. "My boy!" She continued on in Yiddish that Mack didn't understand.

Mack was at a loss. "Congratulations," he said and backed toward the door. "If there's nothing else you can tell me, I want to interview the other offices that were robbed." He grabbed the handle and hurried out the door, shutting it behind him while Mrs. Abrams continued to lecture her son in Yiddish.

Wiping his brow with a handkerchief, Mack turned to the next office. It was a real estate firm. The man in charge described the burglary for him, saying the thieves had gotten only some spare cash from a drawer. Unlike the jewelers, it wasn't the type of business to store valuables on hand.

Mack visited four more offices where safes had been wrecked but not opened. At the Wanda Import and Export company, which dealt in shoes, two pairs of shoes had been stolen and a hole was bored into the safe. Mack figured the thieves weren't professionals. They'd totally bungled the job. It looked like a pickax had been used on the safes.

He left convinced that Mr. Kessler had no enemies and that the fumbled burglaries had nothing to do with his death.

Chapter Seventeen

Fanny entered the North Grove Street Mortuary. The door had been left unlocked. She didn't see Edwin or hear him in his laboratory, so she continued to Jake's office. She heard him grumbling under his breath as she stood in the doorway.

He looked up. "Fanny. We're going to dinner, aren't we?" He continued to read a typed letter he grasped in his hand. "What a bunch of lily-livered bastards." He crushed the paper and tossed it into a metal basket. "Excuse my language."

"Who's it from?"

"Harvard, those snotty sons of bitches."

Fanny was used to Jake's swearing. She ignored it. "Is it about the Legal Medicine courses?" she asked.

"They have no concept of what is lacking. I offered to make the study at Harvard Medical School the best in the world. Nowhere else in the country is scientific medicine applied to the use of the law. The low status of medical jurisprudence and lack of instruction is appalling. Doctors don't recognize signs of illegal practices or unnatural deaths. Police have no respect for the need to preserve evidence. Prosecutors and judges are ignorant. The use of politically elected coroners ensures that no professional advice will be sought out."

Fanny didn't dare interrupt. She guessed he was quoting from his own letter to Harvard. He had that kind of memory that would allow him to repeat it word for word. She sat down in one of the chairs facing him across the desk.

"I've spent years instilling fear of the Lord in local law enforcement so they know to leave the body be until it can be examined in situ. I've used the careful presentation of scientific evidence to educate juries and judges. Still, they prosecute or ignore crimes based on biased assumptions all the time. It's a disgrace. And here I am offering the august institution of Harvard the opportunity to bring science to the table for the sake of justice and they turn up their snotty noses. What a bunch of ninnies."

Fanny completely agreed with Jake. The Harvard authorities were short sighted to refuse Jake's offer to establish a course of study for medical jurisprudence. She knew it was a huge frustration for him to be ignored like this. She had hoped success in a few famous cases would promote Jake's ideas. His scientific approach had solved several murders in the past. The newspapers always praised his contributions, but the police were skeptical. She had pinned her hopes on Peter. If Jake trained Harvard educated Peter Attwood to solve crimes the correct way, the authorities would have to see that his methods were the best. But, so far, Peter's achievements had only led to jealousy and backstabbing. Now, the young police detective was suspended and suspected of negligence in the death of Mr. Kessler.

They heard loud pounding on the front door.

"What the hell," Jake grumbled, rising.

Before he could get out of his office, several men marched into the autopsy room. Fanny and Jake joined them in the big cold room. Captain McKenna, wearing his bowler hat, was in the lead. "Where's Attwood?" he demanded.

"Attwood," Jake said, "I don't know. He doesn't work here. He works for you."

"He's not at his home, at least according to the servants." McKenna peered around as if looking for Peter in a shadowy corner. One of his men opened the door to Edwin's laboratory.

"Stay out of there, or you'll break something," Jake said. He walked over and closed the door firmly. Turning to McKenna, he frowned. "I don't know where Detective Attwood is, so go look somewhere else. What do you want him for anyhow?"

"Patrolman Attwood. We've got some questions about Kessler's death. We got your autopsy report. You say he died from morphine poisoning." The man sneered at Jake.

"That's correct. I don't think Patrolman Attwood poisoned him. It would have happened sometime before he was found."

"How do you know that?" McKenna put his hands on his hips and glared at Jake. "I've got City Hall on my back. Kessler was a big shot with the Jewish businessmen. They're mad about this morphine thing. Don't want to believe it. We know there's drugs being sold in the West End, but Lomasney's Jewish friends are insisting, no, it couldn't be here. Kessler was a saint. No way he was taking morphine. You certainly mucked things up with your report. Why couldn't you just say he fell down drunk and hit his head?"

Jake was furious. "Mucked things up? Got the truth out is what it is. He wasn't drunk. There was no alcohol in his system. That might be the easy answer for you, but it's a lie. He died from an overdose of morphine. He or someone else injected it in his arm. It's all in my report, so stop trying to explain away the facts."

McKenna's eyes narrowed. "Well, in that case, it was Attwood's neglect that got him killed. He said the guy was drunk, and he threw him in the tank. Have it your way, morphine killed him, but Attwood's responsible, and I'm going to get a warrant for his arrest. He can't hide from me. I'll find him." He looked around. "Come on, boys. He's not here." McKenna stomped off, followed by his men.

"Do you know where Peter is?" Fanny asked. "His sister said he had an argument with his father and left the house."

Jake turned back to his office. "He slept on one of the tables last night, but I don't know where he is now."

"Shouldn't we warn him that McKenna plans to get a warrant for his arrest?"

Jake marched into his office. Fanny sensed a wave of anger in his hunched back.

"What's the use? Why bother? The facts of the matter have nothing to do with how Chief of Detectives McKenna will proceed. He'll find Attwood and arrest him, convict him, and wipe his hands of the matter. I've had it with the incompetence, the ignorance, the downright corruption of the system. I'm done." He picked up an envelope and waved it at her. "Do you know what this is? This is my resignation. I'm done with all of this."

Oh no. Fanny knew Jake was frustrated, but she'd never considered he might take the drastic step of resigning. She felt her stomach plummet. Selfishly, she hated the idea that her involvement with death investigations was bound to end if Jake resigned. She was shocked into silence.

Jake dropped the envelope onto his desk. "Let's go to dinner. I could use a whiskey."

"There's something I wanted to tell you," Fanny said as he reached for his jacket. If she could get him to want to know what really happened to Isaac Kessler, she hoped she could keep him from mailing that letter. "I think Rachel Kessler planned to run away before her father died."

Chapter Eighteen

At eight in the evening, Peter was rudely awakened. Apparently, Mack had spent the afternoon roaming the West End looking for signs of morphine sales, before returning to his room to roust Peter.

"Come on. Up and at 'em. We've got things to do after a bite and a drink," he said.

Peter groaned. He sat up and rubbed his face. "I have to go and see Milly," he said. "I have to explain to her."

Mack grunted. "No, you don't. You're coming with me."

Peter was bleary-eyed. "Where?"

"We're going to a party, come on." Mack grabbed his collar and pulled him to his feet.

Peter sighed. He didn't much feel like partying, but he needed to keep Mack sweet, or he wouldn't have a place to stay. In his current predicament, he couldn't be too choosy.

After a meal of meat and potatoes at a local chophouse favored by Mack, Peter followed the big ex-policeman down Causeway Street. Mack turned into an alley across the street from the triumphal arch of North Station. He pounded on a black door and murmured something. Peter heard the latch open and followed Mack down a steep staircase. At the bottom, a big space was filled with lights, music, noise, and dancing.

"Club Garden," Mack muttered.

Peter was impressed. There was a fifty-foot-long bar on one side and small tables on the other. A jazz band played in the rear, with a small dance floor in front. All over the white tiled walls pictures of silhouettes hung. They depicted men in black tie and tails with women in flapper dresses. Shelves behind the bar held bottles of liquor, and the bartender drew fresh beer from kegs mounted against the wall. You'd never know prohibition was the law.

Mack glanced around. He was looking for someone in particular. Peter saw him raise a hand to a man and trot over to talk to him. Meanwhile, Peter spotted a couple of girls he knew sitting at the bar. They were classmates of his sister who'd had "coming out" parties the same time as Holly. Gone were the long gloves and silk ball gowns now. They wore short, sparkly dresses and headbands. Peter was shocked. What happened to them? He thought of Holly and Milly in their low-waisted dresses that were a lot shorter than they used to be, but nothing like this. The girls' legs crossed on the bar stools showed off calves and thighs. They wore sharply pointed high heels and looked like something out of Hollywood. One of the women smoked a cigarette in a long holder.

Peter couldn't ignore their eager beckoning of fingers with blood-red nails. He drifted over to them. Hovering, unsure of himself, he accepted a cocktail glass.

"Gin Rickey," the girl with a dark bob said as she passed it to him. "Peter, so nice to see you. How's Holly these days?"

Peter gulped a mouthful of gin that tasted the way gasoline smelled. He coughed. "She's fine. She's doing woodworking."

The women oohed and ahhed, squealing with fake delight. Peter thought the reaction had more to do with the amount of alcohol they'd imbibed than any real affection for his sister. He tried to tamp down his automatic disapproval. He knew Holly and Milly would never be found in a place like this. At least, he thought they wouldn't. Of course, he'd never have thought to meet these classmates here, either.

Before he could gulp another shot of the vile-tasting mixture, he felt a clap on his back that nearly plunged him into the lap of the nearest girl.

"I see you found playmates," Mack said loudly enough to be heard above the saxophone and piano music. "No time for that. Sorry ladies, I'm going to have to take this boy away now." He grabbed Peter's elbow and drew him through the crowd toward the dance floor. Peter knew it would be useless to resist.

Mack stopped at a round table with three couples. The men wore tuxedos, while the women wore skimpy but expensive-looking dresses. They were all smoking and drinking. A bottle of real Jameson Whiskey sat on the table.

"Mr. Solomon. I hear you're the local supplier for morphine and heroin these days. Could we have a moment?" Mack grinned at the man.

He was slick-looking. He had slightly wavy hair that had been creamed. His crisp white shirt peeked out from a jacket with shiny lapels. He wore a boutonniere on his left breast, and his tuxedo tie was black silk. He held a lit cigar in one hand and cupped a glass in the other. He lifted an eyebrow at Mack's approach but didn't seem to be disturbed.

Two black coated men who'd been leaning on a wall came up behind Mack, right hands stuck into their pockets. Oops. Guns. Peter regretted following the big Irishman tonight. Not as if he really had another option, of course. Still…

Solomon waved away his guards and nodded to the next table. "Pull up a chair," he told Mack. Another black coat with a hand in his pocket got up and shoved the chair at Mack. Peter tried to sink into the background. "You police?" Solomon asked. "I know several deputy chiefs." When he smiled his teeth were so white they dazzled. Peter thought of a vampire book his sister had got him to read.

"Not me," Mack smiled. "I work for Dr. Magrath." He extended a hand. "Michael McNally, call me Mack."

"Ah, the Medical Examiner. That's interesting." Solomon waved his cigar at the other men at his table. This is State Representative Logan and Captain Long. The captain sails boats down to Central America." Solomon's smile made Peter think of the spider luring the fly.

"Interesting," Mack said. "But I'm not talking about rum. It's morphine I'm seeking. You see, a Mr. Kessler was found lying on the ground dead from morphine. Rumor has it you're the man to see about drugs."

Peter's head was still a little foggy, and the drink the girls gave him hadn't helped to clear his mind. It took him a minute to realize Mack was accusing

Solomon of rum-running as well as selling drugs. Peter looked at the next table full of armed men and swallowed. Nothing like an evening out with Mack. He wondered if he'd ever be able to explain himself to Milly Greene now.

Solomon sat back and took a drag on his cigar. "Kessler," he repeated. "Don't think we're acquainted." Peter thought there was a gleam in the gangster's eye. Perhaps he did know the dead man.

Mack pursed his lips. "Hmm. You might not know him personally, I suppose. But do you perhaps know someone who might make morphine available to him?"

Solomon raised his hands to protest his innocence. "Of course not." He flashed the white teeth again.

Mack looked up at the ceiling. "Well, now, I'm not police, but poor Mr. Kessler died in the Joy Street lockup, and those boys were embarrassed. I'd guess they might get a signal from above to crack down on morphine, don't you know." He lowered his head to smile at Solomon. "Can't say that'd be in your interest now, would it?"

Solomon laughed. Peter didn't. Considering that McKenna was out for his scalp, he knew Mack was bluffing. What if Solomon knew, too? Peter clamped his mouth shut and held his breath.

But Solomon seemed to find Mack amusing. He smiled at his companions. "You're quite a persistent fellow, aren't you 'Mack'? Tell you what, maybe I *can* help you. I've heard a rumor that folks have been frequenting the West End House down there for their needs. Not that I know anything, you understand, but as a concerned citizen, we can't be finding men dropping on the sidewalks from drugs, now, can we?"

Peter wondered if Solomon would really betray one of his distributors like that. On the other hand, allowing a customer to die exposed the drug trade in the neighborhood. He might want to punish someone who had put him and his business in jeopardy. Or maybe he was just playing with Mack. There was a glint of mischief in the gangster's eyes. Peter was also suspicious that Solomon seemed to know Kessler had been found on a sidewalk, although Mack had mentioned the jail. Peter was convinced the gangster knew all about Kessler's death before Mack approached him. For some reason, he allowed Mack to question him.

The big Irishman got up, looming over the table. "Well, we'll look into that. Hope we haven't disturbed your evening. We'll be going."

Solomon looked up at him with hooded eyes. "By all means, stay and have a drink on me." Peter thought of a snake he'd seen at the zoo. He was relieved when Mack took him by the arm and led him away.

Outside, it was warm. "Do you believe him?" Peter asked.

"You don't think the man stands on street corners selling heroin and morphine himself, do you?" Mack scoffed. "If he's pissed off at someone putting his affairs in the limelight, he might hand them over as a target. But he's a slimy one. They say he's working on some route for liquor coming up the coast from Cuba and Mexico. The Italians in the North End and the Gustin Gang in Southie are afraid of him. At the rate he's going, he'll be running all the games in this town. He's got brothels and gaming already."

Peter recalled a wild night ride with Mack and his sidekicks to a confrontation with the Gustin Gang the year before. He'd thought he was a dead man that time. You never knew how a night out with the big Irishman would end. He glanced at the man who strutted along, obviously pleased with himself. Mack was enjoying this. Peter was in agony. He hoped it wasn't just an act or hot air. His only hope at this point was for Mack and Dr. Magrath to find something to clear him.

Chapter Nineteen

The next morning, Fanny decided she needed to find Peter Attwood. She was anxious to let him know McKenna planned to arrest him. She felt an obligation to warn him. He was the grandson of her friend and host, and she felt she'd strongly encouraged the young man to continue in his police career. He was part of her own plan to prove Jake's suggested methods of investigation were crucial to police work. Now, it seemed Jake was ready to give it all up. He'd refused to discuss his decision further at dinner the night before. Fanny didn't know how she could convince Jake not to resign, but she was determined to do so.

She'd been encouraged by success in a couple of high-profile, complicated cases where Jake and Edwin's scientific work had led to the killers. But Harvard University and the police force in the form of Captain McKenna refused to recognize the value of their work. It was frustrating. She couldn't see how arresting Peter would benefit anyone. If he could hide from McKenna for the time being, perhaps Mack could continue the investigation, despite Jake's admission of defeat. Where had Mr. Kessler gotten the morphine? Who gave it to him? Why was his daughter prepared to run away? These things needed explanation. If they just convicted Peter for mistakenly putting the man in the drunk tank, they'd never know why Mr. Kessler had died of morphine poisoning.

She was at a loss. How could she warn Peter? She thought he might have contacted his sister by now, so she was determined to find Holly. Fanny was early enough to find her just finishing breakfast at her father's Beacon Hill home. Holly quickly got her things and led Fanny out the door.

"The walls have ears," she said. "My father is already mad at Peter. Better not to discuss him inside."

They walked down the hill toward Cambridge Street. Fanny shocked her with the news that McKenna planned to arrest Peter. "The last I heard Mack took him away, but I don't know where Mack lives, do you?"

Holly frowned. "I have an idea. He shares a rooming house with Edwin O'Connell, I think."

"I don't want to look for Mack at the morgue," Fanny said. "Dr. Magrath might not agree that we should warn your brother and continue to investigate. He's so disgusted, he's ready to resign. But I think McKenna is just out to get Peter."

"I know he is, from what Peter told me."

"I think Mack could convince your brother to avoid the police for now. That's why I want to find him." Fanny also thought Mack was the only one left with half a chance of clearing Peter's name by finding out what really happened to Isaac Kessler.

"Peter might be foolish enough to try to go to McKenna and reason with him. I think Mack would stop him, but if he's alone, who knows what foolish thing he'd think up," Holly said.

Fanny could see that Holly lacked confidence in her brother. But she underestimated him. Because siblings grew up together, they tended to remember each other as children. She'd seen it in her own son and daughters, who didn't realize each of them had grown way beyond what they'd been. As they grew apart, they had separate experiences. They didn't know each other as well as they thought.

Holly had an idea. "I wonder if Milly will know. She works and lives in the West End, and I think Peter would contact her before any of us. She or her brother might know where Mack and Edwin O'Connell live."

Holly led her on a brisk walk to the Peabody House. As usual, the place was bustling despite the early hour. They found Milly at her desk in the first-floor office.

A blush tinted her fair skin when she answered. "No, I haven't seen Peter." She looked a bit sad. "I hope he's all right."

"He's fighting with our father, who threw him out of the house, and he's too ashamed to go to our grandmother," Holly said in frustration. "If you do see him, warn him not to go to the police station. They're getting a warrant to arrest him."

Milly's mouth dropped open. "Arrest him? For what?"

Fanny thought Peter would not thank his sister for dropping this information so bluntly on the woman he was courting. Milly clasped her hands in front of her. She was stiff with tension.

"They blame him for Mr. Kessler's death," Holly moaned. "Because he left him in the jail cell, thinking he was drunk when it turns out he was sick from morphine."

"Peter couldn't know that," Milly said.

"Mr. Kessler's friends are outraged, so there's pressure from City Hall for someone to take the blame," Fanny told them.

"It's my fault," Milly said. "Peter stopped by to see me on his dinner break. Most nights, he came in. We met when he started walking a beat down here. He was interested in our work."

Fanny thought he was probably more interested in the young woman. Two young people with idealistic plans to do good and correct wrongs in the world.

Milly continued. "The people we help bring such backward traditions from their homelands. We try to teach them how to do things in America. Peter appreciates that."

Milly spoke directly to Fanny as if trying to convince her. Holly added her piece. "That's how Rachel and I got involved. Milly told me about the effort to provide work training, and we talked to Mrs. Shurcliff about starting the workshop for building furniture."

"Peter appreciates the work of the settlement," Fanny interrupted. "So he often visited you here. Is that right?" She hoped to get Milly back on what happened the night of Kessler's death and why she felt responsible for Peter's dilemma.

"That's right. Peter was so interested. He'd stop, and I'd get him something from our kitchen for dinner. He was always prompt in returning to his beat." She seemed anxious to excuse Peter's visits. "I think that night I got called away for a while, and he stayed a little longer than usual. A bit beyond his time. I'm afraid if I hadn't kept him, perhaps he might have found Mr. Kessler sooner and helped him."

"Mr. Kessler can't have been lying on the ground when Peter stopped here," Holly said. "Surely, he would have seen him from across the street."

Fanny tried to remember if there was a streetlight near the place where Kessler had lain.

"I'm so sorry Rachel's father passed away like that," Milly said. "But I'm sure Peter would have helped him if he'd known he was ill. There used to be a pub over there, before Prohibition. There have always been drunks outside the place. It's supposed to be closed now, but I think they still serve alcohol somewhere over there. We've complained about it, but the city ignores the problem. See what the result is? Even with the Volstead Act, alcohol is still around."

"Mr. Kessler wasn't drunk, though," Fanny told them. "Dr. Magrath has established that he died from morphine poisoning."

"Morphine? How awful," Milly said, shaking her head. "That is appalling. We've heard about some use of illegal drugs, but it's mostly in the Negro areas. In the illegal jazz clubs. Unlike some of the institutions around here, we don't put up with even a hint of drugs at Peabody House. I thought the problems were confined to the Negro parts of the city. I wonder if the practice is spreading into the Jewish community now."

Fanny caught a hint of something in Milly's speech. "If Peabody House doesn't tolerate these drugs, are there other institutions that do?"

Milly flushed. "I'm not saying that. It's just that my brother has mentioned..." Reluctant to continue, she stood up. "Let me see if I can get my brother Teddy to talk to you." She stepped to the door to call over an older man and ask him to find her brother. "I'll let Teddy tell you if he knows anything. I may be wrong. It was just a hint of something that he said the other day. I'd hate to spread rumors that aren't true." She turned to Holly. "Teddy was going to ask you to join us for our theater group play a week from Saturday. Has he?"

Holly looked surprised. "No. I'm not sure if I'll be around. Mrs. Shurcliff invited some of us out to her summer place. Now that Rachel's in mourning, I'm not sure if we'll go." She looked a bit uncomfortable.

Fanny wondered what brought on the question about a social date between Milly's brother and Holly. Was Milly trying to encourage her brother to court Holly? It seemed an odd concern amongst all the worry about Mr. Kessler's death and Peter's suspension. Curious.

Milly's brother breezed in. He was in shirtsleeves with a polka dot bow tie and suspenders. Fanny had only seen him in passing before. He was a few inches taller than his petite sister. Like her, he had a mass of blonde curls and very pale skin. His eyes were bright, and he seemed a bit hectic, as if he'd been pulled away from more than one activity. He moved with a bounce in his step, as if ready to leave at any moment. Teddy gave them a warm greeting. "Hello. Holly, lovely to see you." Milly introduced Fanny. "You wanted me for something?"

Milly explained about Peter and how Mr. Kessler had died from morphine poisoning. She admitted she thought he might know something about the use of illegal drugs in the area.

"Oh, Milly. I don't, really. I just hear the boys talking sometimes." He turned to Fanny and Holly. "There's a big rivalry in basketball down here. Our team plays the Catholics from St. Joseph's and the Jews from the West End House. They get so enthusiastic they come to blows sometimes. Especially the Catholic boys against the Jews. Not that the West End House is strictly Jewish, it's just that it appeals to a lot of them. Storrow founded the club and he put a Jewish lawyer guy in charge. It's a good place. Fine, really." He stopped for a minute as if he'd lost his place and stared at the ceiling.

"What does that have to do with morphine?" Holly asked sharply.

"Oh, yes. Well, it's probably nothing, but the Catholic boys call the Jews 'dopers' sometimes. It's just boys insulting each other to get their blood up for a game."

Fanny could tell the young man felt a bit guilty about spreading such a damning rumor.

"There's no truth to it," Teddy said. "The West End House is just a bit overly tolerant of more radical views, if you know what I mean. They've hosted strike meetings and anarchist speakers. The Cardinal doesn't like it if the Catholics are radical."

"The West End House held meetings in support of women's suffrage," Holly said.

"Yes. That's right," Milly said. "The West End House is mostly for young men. But they support women's right to vote. Some of them support Zionism, too."

"What's that?" Holly asked.

"The right of Jews to have a homeland in Palestine," Milly said.

Fanny wanted to return to the topic of most interest. "Do you believe illicit drugs are used or distributed in that club?"

"No," Teddy said. "Milly misunderstood me. It was just taunting between rival athletes, that's all."

Holly had her own concerns. "Teddy, have you seen my brother, Peter? He's left home, and we're trying to find him. We thought he'd come to see Milly, but I suppose he's too ashamed of getting suspended. We need to find him, though. He's in trouble."

Teddy turned to Holly. Fanny could see he admired the vivacious young woman. "I'm so sorry to hear that. Last I saw him he was with that big guy who works for the medical examiner."

"Mack," Holly said. "Michael McNally. He used to be a policeman. When did you see them?"

Teddy frowned. "I don't know. Sometime in the past couple of days, I think." Conscious of Holly's interest, the young man pursed his lips and glanced away. He turned back to her. "I didn't see them myself, but someone mentioned they saw Peter and that ex-policeman at a speakeasy. Last night."

"A speakeasy!" Holly's mouth fell open. Milly shook her head in disappointment. Fanny found it hard to believe Peter and Mack would be out drinking after Peter was suspended and kicked out of his father's house. But they were young men; perhaps they were drowning Peter's sorrow.

Fanny thought Teddy took some satisfaction in taking down Peter a few notches in the view of his sister and Holly. Was he jealous of Peter? Did Teddy revel in Peter's fall? She wondered if Teddy's sister Milly had held up Peter as an example and her brother couldn't live up to their old friend. That could explain the satisfaction in Peter's dilemma that Teddy couldn't quite hide.

"Do you know where Detective McNally lives?" Fanny asked. She had a feeling Teddy knew more about the man than he admitted.

"He's got a room over on Warren Street, I think."

Holly jumped up. "I'll bet my brother is staying with him. I'm going to find out."

Chapter Twenty

Fanny walked with Holly through the streets of the West End. They followed Teddy Greene's directions to reach a four-story tenement with a pharmacy on the ground floor. Holly confirmed with a Negro man smoking a cigarette that the side door led to residential apartments. She asked about McNally.

"Mrs. O'Reilly on the second floor," the man said. Then he turned away.

The door was unlocked, and the women climbed a steep staircase and found Mrs. O'Reilly's name on a wide door at the back.

Mrs. O'Reilly was a stern-looking older woman in a flowered dress covered by a white apron. "Mr. McNally, him who was a detective has a room. He's at his breakfast now. I don't allow lady visitors, but as you're only looking to find him, I'll tell him you're here."

Mack showed up, pulling a napkin from his chin and a jacket onto his back a moment later. He looked startled. When Holly demanded to know where her brother was, he frowned. "You're a bold one coming looking for a man in his home." Fanny thought he would have scolded Holly more, but her own presence kept the big Irishman in check. She could see he was irked by their visit. "Come along outside." He waved his big hands, shooing them out the door. Dropping the napkin on a side table, he followed.

At the front door, he nodded to the Negro and continued to shepherd them down the street. The tenement was only a block from the bank of the Charles River. There, he sat them down on a wooden bench and stood before them.

"Where's Peter?" Holly demanded.

"What're you, his keeper?" Mack snapped. "He's a grown man, not a toddler in diapers."

Before an angry Holly could reply Fanny intervened. "Detective McNally…" she knew he liked it when she gave him the title. "We need to warn Holly's brother that Chief McKenna is getting a warrant for his arrest for the death of Mr. Kessler. If he doesn't want to be taken to jail, he needs to stay away from the police station and also from the morgue. Dr. Magrath won't intervene if the police come looking for him there."

Mack thought about that. "He's been sleeping on the floor of my room. I haven't mentioned it to Mrs. O'Reilly yet. If she throws us out, we'll both be bunking at the morgue. I wouldn't put it past McKenna to try to blame Attwood for the death. With the local ward boss, Lomasney, involved, he'll be getting heat from above. You're right about keeping him out of sight for now. Didn't Magrath tell them Kessler died of morphine, not from a fall or a beating?"

"He told them, but I think if McKenna finds Peter, he'll charge him and call the case closed," Fanny told him.

"He didn't get morphine from Peter," Holly declared. "Milly's brother told us there are rumors the morphine comes from the West End House. You need to warn Peter about the arrest warrant. We'll go to the West End House to see if we can find out more about where the morphine comes from."

"Good God, woman. What're you talking about? You'll not be going to the West End House," Mack huffed. Fanny could see Holly's face redden at the rebuke. "I already asked the local kingpin Charles Solomon last night at the Club Garden, and he hinted about the West End House."

"Club Garden?" Holly asked.

"A speakeasy on Causeway Street," Mack said. Fanny understood why Mack and Peter had been seen at the speakeasy. They weren't drowning their sorrows after all. They were tracking down the source of the morphine.

"I'll be checking out that lead," Mack said. "You'll be going home to your sewing or whatever." Fanny cringed. Holly wouldn't take a slur like that sitting down.

In fact, she sprang up from the bench. "Don't you dare tell me what to do.

I'll go wherever I want, and I don't need your permission."

Mack rolled his eyes at Fanny. "Mrs. Lee, can you talk sense into her?"

That seemed unlikely. Fanny stood. "I'm going to the morgue. I want to convince Dr. Magrath to help to exonerate Peter. Arresting Peter will only stop the investigation. I'm sure he'll want to find out how the morphine got into Mr. Kessler's body and whether it was an accident or if someone purposely poisoned him. But he's so angry about McKenna's actions that he's threatening to resign. Meanwhile, Detective McNally, if you would follow up on where the morphine came from, that would help."

"You're not leaving me out of this," Holly insisted.

Fanny turned to her. "Holly, I know you want to help your brother, but Mack is a trained detective. You need to let him work on this problem." Out of the corner of her eye, she could see Mack preen himself.

"I'll get Mr. Johnson to warn Attwood to stay out of sight," Mack said. "When I find out something useful, I'll go back to Magrath's morgue to let you know." He seemed pleased with himself as he tripped away.

"Mrs. Lee, we found out about the West End House. We ought to be able to follow the trail." Holly glared at Mack's retreating figure.

"Holly, we've done what we can. This is a serious and dangerous investigation. We need to let Mack work. He really is better able to find out the truth, and he's already proved he's willing to help your brother." She knew Holly was worried about her brother and Fanny recognized the fever that went with being hot on the trail of information that could solve the mystery of a death. She suspected the man Mack had talked to at the speakeasy was a gangster. It was not a crowd that she or Holly should be involved with. She worried the impulsiveness of youth would get Peter's sister into trouble. She sensed that Holly didn't want to be shown up by an ignorant Irishman like Mack, as well. Her pride was on the line. Fanny could only hope she'd learn sense without having a bad experience. Somehow Fanny trusted that the rambunctious Mack would look out for the impatient girl as well as he had looked out for poor Peter.

Chapter Twenty-One

Mack stopped to ask Johnson to warn Peter about possible arrest. He'd left the suspended policeman dead asleep, and he'd warned him the day before to wait until Mrs. O'Reilly went to the market before sneaking out.

"Avoiding cops?" Johnson asked.

"Aye. They've got the stick at the wrong end, as usual. He needs to stay out of their clutches till we can straighten things out." Mack had no fear that Johnson would tell the police anything. In his experience, Negros with any sense avoided involvement with the authorities better than anyone else.

As he stepped away, Mack saw Peter's sister advancing. Mrs. Lee was gone, and the girl had a determined look. Mack sped away down the street, but he couldn't lose her. When she continued to follow him, he stepped into his favorite chop shop.

The smoky room was full of working men having a big breakfast for five cents. Looking over his shoulder, he saw Holly Attwood stop and hesitate. That would shake her. It was a purely male environment. Mack allowed himself a wicked grin as he took a seat in a booth near the window. He waved provocatively.

The room wasn't as full as at dinner time, so he gave his order to a waiter quickly. The man filled a coffee cup in front of Mack who sighed with contentment. He'd been interrupted at Mrs. O'Reilly's, and he needed his sustenance, especially after a night at the speakeasy. He congratulated himself on the information he'd obtained the night before, and the way he'd gotten rid of Peter's sister.

Just as his full plate arrived and he took his first bite, he was accosted by Holly Attwood. He dropped his fork.

"Here he is," she said loudly. "Look at him, filling his stomach when there are little ones at home with nothing to eat."

Mack choked. He could see the waiter behind Holly looking helpless to restrain her. He couldn't very well put his hands on her and throw her out bodily. He would have done that to a man, but she was a woman, and he was stymied. Holly looked triumphant.

"She's joking," he told the waiter. When the man looked angrily uncertain, Mack added, "go ahead and bring a plate for her, too. She's cranky from hunger." He made a face at her, but she plopped down opposite him.

"The little ones," he scoffed when the waiter went away. "What do you think you're doing? There's no women in the place, did you notice?" He waved his paw around.

Holly wriggled a bit, settling into place. "I know. That's why you came in here to hide from me." She was self-satisfied. She unwound silverware from a napkin and put it on her lap. She thanked the waiter sweetly when he brought a cup and poured coffee. Mack was sure she'd had a fine breakfast in her Beacon Hill home, but he could see she was willing to eat another if he had to pay for it. He addressed his own full plate as the waiter put another in front of Holly.

They ate in silence, and Mack had to admit she had quite an appetite for a skinny Yankee. She wasn't as willowy as her friend Milly Greene anyhow. And she didn't have the deep sunk eyes of Rachel Kessler who had looked driven. She had a sunshiny attitude that could be a burden to put up with and she was too proud of her own cleverness by half. Still, she seemed less stiff than her brother Peter. He imagined she was more rebellious against the banker father than the sons had ever been. But then she was a woman. There was much she could get away with on the basis of her sex. The need to act as a gentleman was the bane of masculinity when it came to dealing with women. You were damned if you gave in to them and damned if you didn't. She'd get along with his only sister, Kate. They'd be two peas in a pod.

While he waited to settle the bill, Mack frowned at Holly. "I suppose now you'll be following me all the way to the West End House."

She smiled. "Of course."

"Look here, they tell me it's a men's club. Mostly Jews, some Lithuanians, Polish, a few Irish. Storrow started it. In case you didn't know, Storrow's a wealthy man from Back Bay."

"I know Mr. Storrow. He's a banker like my father." Holly smiled.

Those Yanks, they all knew each other. "Perhaps you'd like to look him up then and ask him if there's any drugs floating around the place," Mack teased.

"Of course not," Holly snapped.

Mack knew that Storrow had been in charge of a commission that had recommended the city give in to the demands during the police strike the year before, but those recommendations were ignored. When the policemen went on strike, strikers like Mack were blacklisted forever from their jobs. Mack didn't hold a grudge against Storrow, but he was wary of the man's influence and power. "Storrow ran for mayor and city council. He's a bigwig in the city."

"I know, I know. I'll bet you don't even know where the West End House is," Holly said.

Mack glanced at her plate. She'd made fast work of the ham and eggs. "And you do know, I suppose?" He spoke with his mouth full of toast, hoping to put her off with his bad manners. His sister Kate would bop him on the head if she saw his behavior. Luckily, she was over in Eastie minding her kiddies.

"As a matter of fact, I do." Holly wiped her mouth with her napkin and folded it up

Mack considered while he finished the toast. He'd need to find the place, but he planned to just ask on the street. Would he get more cooperation if he showed up with a little missus by his side? She was a friend of Kessler's daughter, after all. "Listen. If you want to tag along, you need to keep your trap shut. This is something they're not going to want to admit, if drugs are being passed around. It takes some finesse."

She stared at him. For a moment, he thought she would laugh, and he felt his neck redden. Finesse. Sure. From a big gorilla like him. He watched for signs she was thinking just that, but she merely said, "Okay." She looked into his eyes. "I know you're trying to help Peter. He's my big brother, but I've always had to look out for him. He's too easy to step on. My father and my older brother have always done that to him, and it's not fair."

Mack was prepared to deny any sympathy for the hapless Peter, but he could see she was in earnest. How did that boy get so much help from the women in his life like Mrs. Lee and Holly? Mack was jealous.

Holly took his silence for dissent. "Look, he's really got a thing for Milly, and to tell the truth, my father would be happy about that. Her father went bankrupt, but she comes from a background he'd approve."

Mack's eyebrows rose. He thought Peter was such a loser his family ought to welcome any woman who would take him off their hands.

"He needs looking after," Holly said. "He's the one that's missed my mother the most."

Women! Mack paid the bill and marched out with Holly at his heels. He sensed that she knew she'd hooked him. He didn't have a way to get rid of her. And he didn't have the heart. "Which way?"

"This way. West End House is on Chambers Street."

Chapter Twenty-Two

Mack and Holly arrived at a trim brick building not far from the river. Inside, it seemed hushed compared to the hullabaloo at Peabody House. A young man at the front desk directed them down a corridor to the office of the director, Jack Burnes.

He was a stocky, middle-aged man with black hair and eyes and bushy eyebrows. He wore a checked shirt and tan slacks with a leather belt.

Mack explained he was an investigator for Dr. Magrath, who was looking into Mr. Kessler's death for the medical examiner. Holly introduced herself as a friend of the family who were currently in mourning.

"Sitting Seder, I've been to see them," Burnes said. "It's a sad thing." He gestured them to chairs beside the desk. "Mrs. Kessler died of the flu. Now Isaac." He shook his head. "What happened? Do you know? I heard he died at the police station. It's hard to imagine Mr. Kessler in a jail cell. He was a prominent member of the community. No one believes he was found drunk on a sidewalk. He wasn't like that at all."

Burnes looked at them shrewdly through half-open eyes as if summing them up. Mack thought he was waiting for a sign that Kessler had been ill-treated because he was a Jew. Holly opened her mouth, but Mack waved her to silence. She'd agreed to let him handle this. He was pleasantly surprised when she shut her mouth and sat back in her chair.

"Mr. Kessler was found on the ground, smelling of whiskey, but Dr. Magrath's autopsy proved he had no alcohol in his blood but a large enough amount of morphine to kill him."

Burnes looked down. Mack was sure it wasn't the first time he'd heard about morphine as the cause of death.

"We'd like to find out more about how Mr. Kessler got the drug. We don't know if it was an accident or something else," Mack said.

"I can't believe Isaac took morphine on purpose," Burnes said. He looked up. "But why are you here? Mr. Kessler wasn't a member. We provide classes and activities for young men. His son participates in some of our programs. But not the father." Burnes looked grim, as if he knew what was coming.

"In asking around about where anyone would get morphine, the West End House was mentioned by more than one person," Mack said.

Burnes had been fiddling with a pencil that he threw down. "That's outrageous. Who said that? We don't allow something like that to go on. This institution was started by young men looking to better themselves. It's been a place for young men to educate themselves and share interests from sports to chess. If anything, we'd help a man get free of something like drugs. We provide alternatives to the temptations on the streets. Our young men are too proud to be involved in anything like that. Who told you that? It's a lie."

Mack considered. He thought Burnes was a straightforward guy. He didn't think the man would cover up for anyone selling drugs to his young men. But these things could happen without someone in Burnes's position knowing. "There's a man called Solomon who suggested we look at your club."

Burnes snorted. "King Solomon? He's a gangster. A traitor to our race as far as I'm concerned. You can't believe him."

Holly stared, open-mouthed. She had no idea a gangster was involved.

"He wasn't the only one to mention West End House," Mack said.

"Who else?"

Mack hesitated to mention the Greenes.

"Peabody House," Holly blurted out.

Mack glared at her, and she shut her mouth.

"Oh, really?" Burnes said. "You should understand, Mr. McNally, there's a certain amount of rivalry down here between Peabody House, us, and St.

Joseph's, as well. But accusing us of allowing morphine or heroin is wrong." He sighed. "Let me get one of our counselors to talk to you. I think he can set you straight about our activities. Excuse me a moment." He left the room.

He returned with a good-looking young man with dark curly hair and the kind of cleft chin and firm jaw that impressed the ladies. Mack saw a look of recognition pass between the man and Holly.

"This is Ari Zellman," Burnes introduced him. "He's a Harvard law student who volunteers as a counselor. "Ari, as I told you, Mr. McNally is looking into Mr. Kessler's death. He says it was caused by morphine poisoning. He's heard rumors that West End House is involved with drugs. I want you to tell him about our efforts."

Chapter Twenty-Three

Burnes left Mack and Holly with Zellman, saying he had to go to a meeting. Zellman took the seat at the desk. He frowned. "What do you want to know?"

Mack noticed that Holly clamped her mouth shut. He saw her nod to the handsome young man. She must know him. "Mr. Kessler died from morphine poisoning. We're trying to track down the source. West End House was mentioned."

Zellman looked up as if searching for patience from the ceiling. "Jack Burnes referred you to me because I run a program to help any of our young men who've gotten into trouble by using morphine or heroin. We get them to stop using any drugs. We don't promote use."

"Where do the drugs come from?" Mack asked.

Zellman shook his head. "I don't know that."

"Baloney. If you don't know, then tell me the names of the guys you helped. They'll know who's selling it."

"I can't do that. It's confidential." Zellman leaned forward over the desk. "Look, these men are often under a lot of pressure. They've got to succeed to support their families. In lots of cases, their families have put all their money into education for a son. They have to go to Harvard and succeed when they get there. If they don't, they've betrayed all the hard work and sacrifice their families made to send them. The families come from Russia and other countries that deny them opportunities. They have to live up to the hopes their families have for them."

Holly spoke up. "They do go to Harvard. You did, didn't you?"

His dark eyes turned to her. "I did. Even though I was an orphan. But you'd be surprised how many obstacles they put in your way." He snorted. "Harvard decided there were too many Jewish students, and so they limited the number. Did you know that? Imagine the pressure to excel when a man gets in despite the quotas."

Holly retreated back in her chair a bit.

"Names. Who knows the sources of morphine?" Mack demanded. He had little sympathy for the Harvard hard luck cases.

Zellman was stubborn. "I won't betray their confidence."

Mack could recognize a brick wall when he bumped his head on it. "What about Kessler's son? He's a member here, isn't he?" Zellman blinked, like Mack had hit a nerve.

"Bernard Kessler. Yes. He's on our rowing team."

"He does painting too," Holly piped up. Mack was surprised and glad for the information that seemed to disarm Zellman.

"Yes. He's a talented artist. We have an excellent teacher who's a pretty well-known artist. Bernie loves those classes."

"Bernie goes to Harvard, too?" Mack asked.

Zellman hesitated. "He did."

"He doesn't anymore?" Mack asked. "Since when? Did he get kicked out? Was he using drugs?"

Zellman looked uncomfortable, and Holly straightened up in her chair. "I believe he withdrew voluntarily," Zellman said. "Quite recently."

"Why?"

Stone-faced, Zellman replied, "I couldn't tell you." He seemed to be searching for an explanation. "His sister told me he had a friend who died last month. She thought he was sad about that and wanted to leave Harvard."

"Rachel," Holly jumped at the reference to her friend. "Of course. You know Rachel. You were at the Kessler apartment when we went to show sympathy for her father's death."

Zellman looked down at the desk.

Holly gasped. "Rachel's father wanted her to marry Mr. Abrams, but she told me she wouldn't do it. I thought she was seeing someone else, but I couldn't get her to admit it. She was going to run away with you, wasn't she?" Holly turned to Mack. "Rachel Kessler had bags hidden at Mrs. Shurcliff's house. She was going to run away."

Zellman looked grim. "You're mistaken. Miss Kessler is engaged to Mr. Abrams. You can ask her if you don't believe me."

Holly looked flabbergasted. "But… "

"It was her father's wish," Zellman said. "Now, if that's all, I have work to do."

Chapter Twenty-Four

Later that morning, Fanny was packing her trunk in the spacious bedroom at her friend Cornelia's house on Beacon Hill. Her seventeen-year-old daughter and namesake, Frances, was coming by train from her boarding school. They were to spend some months in northern New Hampshire, where Fanny had started a business the previous summer.

But how could she leave now? Jake had already written his resignation letter. And Peter Attwood would soon be arrested for Mr. Kessler's death. Fanny knew she ought to leave on time and keep her promises to her daughter. But could she really abandon Jake? During the winter, she'd become even more involved in his work to unravel the mysteries of unexplained deaths. She'd become fascinated with the details of his work. She felt ambitions growing.

Of course, who was she to have ambitions to solve crimes? She was a moderately wealthy woman with no education or experience who had opinions on how death investigations should proceed. She was gaining experience by offering her services and support to Jake Magrath, but to what end? Her organizing mind had been planning out a course of action where Jake could use a young detective, open to new ideas, to improve investigation techniques. But those plans were wiped out by Peter Attwood's troubles, and Jake's threat to resign his position as medical examiner. If she left now, there would be nothing to come back to in the fall.

Fanny refused to relinquish her well-laid plans. There had to be a way to exonerate Peter. Jake had given up. He couldn't help Cornelia's grandson if he quit his job. Holly was worried about her brother and determined to do something, but Fanny knew her amateur attempts to help could well backfire. Cornelia was going to approach Peter's father, demanding he help his son, but he'd never wanted Peter to join the police, so his assistance might be conditioned on Peter giving up his ambitions and returning to Harvard. Mack was investigating but he would need Jake's support to disprove McKenna's accusations. Fanny couldn't leave Boston with so much trouble swirling around. She didn't feel she was as much an amateur as Holly. She'd worked with Jake, Edwin, and Mack. She knew she could help, if only by spurring them on to find the truth.

She stopped folding the frock she held. She would stay. Her daughter could carry on. Frances disliked her school and had no ambitions to marry or attend college. The one thing that she loved was treasure-hunting antiques. It roused her enthusiasm. Fanny worried about her middle child's health as she was subject to colds and fevers. But she wanted to encourage her in the antiques business. It might be a good thing for her to be in charge without her mother giving all the orders.

Fanny dropped the frock and prepared to meet her daughter at the train station. She'd send her on to New Hampshire, like a mother hen pushing a chick out of the nest. Frances would understand.

Chapter Twenty-Five

When Mack ushered a stunned Holly out into the sunshine, the street was crowded and noisy with the cries of street peddlers. West End House was on a block that ended at the banks of the Charles River. He guided her to the riverbank.

"I'll go find out about this engagement," he said. He planned to find Rachel Kessler and confront her. Holly seemed deeply troubled by the news of Rachel's engagement. He wondered why.

"No, you can't." Seeming to wake from a dream, she grabbed his arm. "They're still mourning her father. You can't disturb them."

She was right. It would be a gaffe to barge in on their Jewish mourning period. But Mack wasn't sure how long he could hide Peter from the police. If he could find the source of the morphine, McKenna and his crew would have to pay attention.

"Rachel was in love with Ari Zellman," Holly said. "I know she was. It's true her father wanted her to marry Leonard Abrams. She told me he's part of their Orthodox congregation. I'll bet Zellman isn't. But Mr. Kessler knew she was against marrying Abrams. She told me her father insisted Abrams would need to have enough money to support his own home before they could marry. She didn't think he was capable of raising the money. Her father wouldn't have abandoned Rachel to Leonard's mother. She's a terror. Rachel told me how much she detested her."

Having met Mrs. Abrams, Mack could agree. No loving father would curse his daughter with the likes of the pushy widow. But he shrugged his big shoulders. Romance wasn't his area of expertise. "Maybe she feels obliged to obey his wishes now that he's dead," he suggested.

"She wouldn't," Holly said, stamping a foot. She certainly was riled up at the thought. Mack tried to think of a way to distract her. He was appalled to sense she was on the brink of tears. He needed reinforcements.

"I have to go report to Dr. Magrath," he said. When faced with female tears, his impulse was to flee.

"I'm coming with you," she announced.

Mack tried not to demonstrate his disappointment as he walked away. He couldn't stop her. He hoped Mrs. Lee would be present at the mortuary. She could cope with Peter's sister.

At the morgue on North Grove Street, they found Peter arguing with Dr. Magrath. Edwin stood silent in the background. Mack asked after Mrs. Lee and was told she was meeting her daughter at the train station.

"Peter," Holly rushed to her brother. She grabbed his shoulders. "The police want to arrest you!"

Peter struggled to free himself from Holly. Mack looked at Dr. Magrath, who shook his head of white hair. He scowled at the siblings. Was he going to tell Peter to turn himself in? Mack didn't want that. McKenna would use an arrest to abandon the investigation. He refused to credit the medical examiner's report that Kessler died of morphine poisoning. He would crucify Peter to be able to tell the local ward boss, Lomasney, and City Hall that someone would pay for Kessler's death.

Peter looked at Mack beseechingly.

"Did you find the source of the morphine?" Dr. Magrath asked.

Mack hated to admit failure. "Not yet. I'm sure it came from King Solomon, but I don't know who gave it to Kessler." He recounted his trips to the Club Garden and the West End House. Dr. Magrath scoffed at the idea that a settlement house supported by James Storrow would be the site of drug sales. Mack thought Dr. Magrath was too quick to defend prominent businessmen and politicians just because he knew them from his clubs and other activities. Mack had a more jaundiced view of those characters.

The air split with a series of imperious rings of the doorbell and a banging on the door. Mack thought he heard a familiar voice. Dr. Magrath nodded at Edwin to go and answer the summons.

Mack grabbed Peter. "Take off your shoes and socks." When Peter stared, uncomprehending, Mack clapped him on the back. Holly stepped away, looking at Mack as if he were a madman. Mack lifted Peter onto an empty metal table, pulling off his shoes and socks to shove them under some shelving. He grabbed a sheet and whipped it into the air, dropping it over Peter and draping it until the bare feet were the only thing visible, then he took a tag from a box on the shelf and tied it to Peter's bare toe as Edwin returned followed by Chief McKenna and one of his henchmen.

McKenna ignored Mack and the wide-eyed Holly and confronted Dr. Magrath. "Where's Attwood?" he asked.

Mack held his breath. He knew Dr. Magrath might not agree to hide Peter, but he hoped the doctor wouldn't expose the lad. Luckily, McKenna did everything he could to prevent Dr. Magrath's cooperation. The chief of detectives launched into a tirade about what he'd do to Dr. Magrath if he found out he'd been hiding Peter Attwood. Then he barked at Holly. "You're Miss Attwood, aren't you? You claimed your brother wasn't at your home. I've spoken to your father. He says he threw your brother out." He took three steps over to intimidate Holly. "Now, you look here, missy. If I find out you're hiding your brother, he won't be the only one visiting the inside of a jail cell. Aiding and abetting. You heard of that? I can arrest you for that, so you'd better tell me if you know where he is."

As Mack took a step towards the loud bully, Dr. Magrath's deep voice rang out. "Get out of my morgue, McKenna."

McKenna turned around to glare at the medical examiner. Mack stopped in his tracks. He could see that Holly was shaken. He wanted to smash the guy, but Dr. Magrath's voice stopped him. "Detective McNally, please escort Chief Detective McKenna and his man to the door. McKenna, if you ever barge into my examination room again, I'll have your badge."

Red-faced, McKenna looked ready to burst. But Mack could see the gears grinding in his head as he weighed Magrath's influence against his own. McKenna had survived the police strike by betraying his fellow officers, and the Yankee sticklers in charge had promoted him, but he knew his political connections were nowhere near as strong as Magrath's. Dr. Magrath was an old Yankee himself with all the power and influence that came with that status. McKenna could only go so far when he irritated the well-known medical examiner. Mack could see him calculating the odds.

Mack felt his temper cool down as he watched McKenna grunt and head for the door. He followed the men out and locked the door, taking a big breath.

Back in the autopsy room, Peter peeked out from the sheet over him. Mack motioned for him to sit up. Before Peter could thank them, Mack said, "McKenna is one of the biggest jerks on the force." He knew Dr. Magrath would agree. But his comment didn't lighten the doctor's expression. He looked like a thundercloud about to burst.

Edwin spoke up. "At least we'll have a full crew for Sunday," he said.

"What?" Holly asked. She appeared to still be worried.

"The race," Mack said. Of course, Edwin knew Magrath better than any of them. The medical examiner was an enthusiastic amateur rower. He belonged to the Union Boat Club on the Charles River. In May, he had recruited Mack, Peter, and Edwin to row in his four-man rowing scull. Magrath himself both rowed and steered. Practice was held in the early morning before work hours. Peter had rowed at Harvard, and Edwin would do anything for the medical examiner. Mack felt obliged to go along, and many an early morning, he'd taken a head heavy from drinking the night before to the boathouse. He'd have preferred boxing as a hobby, but he was so grateful for the job at the mortuary, he'd managed the practice sessions even when he still lived in Eastie. Magrath had been training them for a race coming up the following Sunday. Practice was suspended when Magrath decided to have the rowing scull painted before the race. Mack had secretly hoped the race was forgotten, but now he saw a use for it. "We need Peter for the crew, don't we?" He glanced at Edwin, who nodded.

Dr. Magrath frowned and folded his arms over his chest. Mack thought he knew they were manipulating him. He glowered at Peter, who bit his bottom lip. "All right," Dr. Magrath said. "You can hide from that clown McKenna a little longer. But I'll expect you all at the boathouse tomorrow at six."

Mack considered that Peter was going to owe him a lot for the sacrifice of sleep. With Peter sleeping on his floor, he supposed he could prevent the Harvard man from forgetting his debt. Seeing relief in the eyes of Peter's sister, he knew he could survive the race. He wasn't so sure he could find Kessler's killer, though.

Chapter Twenty-Six

On Sunday, Fanny joined Holly and Milly at the riverbank to watch the races. There were rowing sculls from Peabody House, West End House, and St. Joseph's, as well as from the Union Boat Club. Temporary floating docks had been placed around the Charles River Basin for each of the competitive teams. They watched as the lightweight boats were carried to each dock.

"Teddy coaches the boys," Milly said, waving to her brother, who walked beside four young men carrying a yellow hull. He veered toward them.

"Ladies, it's a lovely day for it," Teddy said. With their golden curls, he and Milly could have been twins.

Fanny had to agree about the day. It was warm in the sun, where the women sat on plaid blankets with two picnic baskets. Teddy sat down beside Holly, stretching out his legs and leaning back on his forearms.

"Don't you need to go with them?" Holly asked.

"I've done my best," he said with a grin. "It's up to them now. And I can watch and picnic with you ladies." He pulled a cloth cap from his pocket and put it on his head. The women wore wide-brimmed hats to protect them from the sun.

Fanny heard a gasp from Milly.

"It's Peter," Holly said. She grabbed Milly's hand. "He's been keeping out of sight, but they must think the police are unlikely to turn up at the race."

Fanny could see that Milly looked relieved to know where Peter was. She waved. Peter had part of the boat on his shoulder, but he looked over longingly and waved back. Mack held up the back of their boat while Edwin and Jake strolled along, holding the long oars. They dropped the boat on their dock.

Teddy kept up a commentary on the crews. He rated his own group as primed to win. He'd recruited some college men. He frowned at Dr. Magrath's team and told them the doctor was a five-time medal holder for the single scull, but not as proficient with a team of four. He scoffed at the broad-shouldered group representing St. Joseph's. "Strong but heavy," he told them. "The West End House has won in the past, but we beat them last year in the four-man."

Fanny looked across at the farthest dock. "Is that Mr. Kessler's son?" she asked. Holly peered at them.

"Yes, that's Bernie. And Mr. Zellman is their coxswain," Holly said. "The mourning period must be up. She stood and glanced around. "I think I see Rachel with Leonard Abrams." She sat back down, and Fanny sensed she was unsure about approaching her grieving friend.

"I can't believe Rachel is engaged to Leonard Abrams," Holly murmured.

Milly took her hand. "I think she wants to honor her father's wishes. Don't you?"

Teddy sat up. "It's spring. Love is in the air. Don't you agree, Miss Attwood?" He smiled, and Fanny had to admit to herself he was an attractive young man.

Holly rolled her eyes, but she smiled. "Poor Milly," she patted Milly's hand. "It'll be all right in the end, you'll see. We'll get Peter out of this."

Milly blushed under her hat and pulled one of the baskets over to start handing out sandwiches wrapped in wax paper.

Fanny watched as the boats slid into the water, and the men carefully climbed in. The boats looked like thin shells, and she noticed the men were careful to balance on the ribs before lowering themselves and taking the long oars passed to them from the shore. Teddy leaped up to help his team get off, then returned. He pointed out the pontoon boat and floating marks that formed the racecourse.

While Teddy teased the young women, Fanny watched Jake's team. They seemed slightly disjointed as they rowed out. Teddy's young men were like a machine and rowed as if tied together for synchronization. The West End House team, with Ari Zellman in the stern, had a little competition with the Peabody House boat, but they both broke off when the St. Joseph team passed them with long strokes.

"Lots of power but not so much speed," Teddy commented on the Catholic boat.

Jake's team lagged. Edwin was in the bow, with Peter next, his oar on the opposite side, then Mack rowing on Edwin's side and Jake at the stern, rowing and steering with one foot, as Teddy had explained. Fanny thought Jake looked quite relaxed. He eyed the other teams from under his bushy eyebrows, and he steered his boat to a place beside the pontoon boat. He spoke to his men, and they laughed.

Fanny was glad to see that reaction. It had been a stressful week. Mack continued to try to find the source of the morphine. Peter continued to hide from the police, faithfully attending the early morning practice rowing sessions. Fanny had worked with Jake and Edwin on two other unrelated deaths with simple explanations. Jake never mentioned his letter of resignation. Fanny hoped he'd put it aside. Mack continued to report on the investigation, but Jake still wasn't satisfied with the explanation of Kessler's death. He encouraged Mack to try to find out who had provided the dead man with morphine, and they discussed and followed every lead they could think of. Meanwhile, Holly had spent a lot of time at Peabody House. Fanny wondered how close she was becoming to Milly and Teddy. Perhaps Holly met Peter in secret and passed messages between him and Milly. Fanny wouldn't be surprised.

A gunshot broke her concentration. Fanny jumped at the sound, but it was only the starting gun. There were six boats rowing toward a bridge where, as Teddy explained, they'd round a floating mark and return to the boat, marking the finish.

Picnicking crowds cheered on their favorites. Teddy was loudly urging on the yellow boat while it was neck and neck with the blue boat from West End House. Fanny noticed the thick-necked young men in the St. Joseph's boat were falling behind a bit. "Extra weight," Teddy commented. Jake's boat slid past them and between another boat and the dueling yellow and blue. The two boats were so engaged with each other they went slightly off course.

Jake and another boat rounded the mark first. Milly and Holly screamed encouragement while Teddy scolded his team from afar, shaking a fist at them for letting the two boats get by them. Blue and yellow were third and forth to round and head back. On the stretch, the boats flew along the water. They could hear the coxswains yelling, "stroke, stroke." The crowd shouted comments, and some people stood up as the four boats in front got closer to the finish line.

Fanny stood. The blue boat was gliding fast. The men's heads were down as they bent to the task. Teddy screamed to his men who were close behind. Fanny could see the boats had to be careful to steer away from each other, so oars didn't tangle, as they did for two of the boats that were far behind the leaders. St. Joseph's got tangled up, and the boat nearly capsized. The extra weight was harder to keep balanced she thought. Then she saw Jake's boat heading straight for the blue West End House boat. Ari Zellman's head shot up as he saw Jake's boat approach, but at the last minute, Jake turned the boat and crossed the line to the sound of a gun.

Milly and Holly jumped up and down, clapping. Teddy complained, but he was smiling. Fanny smelled something. It was a cigar. She looked around. Chief Detective McKenna stood with a hand shading his eyes as he stared out at the riverboats. *Oh no.*

McKenna yelled at a couple of uniformed patrolmen and waved them over to Jake's dock just as the rowing scull landed. Hands on his hips, McKenna gloated. He looked at Fanny. "Got him now," he said.

Chapter Twenty-Seven

Jake saw McKenna and his men as he steered the boat to the dock. Too bad. He hoped Mack wouldn't blow his stack. The big Irishman encouraged Jake to support Peter every time they showed up for practice. He was nothing if not persistent. And they'd won in a spurt at the end. But Jake couldn't do anything about Peter's arrest. McKenna had a warrant. The law was on his side.

Hands reached out to pull the rowing scull in. The uniformed policemen nearly capsized the boat when one of them grabbed Peter and tried to pull him out.

"Hey," Mack shouted. He stood up and bent to grab the dock, spreading his weight to bring the boat back into balance. "You stupid sons of…" He stopped when he saw Fanny, Holly, and Milly on the unsteady dock.

While the policemen arrested Peter, Jake remained sitting in the stern till the boat steadied. He saw McKenna gloating on shore, reluctant to set foot on the floating dock. Edwin jumped out gracefully and offered Jake a hand. It made him feel his age, but he took the help. He purposely stood in Mack's way as the big man cursed the policemen and yelled an insult at McKenna, who gave him a finger salute.

"Stop, Mack. He's got a warrant. There's nothing we can do now." Jake gestured to the boat, and Mack helped lift it out and on to the dock. The women huddled at the shore side of the dock watching the police handcuff Peter. "Out of the way," Jake yelled at them as Mack and Edwin picked up the scull, and Jake gathered the long oars. Teddy Greene stepped forward to help them.

The women scurried out of the way but followed the men to the Union Boat House, where they put the boat on a rack. Teddy passed oars to Mack and turned to his sister and Holly. "It's too bad Peter came out of hiding for this."

"How would McKenna know to look for Peter here?" Holly asked. Jake noticed that Teddy Greene put an arm around the girl's shoulders to comfort her.

"Someone squealed," Mack grunted. He loomed up from the boathouse shadows. "When I find out who, they'll regret it."

Jake knew Peter could have been spotted when they practiced rowing in the early mornings. That fool, McKenna, was intent on blaming Peter Attwood for Kessler's death. No matter that the man had been injected with morphine. That fact didn't register with the thick-headed Chief of Detectives McKenna. This is what he had to contend with. Profound ignorance.

"Where did they take Peter?" Milly asked. "Can't we do something to help him?"

Jake thought Peter would be pleased with the concern from his ladylove if he hadn't been arrested and taken away. Too bad he missed it. Fanny was looking at Jake with raised eyebrows. She expected him to do something even though she knew he planned to resign. He was surprised to see her at the race. He thought she'd left for New Hampshire with her daughter. The Kessler mystery was keeping her in town.

"You know that blockhead McKenna will never follow up on the source of the morphine," Mack said. He wanted to get back on the case.

"All right, all right," Jake succumbed to the pressure. "Let's meet back at the mortuary after the ceremonies. We can decide what to do next." He turned to Holly and Milly. "You ladies might want to see if Mr. Attwood senior can bail his son out." Holly grimaced as if in pain. "If he won't, then Peter will just have to wait for a hearing. You might find him a lawyer."

"I can go to Joy Street and find out what's become of him," Teddy offered.

Milly stood wringing her hands. Her brother pulled her away.

As Jake headed back for the awards on the riverbank, he saw Fanny attempting to soothe Holly. They had their heads together. He felt a twinge of guilt. He knew Mack had convinced Peter to do the rowing in an attempt to get him into Jake's good graces. The fact that winning the race had put Peter in jail didn't escape Jake's notice. Jake was frustrated that the powers that be didn't care for the truth about Kessler's death. They only wanted a solution that would make the problem go away. Jake felt he owed it to his team to find out the truth before he turned in his resignation. He knew it was what Fanny wanted, and he had to admit she was right.

Chapter Twenty-Eight

Fanny gave Holly the names of two criminal lawyers. Holly recognized the family name of one. "You're sure your father won't help him?" Fanny asked.

"He'll be furious that Peter has gotten into such serious trouble. Maybe I should bring Milly to plead for Peter. My father likes Milly. He knew her father pretty well."

Fanny wondered if the elder Mr. Attwood also liked Milly's brother, Teddy. He was, after all, a Harvard student, and Peter's father was angry when his son left that august institution for the police. Perhaps he could see a way to force a return to Harvard by helping Peter. Fanny would be disappointed, but it might be best for the young man. From the father's old-fashioned point of view, the marriages of Milly to Peter and Holly to Teddy might bring his whole world back into balance. Fanny knew the pull of society's expectations for obvious life choices. She'd tried that for herself, but the real world was no longer the predictable, constrained society of her parents' youth. She hoped the young people would successfully release themselves from the expectations of the older generation. But they had to live, and the real world could be a bruising place, as Peter was finding out.

Fanny spotted Rachel Kessler walking with an awkward young man and a bulky older woman. "That's Leonard Abrams and his mother with Rachel," Holly said.

They were all in black. "They must have come to see her brother Bernie in the West End boat," Milly said.

"I can't believe she's going to marry Abrams," Holly said. "Even her father held off allowing the engagement until Abrams had enough money to support a wife. Rachel told me Leonard Abrams' mother is unbearable, and she'd shoot herself before she'd live in the same house with her." Holly looked at Fanny. "She was kidding. But I'm sure Rachel was involved with someone else. I think it was Mr. Zellman. I really don't understand. I have to talk to her. Rachel! "Rachel!" She hurried away and caught her friend by the arm.

Fanny followed.

"Rachel, you remember Mrs. Lee? I've been hoping to talk to you. Mrs. Abrams, Mr. Abrams, this is Mrs. Lee."

Fanny chatted about the weather and the races while Holly pulled Rachel away from the group. Fanny could see Mrs. Abrams was keeping an eye on the young women who had their heads together. Bernie Kessler, who had been pointed out to her as Rachel's brother, joined them. He was in rowing shorts and tee shirt. He had shadows under his eyes and was stick thin. His dark hair was in need of a cut, and he had a small moustache. He'd come out for the race, despite mourning his father. Fanny noticed a frown of disapproval on Mrs. Abrams's face.

"You're done with your boating?" Mrs. Abrams said. Bernie looked away. "I don't know how you could do this race business so soon after your father is buried. It's not proper."

Abrams attempted to wave her comments away, but she wasn't to be ignored. Bernie Kessler stepped away just far enough to pretend not to hear Mrs. Abrams.

"No, Lenny, it's not right," she told her son. "We don't do that in our family. He's under the influence of the Zellman character." She turned to Fanny. "He's a radical, you know. He's giving other Jews a bad name with his strikes and his Zionist meetings. He's a bad influence. I don't let my Lenny hang around that West End House. There's all sorts of bohemians and others there."

"Now, Mother, stop it. Bernie's an athlete, you see? He rows. That's a manly sport, isn't it?" Leonard Abrams insisted.

Mrs. Abrams grumbled. "It's something those Harvard men do. All trying to be alike. No need for that. My Lenny doesn't need all that bookish nonsense at Harvard. We told Bernie he needs to do business, like Lenny. And now they can do his father's jewelry business. Much better than all that studying for nothing over in Cambridge."

Fanny remembered hearing that Rachel's brother was no longer enrolled at Harvard, according to Mr. Zellman. She thought she saw a look of utter desperation on Bernie Kessler's face. He returned to Leonard Abrams' side. "Len, I need to talk to you about the Securities Exchange Company. Teddy Greene told me something today."

Abrams stepped over to put an arm around Bernie and lead him away, excusing them both to talk business.

Fanny was left with Mrs. Abrams, who frowned at their backs. "My Lenny is turning into quite the businessman. He knows what he's doing. Before you know it, he and Bernie Kessler will own that building they work in. Rachel won't have to work at that dress place when she marries my son. I always knew Lenny would be a success."

Rachel returned to them looking flustered. Fanny could see Holly left behind, talking to Mr. Zellman from the West End House. She wondered what had brought Rachel back to her future mother-in-law without Holly. Rachel was unusually quiet, letting Mrs. Abrams chatter on. Fanny wondered if the death of her father had completely buried the young woman's spirits.

When Holly came to rescue Fanny and led her away, Fanny sensed a coolness between Holly and Rachel. They said goodbye, promising to meet at Mrs. Shurcliff's house the next day, but after they moved away, Holly told her Rachel was quitting the apprenticeship.

"I can't believe how she's changed," Holly said. "She's actually going to marry that Abrams wimp. How can she? And she says she can't work anymore. I don't understand it. Rachel's been more enthusiastic about the Pegleggers than even me. Mrs. Shurcliff will be devastated. We've got several commissions Rachel and I are helping with. How can she give it all up for that man?"

"The death of her father seems to have hit her very hard," Fanny said.

She didn't know Rachel, but the changes Holly mentioned seemed extreme. "Doesn't she want to know how her father died?"

"I tried to bring it up, but she blanked out completely," Holly said. "She didn't want to hear about it. She's deeply sad, I could see that, but why won't she do something about it?"

"Does she think her father took the morphine by accident? Or on purpose?" Fanny asked.

"I don't know. I don't understand. She wouldn't talk about it. It's so unlike her."

Fanny wondered if Rachel had found out something about her father's death that she didn't want to reveal to her friend.

"She doesn't even care that Peter was arrested," Holly moaned. She was hurt by her friend's lack of sympathy. Fanny wondered if Peter's failure to see that Mr. Kessler was ill made Rachel believe he was somehow responsible for the death. It was sad to see the break between Holly and Rachel, who had been such good friends. She thought of a way to distract Holly and help with the investigation.

"Holly, after you find a lawyer for your brother, perhaps there's something else you can do to help with Mack's investigation." Fanny hoped Mack and Edwin would be able to get Jake to support a continuing inquiry into Kessler's death.

She explained how, in two previous cases, they had used a miniature construction of the crime scene to help with the investigation. Holly jumped on the suggestion. Fanny told her she would supply her with the sketches she had made on the street where Peter found Kessler. "And the jail cell, too," she said. "We think he was injected with the morphine elsewhere, but he actually died in the cell. The scale should be one inch to one foot. Do you think you can do that? Just the buildings. I'll supply the dolls for the bodies at both places, and we can work together on other details."

"Yes. I can do it. I can work at Mrs. Shurcliff's studio, and I can go look at the buildings again, too. Maybe I can see Peter if I can get into the jail."

Fanny was glad to provide Holly with something to do. They agreed to meet after Holly found the lawyer for Peter. Fanny suggested that their grandmother, her good friend Cornelia, would be happy to pay the lawyer.

Chapter Twenty-Nine

After accepting the trophy and cleaning up, Jake returned to the morgue, where he found Edwin and Mack. In his office, the envelope containing his resignation was centered on his desk. He moved it under a pile of autopsy reports and pulled his chair out to the big examination room. Mack and Edwin were already seated. The front door opened and closed. Fanny joined them. Jake was glad to hear she'd sent Holly to find a lawyer for her brother. Not an easy task on a Sunday.

"I thought you'd have left for New Hampshire by now," he said to her.

She sat on a stool. "I couldn't leave. You can't let McKenna get away with this, Jake. It's not right. You know Peter Attwood is not responsible for Mr. Kessler's death. McKenna is just lazy!"

He'd told her he planned to resign. With typical stubbornness, she refused to accept his decision. She'd be bitterly disappointed if he turned his back on the situation now. Jake resigned himself to picking up the pieces of this tattered investigation and trying to put them together. It wasn't just Fanny's disappointment that spurred him on. He knew he wouldn't be able to live with himself if he left Peter in jail and Kessler's death still unexplained.

Mack grinned at Fanny's description of McKenna. "You're right, Mrs. Lee. McKenna is a lazy bum. With Attwood under his thumb, he won't move his ass out of his chair to find out where the morphine came from. He'll ignore it. I haven't been able to track down who's distributing drugs. Nobody's talking. They're afraid of King Solomon."

Jake considered McKenna a drunken sod. The man was clearly determined to rid himself of Peter. Yet, if Peter showed any signs of having support from his politically influential Brahmin family, McKenna would stop persecuting Peter. An idealistic young man might be outraged at the thought of influence, but it was the way of the world. Jake hoped Peter's sister would convince their father to intervene.

Time to go back to the beginning. "Who benefits from Kessler's death?" Jake asked.

"His children, Rachel and Bernie," Fanny said.

"Abrams," Mack said. "He gets to marry Rachel and gets control of her half of the inheritance. Bernie wasn't involved with the jewelry business. Abrams will get that."

Edwin had a different idea. "If Kessler knew who was providing the morphine, He could have been killed to prevent him from going to the police. There must have been a reason for Mr. Kessler to be near where he was found on the street. Somebody in that speakeasy must know how to get drugs."

Jake turned to Fanny. "Do you really think either of the Kessler children would kill their own father?" he asked.

"Mr. Kessler apparently wanted his daughter Rachel to marry Leonard Abrams," Fanny said. "Holly thinks she was in love with Mr. Zellman, and she was going to run away to avoid the marriage." Fanny was very disturbed that a young woman would take such radical action. Jake trusted her judgment about how extremely fraught the girl's home life must have been to plan to run away.

"If Miss Kessler injected her father with morphine to avoid marrying Abrams, she didn't succeed," Mack said. "They're engaged now, according to him and his mother. That Mrs. Abrams is enough to give you the heebie-jeebees, I've got to say."

"Perhaps she accidentally killed her father, and now she regrets it," Fanny said. "Why else would she agree to marry Abrams now?"

Jake remembered the grieving young woman who had identified her father. He was sorry to hear the death seemed to have thrown her into the arms of a man that neither Mack nor Fanny approved. "Where would Miss Kessler get morphine? Do you think she was addicted?"

"More likely the brother," Mack said. "Bernie Kessler resigned from Harvard," he told them. "Sounds like he may have left under a cloud. Maybe he was caught using drugs over there and got kicked out. Teddy Greene mentioned some friend of Bernie's recently committed suicide." Jake wondered if they should follow up on the Harvard connection. It was too bad Peter was unavailable to help. He would know people over in Cambridge. It wasn't a place to send Mack, but they might have to.

Fanny mentioned that Rachel's brother Bernie had accosted Abrams about some business deal that Teddy Greene also was involved in.

"My money's on Abrams," Mack said. "He gets the business by marrying the daughter. There's something fishy going on there. That botched robbery is suspicious. I don't believe Mr. Kessler would have let him marry the girl. He was supposed to need money to get the father's approval. Suddenly, he doesn't have to anymore."

Clearly, Mack was suspicious of Leonard Abrams. "It would help if we knew where Kessler was when he was injected," Jake said.

Edwin's research led him to believe that Kessler had been injected with the drug four to eight hours before his death after midnight in the jail cell.

"He got stuck with the stuff, then put on his coat and went out?" Mack asked.

"Could be," Edwin said. "He wasn't found near his own apartment, however. He was in front of the speakeasy joint. He couldn't have gone far alone. The drug took some hours to kill him but only twenty minutes to make him too drowsy to navigate."

Jake blew out a long breath. Mack, Edwin, and Fanny were spread around the autopsy room. The tables were empty of bodies but ready for customers when the work week started on Monday. Since the police refused to go any further with their investigation, it was left to the medical examiner's office to find out the truth. Who had given Isaac Kessler morphine? Had he injected himself, or had someone stuck him before he could fend them off? There were no signs of a struggle on the body, which had already been released and buried. He didn't believe the man had stuck himself with a hypodermic needle.

"The speakeasy seems the logical place to buy drugs," Edwin said. "You couldn't find anyone who knew anything about it there?"

"They denied it," Mack said. He clearly thought if they wouldn't tell him, they wouldn't spill to someone else.

"Of course they did. Nobody would believe you'd look for drugs," Edwin pointed out. "I've got friends who were fellow soldiers who got stuck on the stuff." He grimaced in disgust. "I'll bet they'd be more willing to believe that someone with a face like this would be looking for drugs." Jake realized that Edwin wanted to go to the speakeasy himself to investigate the drug sales. Edwin never willingly brought up the burn scars that ruined half his face. Jake was surprised that he was willing to use his injuries to find the source of the morphine. As a medical student, Edwin had access to drugs. Jake hoped he didn't fall into the trap of using them. He didn't believe Edwin pretending he used morphine would tempt him to try the drug. He'd suffered through so much the past few years. Jake trusted Edwin's attachment to the young Irish widow he was seeing would protect him from temptation.

"It seems like the speakeasy might be worth another look," Jake said. Before Mack could object, Jake gave him a task. "Mack, you need to find out what's really going on with Leonard Abrams. He does seem to benefit from Kessler's death. Find out about his finances. And what does that robbery at the building they're in have to do with Kessler's death, if anything?"

Mack nodded enthusiastically and prepared to leave.

"This can all wait till tomorrow," Jake said. "I'll be at the Hendrick's Club in the morning. Lomasney wants an update."

Chapter Thirty

Fanny waited until Mack left before telling Jake and Edwin that she had recruited Holly to build a miniature of the sidewalk where Peter found Kessler and the jail cell where he'd died. Mack would probably think it was a waste of time. But Fanny thought it helped to focus the investigation by concentrating on the details. In any case, she hoped it would keep Holly busy and away from more dangerous aspects of the investigation. She didn't want Holly running to Club Garden to confront a gangster. Much as she admired the young woman's efforts to find a place for herself that was not constrained by her family background and society's expectations, she knew that Mack belonged in places like a speakeasy and Holly did not.

Fanny would create the dolls that represented Kessler, so she wanted to see the clothes he'd worn.

Edwin found the paper bag with the dead man's belongings and spread them out on one of the examination tables. There was a plaid cap and a rough brown wool jacket. In the pocket, Fanny found a worn pipe and a small package of tobacco. When she moved on to the white shirt, silk tie, and trousers of a fine gray wool, she frowned.

"The shirt and pants are good quality. What I'd expect from a prosperous jeweler. And look at the shoes. Good leather. But the jacket and cap don't match. Those pants look like part of a suit. Why wasn't he wearing a matching suit jacket, I wonder."

Edwin tried to help. "Perhaps he wore a suit to work, but afterwards, when he went out, he wore something not so formal."

"Assuming he'd gone home after work and before he met his death," Jake said.

Edwin lifted another bag onto the table and spilled out its contents. "We picked these up from the sidewalk where Kessler was found. That was when we went back the next day."

There was a metal lunchbox and a blackened banana peel. Fanny assumed Peter had left them behind when he'd transported Mr. Kessler to the jail. He wouldn't have considered them important, but Fanny was scrupulous about every detail when she constructed a miniature.

Jake considered the banana peel. "What a bad joke. As if he slipped on the banana like a scene from the Chaplin movie." He shook his head. "Poor Mr. Kessler to suffer such indignities in death."

Fanny opened the lunchbox, but it was empty. "Why would he have a lunchbox? If he'd brought it from work, why was he not still wearing the suit jacket? If he'd gone home, surely he'd have left his lunchbox behind when he went out again."

Edwin's face lit up. "Perhaps he wanted to look like a workman. And he brought the lunchbox on purpose. What if he was trying to buy the morphine, but he was recognized, and he got stuck with the morphine instead?" He tapped the lunchbox. "I think there's drug selling in that speakeasy."

Jake looked concerned. "It's possible, but, Edwin, if you pursue that on your own, be very careful. King Solomon has a gang. They won't be happy if they think you're snooping around their drug trade. Look at what you're theorizing about Kessler's death. If they killed him to keep him quiet, they'd do the same to you. Maybe you should bring Mack if you want to check out the speakeasy."

"They've already seen him as an investigator. They probably think he's police. They've never seen me."

Fanny sketched the pieces of clothing, thinking about how she would make a doll dressed like Kessler. She wasn't sure a miniature recreation of the crime scene or scenes would help to solve the mystery, but it couldn't hurt. She wondered whether the sidewalk or the jail cell was the real crime scene or was it somewhere else. Where had Mr. Kessler been stuck with a hypodermic needle full of morphine? And by whom? And why?

Chapter Thirty-One

Monday morning, Jake found the Hendricks Club in an uproar. When he entered Lomasney's office on the second floor, he found three men confronting the politician, who sat back in shirtsleeves on his rolling wooden armchair beside his desk.

"Please, boss. Look at this." The bowler-hatted man thrust a newspaper at Lomasney. Jake could see it was The Boston Post opened to the second page. He'd seen the story earlier. It was about a local investment company that was making huge amounts of money every day. Jake had read the article, but his own money was in a long-running annuity that supplemented his meager county salary.

"We could have been part of this," another man spoke up. "We could have been rich, Martin."

Lomasney shook his head. "When a deal looks too good to be true, it's too good to be true. A fifty percent profit in a month, one hundred percent in three months. On discounted postal coupons, come on, boys, you know it ain't true."

The men fell back in disappointment. Jake suspected Lomasney was doing them a favor. He'd heard drinking and pool were activities in the Hendrix Club, but gambling was forbidden. He'd also heard that Lomasney himself didn't even drink. He just played at politics.

"What can you tell me, Dr. Magrath? Have you found out what happened to our Jewish friend who died in a jail cell? I promised I'd find out for my constituents."

Jake reported that Kessler had died from morphine poisoning, making it clear there was no evidence he'd been mistreated by the police. He emphasized that the dead man's clothes had been soaked in whiskey. "That's why the patrolman thought he was just drunk. Chief Detective McKenna has arrested that young officer. But he hasn't tried to find out how or why Mr. Kessler was injected with morphine."

"What's the officer's name?" Lomasney asked.

"Peter Attwood," Jake told him. He thought Lomasney would be more interested if one of his Irish constituents was implicated. Jake figured Peter's Brahmin upbringing wouldn't help him in Lomasney's eyes. Still, he hoped to recruit the politician to help the young officer.

"We can't have drugs like morphine or heroin being sold in the West End. We won't stand for it. Do you know where it came from?" Lomasney demanded.

"The police have stopped investigating, but I have my people looking into it. We don't know where it came from. There's a speakeasy near where he was found, but we can't prove they're selling drugs." Even though Lomasney didn't drink himself, Jake knew he'd been vehemently opposed to the Volstead Act. He would have no problem with speakeasies in his precinct. It was the drugs he objected to.

"I can't believe Mr. Kessler would have gone to a speakeasy to buy morphine. His fellow businessmen all vouched for him." Lomasney sat back and scratched his head. "If the officer was negligent in Kessler's death, the police should follow up on that. But if he died from morphine and there's someone selling drugs on my turf, I want to know. I'll support your investigation, and I'll send out some of my men to see what they can find. Where is this speakeasy?"

Jake gave him the information. He was disappointed Lomasney wouldn't help Peter Attwood, but if anyone questioned him about Mack's investigations, Lomasney would support the medical examiner.

Just as Jake was leaving, a Catholic priest in a black cassock and white collar marched into the room, followed by one of Lomasney's minions. Jake saw a look of annoyance flash across the politician's face, but Lomasney pasted on a big smile when he rose and extended a hand to the priest. "Fr.

Kelly, how are you this fine morning? Here's Dr. Magrath, our revered medical examiner. Are you acquainted?"

Jake was forced to greet the priest. He suspected Lomasney didn't want to be left alone with the man who had an angry look on his red face. Jake thought the face probably always looked angry like that.

"Yes, of course. Congratulations on your trophy yesterday," the priest said. He would have been cheering on the St. Joseph's team and was clearly disappointed in their defeat.

Before Jake could thank him, the priest turned on Lomasney. "Martin, you need to do something about the Hebrews. Have you seen what Ford says in his latest article?" He held out a newspaper. The headline read "The International Jew: The World's Problem." Jake was startled. What was this all about?

When Lomasney returned to his desk and chair, Jake heard a sigh escape from his mouth. "Well, now, Fr. Kelly, that's a Michigan newspaper, isn't it? Seems like Mr. Henry Ford has strong opinions about many things. He's against the Jews now, is he?"

"You need to read this, Martin. You need to hear the truth. It's a conspiracy, a worldwide conspiracy." Fr. Kelly attempted to thrust the paper at Lomasney, but the canny politician wouldn't take it.

"This is the same Mr. Ford who was against the war in Europe, now wasn't he?" Lomasney said. Jake wanted to extract himself from the unpleasant discussion, but he didn't want to draw fire from the animated priest, so he kept quiet. He'd wait for a break to announce his departure.

"That's because the Jewish bankers were behind it," Fr. Kelly insisted. He slapped the newspaper onto Lomasney's desk. "You've got to read this so you can see why you need to stop supporting Jewish candidates for political positions. It has to stop, Martin. How can you support a candidate like that against an Irishman who's supported you for years? You're being manipulated by the Hebrews."

Lomasney frowned. "If a man takes a position and then doesn't show up and do the work, I've no obligation to see him reelected or reappointed. I know who you're talking about. The man didn't live up to his obligations and then he moved to Dorchester. The candidate I support is an active precinct captain who delivers the vote. I don't care what religion the man adheres to as long as he's good at the job. If he's not, then being Irish won't help him."

Jake knew that Lomasney's West End used to be primarily Irish. But as the Irish had moved up in the world, they'd moved out to other areas, and Italians, Jews, Polish, and others had filled the tenements they left behind. Lomasney was a man who moved with the times. Fr. Kelly apparently wasn't.

"You endanger your soul with such attitudes, Martin. You endanger your soul!" the priest murmured as he stomped out of the room, defeated by Lomasney's intransigence.

The politician looked at Jake. "I take it St. Joseph's didn't do well in the rowing races?"

Chapter Thirty-Two

The same Monday morning, Holly found Milly Greene on her doorstep. She'd asked her friend to plead Peter's case with Holly's father. The senior Mr. Attwood had heard of his son's arrest and was furious, but at Peter, not the Chief of Detectives who had arrested him.

Milly wore a low-waisted chiffon dress in a pale blue and green print. Her snug hat framed her face with blonde curls peeking out. Gloves and a long pearl necklace completed an outfit Holly knew would impress her father. She thought her friend had done well in choosing her dress. She looked the way Holly's father would have liked his daughter to look, Holly thought, self-conscious about the wrinkled walking skirt she'd chosen to wear.

Holly left Milly in her father's study and went to get him from the breakfast table. Luckily, he was just finishing his coffee and newspaper. He raised an eyebrow at the news that he had a guest, but he dropped his linen napkin and followed Holly back to the study where he seated Milly on a straight-backed chair in front of his desk and took the place behind it. Holly drew up a small, cushioned chair. She wasn't about to leave her friend alone with her often brusque father.

"What can I do for you, Miss Greene?" He leaned his head back and looked down his nose at Milly. Holly could have pinched him for intimidating her friend, but Milly was firm.

"I've come to plead with you to help your son Peter. He's been arrested by the police, and it's very unfair. The policeman in charge has some sort of vendetta against your son. Peter tried to help the man who died; he didn't harm him."

Holly thought it was shrewd to appeal to her father's family pride, and she knew the wispy feminine figure Milly cut perched on the edge of her big chair would appeal to her father. He was probably thinking Milly always appeared this elegant. Of course, at Peabody House every day, Milly didn't put on such airs. Holly's father never visited the settlement house.

"My son joined the police force against my express wishes. He should have continued his studies at Harvard. I am deeply disappointed in him. In fact, after a particularly disrespectful argument, I washed my hands of him."

Milly sighed and fiddled with the small purse in her lap. "I know you've disagreed about Peter's choice of profession."

"Profession, is that what he calls it?" Peter's father scoffed.

Milly bit her lip. "I've become very good friends with your son in the past few months," she told him. "He confided in me about your disapproval, and you should know that he is deeply distressed at the gulf that has grown between the two of you."

Holly blinked. She thought Peter was deeply angry with her father, not so much distressed. Perhaps Peter showed a different side of himself to Milly, but Holly thought her brother detested many of their father's beliefs.

"We've talked about why you were disappointed that he left Harvard," Milly said. "I could understand your point of view. I told him how we've struggled to fund my brother's studies at Harvard because we know it's what my father would have wanted had he lived."

Holly's father looked sympathetic at the unspoken reference to the suicide of Milly's father. She knew how to soften up a hard case. Holly pursed her lips to restrain herself from uttering a word. Milly had the man in the palm of her hand.

"I believe that, after this experience, Peter will rethink his plans. The man who is his superior, named McKenna, despises Peter. I believe it's because your son was a Harvard student, and because he is from a Brahmin background. He holds that against Peter, whether from jealousy or some other reason."

Good tack, Holly thought. Milly was positioning Peter against an Irish cop. Holly's father despised the immigrants he saw flooding his city. Especially those Irish who had snatched the reins of the city from Brahmin hands. But the Irish weren't the only ones Milly was presenting as foes of Peter.

"You might not know that Mr. Lomasney, who has a lot of political power in the city, has demanded action because some of the Jewish businessmen who were friends of the dead Mr. Kessler have gone to him to intercede," Milly said. Holly's father grunted and moved in his chair. Holly knew he despised Jews, especially if they competed with him at banking. "From what Peter has said, I believe that is one reason McKenna arrested Peter, to respond to influence from Mr. Lomasney."

Milly knew how to appeal to the prejudices of Holly's father. Holly thought Milly must have spent a lot of time in heart-to-heart talks with Peter to know so much about the elder Attwood's opinions and dislikes. She also must be very attached to Peter to approach their father so fearlessly. Holly thought Milly might be the very one to take over the task of protecting her brother. She clearly cared deeply about him. Holly held her breath, hoping Milly had somehow pierced the thick skin of her father.

"You are very generous in your defense of Peter," Holly's father said. "I confess, I did not plan to help him this time." *As if he had ever helped him,* Holly thought. "Of course, I love my son, Miss Greene. But he has been so stubborn, and he won't listen to me."

Holly's father exasperated her. She knew he loved his children, but since her mother's death, he had become rigid in his thinking. She remembered how her mother had managed to coax him from harshness by teasing him. Sometimes, Holly succeeded in this approach herself, but with her brothers, he'd become more and more stiff and intransient. She saw a glimmer of hope that Milly might be able to intercede for Peter as their mother would have done.

Holly's father cleared his throat. "I understand, from your description of the circumstances, that this McKenna is some kind of bullying oaf. Unfortunately, this type of man has been appointed by the recent administrations at city hall. I'd hoped with the breaking of the police strike such obnoxious officers had been purged from the ranks. And for him to attempt to sully our family name for the sake of a dead Jew is too much. Too much."

Holly was offended by her father's reduction of Rachel's father to a "dead Jew," but for the sake of her brother, she bit her tongue. Milly sat staring up at Holly's father, hopefully.

"I will do what I can, Miss Greene. Peter should be sincerely thankful to you for your kind words on his behalf. I can't promise he will be, since his attitudes and beliefs are beyond my comprehension these days. But I thank you for him. I will see what I can do." Holly could see he was definitely softened up. "As a matter of fact, my mother-in-law contacted me today to get me to pay for a lawyer for Peter's defense. The woman has no notion of who to hire, so I will have to look into it. I will. I only hope my son will be suitably grateful."

Holly walked her friend to the door, squeezing her elbow to let her know she'd done a super job of convincing her father to help Peter. Holly wasn't at all sure Peter would be on board for Milly's implied promise that he would rethink Harvard, but at least he'd get a good lawyer. She knew her grandmother's intervention had helped to push her father to support Peter as well. She figured the women were winning, at least at the moment.

Chapter Thirty-Three

Mack found Leonard Abrams at the Kessler Jewelry Company. Glancing around and listening closely, Mack was glad to see and hear no sign of Mrs. Abrams. He remembered her only too clearly from his earlier visit. Abrams didn't look happy to see him.

"What can I do for you? I don't suppose you've come to look for a ring for your fiancée, or something for your mother?" Abrams asked.

Mack was momentarily distracted by the idea of looking for an engagement ring. Was he being facetious? As if Mack'd ever be faced with that task. Not very likely.

"Dr. Magrath has determined that Mr. Kessler was poisoned with morphine. Was he with you here at your workplace that day? Did you see him take any medicine?"

"He was here, of course, but I didn't see him take any medicine. He wasn't sick."

"What did he do that day? Any detail may help," Mack stared at Abrams. He hardly knew what to make of the little man with his full beard and the top hat he wore even inside. He made Mack impatient.

"Mr. Kessler was the same as always until late in the day. He received a letter in the mail. When he opened it, he appeared upset. He left right after that."

"Where's that letter?" Mack asked.

"He took it with him." Abrams seemed self-satisfied.

Mack wanted to shake him up. He leaned across the counter and said, "How is it that suddenly you're engaged to Miss Kessler? I thought her father demanded you have enough money to support her in a home away from your mother. Where'd you get the money?"

Behind the counter, Abrams backed up to the wall. "That's no business of yours. Miss Kessler has accepted my proposal. I've picked out a very fine diamond for her. We'll just wait a decent time for mourning and then marry."

"I see. Did you inherit money from Mr. Kessler? Did he leave you the business?"

"No, no, of course not. He left it to his children, but they depend on me to help them run it."

"So, you don't get the money."

Abrams looked flustered. He reached under the counter and came up with a newspaper opened to the inside. "As a matter of fact, I've had a good return on my investments. If you don't believe me, look at this." He pointed to an article about a local firm that was giving unusually high returns.

Mack had no knowledge of finance, but he did smell a problem. "Where'd you get money to invest? Did you take it from the Kessler company?"

"Of course not. I used my savings. I have savings from my salary." Abrams could see Mack was skeptical. "I live with my mother." His face reddened. "That allows me to save money. That's what I used."

At that moment, a bell jangled behind Mack. He turned and saw Bernie Kessler enter the room. He looked pale and drawn, skittish like a nervous horse. Mack felt waves of anxiety from the slight young man.

"Did you do it?" Abrams demanded.

"Yes," Bernie said.

"All of it?" Abrams asked.

Mack thought Bernie quailed a bit at the questions. "Yes. All of it."

Abrams turned to Mack with a satisfied expression. "Our investments are doing so well, Mr. Kessler and I decided to put in more of the money from the company. We used some of our diamonds as collateral. As you can see, I'm very close to Mr. Kessler and his sister. They depend on me now that their father has passed away."

Mack detected fear, not gratitude, in Bernie Kessler's attitude towards

Abrams. Why was he afraid of the man? The big Irishman turned and held out his left hand to Bernie. "Mr. Kessler? I'm McNally from the office of the medical examiner." Doubtfully, the young man put his bony left hand into Mack's big paw.

Mack grasped him firmly and shot out his other hand to push up the man's sleeve, exposing tracks of hypodermic marks.

Bernie pulled away, clutching his left arm to his stomach. "What are you doing?"

Abrams rushed from behind the counter to put himself between Mack and Bernie. "What's this all about?" he demanded.

Mack leaned back against the counter. "I see you're not surprised to see those marks on Mr. Kessler," he said to Abrams, who stood upright, flustered by the situation.

"It's none of your business. Mr. Kessler has a condition. A medical condition."

Mack lifted a skeptical eyebrow.

Abrams pulled Bernie by the arm, then pushed him through a doorway. "Stay in there." When he turned back to Mack the investigator saw a look of cunning in the jeweler's eyes. "Please, have some pity. He's just lost his father. Mr. Kessler's in a bad way."

"Does Mr. Kessler use morphine?" Mack demanded.

"Oh. It's a sad case." Abrams's shifty eyes were all over the place as he decided what to say. "It's like this. Bernie was under a lot of pressure at Harvard. With his studies. His father expected so much of him. He got in with a bad crowd. He was weak. He became dependent on morphine."

Mack couldn't help wondering if Abrams was making this all up as he went along. "Did his father know?"

"Not at first. But he found out."

"Is that why young Mr. Kessler left Harvard? Was he thrown out?" Mack had little understanding of the intellectuals over in Cambridge, but he supposed if they found out about the young man's drug dependency, they might expel him. Or they might not.

"I think so. I think so." Abrams twiddled his hands in front of him, revolving as if he were knitting or something. Mack wished he'd stop. Abrams rushed on with his explanation. "You can't think Bernie had anything to do with his father's death, though. His father would have been furious, but Bernie was just terribly ashamed." He glanced at the doorway and lowered his voice. "We were afraid Bernie might hurt himself. But never his father. Never."

"There was talk of some friend of Mr. Kessler's who committed suicide. Is that what you're talking about?" Mack asked.

"Yes, yes. That's it. He was addicted, too, I guess. But Mr. Kessler wouldn't blame Bernie. We all just wanted to keep him safe. Mr. Kessler, Rachel, and me. You see?"

Mack wondered if Abrams had used the information about the brother to blackmail Rachel Kessler into marrying him. Could he have threatened to turn Bernie in to the police? Before he could ask, Abrams' eyes lit up, and he rumbled on.

"Mr. Kessler would have been furious at whoever was providing Bernie with the drugs, don't you see? He tried to stop Bernie from going to the West End House anymore. He forbade it. But Bernie couldn't stop."

"You're saying someone at the West End House was selling morphine to Bernard Kessler?" Mack was blunt.

"I don't know. That's what I think. That's what Rachel and I thought. I don't know if Mr. Kessler knew, but I think he suspected."

Mack glanced at the doorway. He needed to talk to Bernie Kessler. Ignoring protests from Abrams, he marched through the door. When he confronted Bernie with the story Abrams had told, the exhausted-looking young man meekly agreed. He didn't add any information or dispute anything Abrams had said. The only thing he denied was that the drugs came from West End House. When asked where he got the morphine, he stared blankly into space. Finally, Mack gave up on him.

He certainly didn't seem capable of running his father's jewelry business. Mack could understand why Abrams was allowed to step up and take over. He could even imagine why Rachel Kessler might come to depend on Abrams to take care of her and her brother. But would she give up the much more handsome and impressive Ari Zellman, Mack wondered? Perhaps she'd learned something more about the West End House lawyer that made her turn to the unimpressive Abrams and his irritating mother.

Chapter Thirty-Four

Mack found his way back to the West End House, where he asked to see Ari Zellman. He found him in a small, crowded office on the first floor. Zellman heard him out and admitted that he knew Bernie Kessler had a drug problem. But he insisted his involvement had been confined to an attempt to help Bernie kick the habit. He admitted his efforts were ineffective.

"Is that why Bernard Kessler left Harvard?" Mack asked. These Harvard people were a close-mouthed group. He hated how they stuck together, as if mere association with the august institution layered them with a steel coat of protection from any accusations. Even Dr. Magrath was guilty of assumptions of innocence when it came to Harvard men.

Zellman wasn't willing to confirm that Bernie's drug problem was what made him give up his studies. "I don't know. I can't say that for sure."

Mack could see the man was struggling with something. It seemed like Zellman wanted to say something more but felt obliged to hold his tongue. What was it about these guys? Did they take a blood oath, or something?

"There are accusations that you or someone else at West End House is supplying morphine and heroin," Mack told him bluntly, hoping to get under his skin. "There are also rumors that some friend of Bernie Kessler's committed suicide because he was addicted to these drugs. If you're involved with Charles Solomon and his drug sales, sooner or later, we'll nail you for it."

"West End House has nothing to do with Solomon's drugs. And nothing to do with Bernie Kessler's problems or the suicide of his friend. All we ever did was try to help Bernie give up the drugs."

"You knew about this friend who committed suicide then?" Mack asked.

Zellman sighed. "Cyril Wilcox. He was a good friend of Bernie's. His death drove Bernie to nearly killing himself as well. But morphine was only the method Bernie might have used if he got up the courage. Luckily, he confessed to Rachel, and she didn't let him use the drug that way, to kill himself. I think he's still using it to deaden his emotions, though."

"So, you do know about who's selling drugs. You know about this Cyril Wilcox."

Zellman looked weary. "Not really." He closed his eyes as if struggling with his conscience. "I can't tell you about Cyril. But you could talk to Harry at Café Dreyfus on Beacon Hill." Having given Mack that much, Zellman stood up. "I can't help you with anything else. Please let me get on with my work."

Mack wasn't sure what to believe. It was clear that Bernie Kessler had a drug habit. How that had led to his father's death was a different question. Could Bernie have fought with his father and injected him with morphine? On purpose? Or, by accident? Surely not. It seemed to Mack more likely that Edwin was right. Isaac Kessler must have found out something about who was selling drugs to his son. Mack decided he should check out this Café Dreyfus. But he was irritated by the attitudes of these people with Harvard connections, be they Brahmins or Jews. They made him uncomfortable. He had a hard time reading their expressions. Give him a drunk or stubborn Irishman, even a garrulous Italian, and he'd know where he stood. These supercilious Harvard types stumped him. He needed to visit the café, but perhaps he should bring an interpreter. It was an idea.

Chapter Thirty-Five

Monday night, Edwin found his way to the speakeasy in the basement of the ice cream shop. As he expected, no one questioned his entrance. The waitress upstairs nodded at the door to the basement steps, and the men at the long bar in the damp basement barely looked at him. He found a seat in the shadows, and the barman filled his order for a beer.

He couldn't hide the scars on his face. The barman wiped the unvarnished wood of the counter. "You get that over there?" he asked.

Edwin was used to the question. He nodded.

"I was there. Belleau Wood," the barman said. "A real nightmare."

Edwin gulped down the whole glass and prepared to talk about things he usually avoided. "Got blown up. You can see." He motioned for another beer, and the barman pulled one for him.

"That's got to hurt," the barman said. "Got a pal lost his leg. Says he still feels it. Never goes away." He looked sympathetic. He nodded at the drinkers at the other end of the bar. "These civilians don't know." He set the glass mug before Edwin. "On the house. For your service. God knows Solomon can afford it."

"Solomon owns this place?" Edwin asked.

The barman glanced around to be sure they weren't heard. "Yeah. Not a bad boss, even if he's a Jew."

"I heard he's into more than alcohol," Edwin said, then took a sip.

"Yeah, women in a couple of buildings, other stuff."

"Does he do drugs? I heard something," Edwin said.

The barman bristled. He started wiping the counter again. "Not in here. No such stuff. Booze, you just pay up to the cops. Give 'em a free drink if they threaten a raid. But ain't nobody going to turn a blind eye to drugs. Especially as Lomasney'd be on them like a hawk. No drugs here."

Edwin could see he didn't want to discuss drugs. When the barman started to move away, Edwin reached out and grabbed his sleeve. "It's the pain," he said. "They gave you stuff for it in the hospital. But now you have to find it on your own. You wouldn't believe the pain." He reached up and touched his scars, causing the barman to look away. Edwin had him now. "I had a supplier over on the Common, but he's disappeared. I'm desperate, man. I heard there's some down here in the West End. Help me, can't you?"

He'd worn a threadbare old uniform jacket and gone unshaven to help look like he was in bad shape. He faced the barman full-on, while still clutching the man's sleeve, so he had to look at the scars. Edwin knew how ugly they were. He avoided his own mirror. God only knew how his fiancée endured it.

The barman pulled away. "Not here," he said. He stretched the rag in his hands. "Solomon has some business, but never in the speaks, like I said. I've heard something."

Edwin looked as pitiful as he could, tears welling in his eyes.

"Look," the barman said in frustration, "I don't do drugs. It's only what I heard. They say he's got contacts in the houses."

"The settlement houses? Which ones? Peabody House? West End House? Isn't there another?"

"All of them," the barman said.

Chapter Thirty-Six

Mack convinced Holly Attwood to accompany him to the Café Dreyfus Monday evening by agreeing to finish up the night at a performance in the Peabody House theater. When he telephoned, she told him in hushed tones how Milly had convinced her father to find a good lawyer for Peter and how Holly had agreed to join Milly and Teddy Greene for the amateur production of *Midsummer Night's Dream*. Mack planned to make a speedy retreat after delivering Holly to the settlement until he heard that Ari Zellman had a part in the play. His suspicions of the Harvard law student ran deep. He suspected Charles Solomon could have corrupted the prickly young man if he tried. And why wouldn't he? Like all gangsters, Solomon needed a lawyer.

Holly had never visited Café Dreyfus, but she met Mack at the front door on Beacon Street. The café was housed in the bottom floor of a brick rowhouse. There was a discreet sign in tiny flowing gold on black. You stepped down a few steps to the door.

Inside, the room was dark and smoky. Small round tables with dainty iron chairs were packed into the room. Heavy velvet curtains shrouded tall windows, and wallpaper in deep red satin ran up the walls and across the ceiling. Chandeliers and light brackets were formed of twining branches and leaves in black iron. Dark cherry furniture lined the walls.

As Holly bravely marched across the room to an empty table, Mack was shocked to see that the room was filled with young men, and only men. He'd assumed it would be a place that served coffee and tea and was frequented by ladies of Beacon Hill. Now, he wondered if this was some sort of men's club. He regretted recruiting Peter's sister. When they sat, Holly looked around, pursing her lips and nodding to herself. Mack was about to ask her what she was thinking when a waiter approached.

"Good evening, dears. Can we get you something? We have a lovely Bordeaux in a coffee cup, or a mellow whiskey in a glass mug. Slumming, are we?"

Holly spoke up. "Just dropping in before we go to a play," she said. "I thought I might see my brother here, but I'm wrong tonight." She smiled.

The waiter, who had seemed a bit on edge, settled down. "Perhaps he'll be along later. Do I know him?"

"His name's Peter, but no worry. We'll have the whiskey, thanks."

Mack frowned. "You think Peter comes here?"

"Not likely. Just making conversation." Holly looked like a cat who had swallowed a family parrot. Mack decided not to humor her.

"I need to speak to a man named Harry Dreyfus. He must own the place," Mack said.

"Son of the owner, I think," Holly said. "I remember hearing of this place before, but I've never been here."

Mack wondered at that. Maybe that was why she mentioned her brother. He felt warm and ran his finger around his collar. The air smelled as if laden with perfume. The young men sat elbow to elbow, speaking with animation. Many of them seemed dressed up. Perhaps this was a meeting place before people went to the opera or symphony, or other rarified entertainments that Beacon Hill denizens haunted. Even if Holly was the only female in the place, it was probably a good thing he'd brought her. Mack had a hard time understanding Brahmin culture.

When the waiter brought the glass teacups with whiskey, Mack asked for Harry Dreyfus. They sipped from the unlikely vessels while the waiter disappeared behind a curtain. Mack supposed, like other places, the Café Dreyfus made a nominal effort to pretend they weren't serving alcohol. A man joined them at the tiny table.

Harry Dreyfus was in his thirties, older than most of the men in the room. He wore a pencil-thin moustache, and his hair was oiled back like a matinee idol. His trousers had a sharp crease, and his brown shoes were shiny. Quite the dapper, Mack thought.

Mack got to the point immediately. "Ari Zellman at the West End House told me you could explain about Cyril Wilcox's suicide. I'm investigating the death of Isaac Kessler for the medical examiner. Kessler died of morphine poisoning. His son Bernard was a friend of Wilcox. Was Wilcox a user of morphine? Was that behind his death?" Mack glanced around the room as if to suggest there might be trade in morphine going on in the café.

Holly gulped a mouthful of whiskey, then made an effort to suppress a cough.

Dreyfus had a hurt look on his face. "Mr. Zellman gave you the wrong idea. There are no drugs here. As you can see," he waved a hand. "We have a bohemian set of customers. If some of them indulge in mind-numbing drugs, they do not do it here, and they certainly don't buy drugs here. We'd never allow it."

The smells tickling Mack's nose weren't from heroin or hashish. He looked around at the "bohemian" crowd and thought of his cousin Francis Xavier. Of course, they were like him. Francis Xavier was fussy and considered a sissy, but he took good care of his old mother and went to mass with her all the time. "Fairies," some guys called them, but Mack didn't see any harm in Francis Xavier and his like. Each to his own. He didn't believe Peter Attwood spent time here. Holly was pulling his leg. Why had Zellman sent him here? "You knew Cyril Wilcox? Did he use drugs? Morphine in particular."

Dreyfus looked down at his hands, clenched in his lap. "Cyril was a friend. That is true. And he came here." He shook his head in sorrow. "I am devastated by his death, especially if he really did take his own life, as they tell me."

"Was it morphine that killed him?"

"No, gas. He opened the gas valve in his bedroom."

"Why'd he kill himself? Was he addicted to drugs?"

"I don't know. The pressures from Harvard, I think. He said goodbye to me before he went home to his parents. I didn't know he was so unhappy. I would have helped him if I did."

Mack wondered how the man could not know if the dead student had been dependent on drugs. It must have shown in his actions. He still suspected Dreyfus was lying.

"What about the drugs?"

"I don't know. I think perhaps he may have used some drugs. Perhaps smoking hashish. Some of the students do that. I don't know. You would have to ask Mr. Zellman and the other Harvard students."

Mack was frustrated. Why had Zellman sent him to Dreyfus? If the man was selling drugs, Mack couldn't get him to admit it. He thought of Edwin and wondered if he sent Edwin to Café Dreyfus, perhaps he could get them to sell him drugs. Mack was sure Edwin was wrong about the speakeasy. He'd been in the place, and it was like every other pub that had gone underground. There was nothing suspicious about it. This place, on the other hand, was unlike anything in Mack's experience. He was highly suspicious of it.

Holly put a couple of dollar bills on the table. "We'd better go, or we'll miss the first act," she said, standing. When she headed for the door, Mack had to follow. He took a last look over his shoulder and the overly stuffed room with its crowded tables and he heard shivery laughter in the background.

Chapter Thirty-Seven

At Peabody House, they met Milly and Teddy Greene. Milly wore a lush maroon velvet dress with a white flower pinned to the bodice. Teddy was in a fine wool jacket over a linen shirt, silk cravat, and dark pants. Mack wondered if he was expected to dress up for this amateur performance. He wore his second-best brown wool suit. It would have to do.

The way Teddy put his arm around Holly's shoulders, Mack got the uneasy impression he was supposed to be Milly's date for the evening. Was he stepping in for "poor Peter." Milly told him how she'd spoken to Peter's father, and she hoped he would help his son. "Mmm," Mack said. Not everyone had a rich banker father to find them a slick lawyer and impress the likes of McKenna with their influence. Peter would land on his feet. Though whether he'd ever go back to the force was an open question. It seemed unlikely from what Milly was telling him about how the father wanted Peter back at Harvard.

Mack was going to excuse himself and go home until he was reminded that Ari Zellman had a part in the play. He wanted to confront Zellman after the play. Why had he sent Mack to Café Dreyfus? What was he playing at?

As Milly herded them towards the stairs, a rattled-looking Bernie Kessler blocked the way and grabbed Teddy's sleeve. "I have to talk to you. Did you see the papers? We're ruined." Sweat glistened on his forehead.

Teddy let go of Holly and pulled away from Bernie, frowning. "Get off, Bernie. We've got the play to see."

"But I've got to talk to you." Bernie seemed to notice the others in their group. "I'm sorry, but I have to talk to Teddy. Please, Milly." He extended his hand to Teddy's sleeve again and rubbed it as if interested in buying it. Mack thought he was in a very odd state. Had he taken drugs that night? If he was so addicted he could inject himself after his father had died of an overdose, could he have been the one who caused the older Kessler's death? Or was he so desperate to get more of the drugs that he'd come looking for his supplier? Zellman, perhaps?

"Teddy, talk to him, then join us, will you?" Milly briskly led the others up the steps, obviously put out by the interruption. Holly ran after her, and Mack followed, glancing back at the two men. He decided to find Bernie and make him talk. But it could wait until after the play and after Mack talked to Zellman.

Milly explained to Mack that the theater took up two floors, and above were a gym, classrooms, and workshops like the one Holly and Rachel used to teach woodworking. At the very top was a refectory and rooms for residents like her and her brother.

The theater in Peabody House was very professional looking. Milly led them to red plush seats near the front. She introduced them to the director of Peabody House, a businesslike woman in a smart walking suit. She made a point of thanking Milly and Teddy for their work. She recognized Holly as an instructor in woodworking and expressed her happiness that Holly and Rachel had attracted the interest of Mrs. Shurcliff. On that note, she stepped away to greet an older couple dressed for an evening out, who Milly said were donors. Beyond them, Mack spotted Leonard Abrams and his mother. He craned his neck but didn't see Rachel Kessler. Apparently, the theater was a big event for the whole community in the West End.

Just before they sat down, a young girl pulled Milly away. She promised she'd return immediately.

"Have you seen *Midsummer Night's Dream* before?" Holly asked.

Mack thought she probably judged him to be illiterate. "No. The brothers at my school were more likely to make us read the histories. *Julius Caesar, Henry V*, that weasel Richard who was forever whining."

She sat up and looked at her program, a mimeographed sheet. "You're in for a treat. It's a wedding, in ancient Greece. Theseus is marrying an Amazon, a woman warrior." Mack knew what Amazons were. He bristled a bit at being lectured but he kept his silence. "But it's really about two pairs of young lovers who run around, bewitched by the fairies, so they're after the wrong lover."

Mack thought he was in for a boring night.

Holly noticed his lack of enthusiasm. "Then there's the peasant who becomes an ass."

That woke him up. "What?"

"You'll see."

Teddy appeared and forced his way into the row to sit beside Holly. "Sorry about that. Bernie was upset. Had to calm him down."

"Where's Milly?" Holly asked.

"Ah, looking for Zellman, I think. He plays Theseus, and they couldn't find him. Oh, guess they did, they're starting."

The curtain rose, and the play began. At the first break in the action, Milly slid into the aisle seat.

As usual, Mack found the Shakespearean dialogue hard to follow, but the action explained more than the words. He was quickly caught up in the high jinks, as the young lovers ran around the enchanted forest being tricked by fairies. He forgot all about Zellman who he recognized as a stately Theseus at the beginning but disappeared for much of the play. Queen of the Fairies, Titania, was a tall, buxom woman whose charms were on full display. Mack squirmed when he saw how Bottom was being tricked into believing such a beautiful woman could be interested in him. Couldn't Bottom see he was no match for the luscious creature? Only the cruel love potion could make her look at the crude peasant. Mack was worried for Bottom when he fell asleep in Titania's bower. When the peasant woke with the head of an ass, Mack gasped. When Tatania threw herself on him and lavished the braying Bottom with caresses, Mack was mesmerized. At the end of every statement, the ass-headed Bottom honked, and the audience broke out in laughter. It was a relief when the two tricked lovers retired to the hammock that was lowered through the floor of the stage. Something bad was going to happen to that ignoramus.

The hammock had almost disappeared when a scream cut through the air. Then, more screams. That couldn't be part of the show. "Help, help!" The screams came from the pit where the lovers had been lowered through the floor.

Chapter Thirty-Eight

At first, people thought it was part of the play, but when actors on the stage knelt to see what was happening, everyone held their breath. One of the fairies yelled for a doctor. Mack heard someone shout from below, "He's dead, he's dead."

"Stay here," he told Holly and Milly. The audience was on their feet. The director of Peabody House hurried to a set of stairs leading to the stage with Mack close behind. He showed her his investigator identification card from Dr. Magrath. He grabbed a man not in costume to lead him down to the area below the stage.

In the low-ceilinged wooden structure under the stage, the actors stood in a circle around a figure on the floor. Mack pushed his way past Titania and Bottom. He was followed by a man in evening dress who said he was a doctor.

Bernie Kessler lay sprawled on the floor. His eyes were open, but Mack could only see the whites. His arms and legs were splayed. A hypodermic needle was beside him. His jacket was tossed on the ground, and the sleeve of his left arm was rolled up.

The doctor tsked. "He's gone, I'm afraid." He picked up the needle. "A drug of some kind."

"That's it," Mack stood up, angry that this had happened while he sat out in the auditorium. "You," he pointed at Bottom. "Call the police, then call the medical examiner, Dr. Magrath. Tell him McNally says he's got to come quick. Go, man, now. The rest of you sit down over there. We'll need to talk to you." He turned to the man who had led him down. He said he was the stage manager. "Keep everyone here until the police come." It appeared that Bernie Kessler had injected himself, but Mack wasn't sure. Dr. Magrath would want to see the scene.

The actors were too shocked to complain. They retreated to a corner and sat on boxes. Above them, Mack heard the Peabody House director address the audience, asking them to remain in their seats until the police told them to leave. There was a roar of conversation after that.

Soon, police arrived, and Chief Detective McKenna clomped down the stairs to the space under the stage, followed by two plainclothes detectives. "McNally, what the hell are you doing here?"

"I was watching the play. The dead man is Bernard Kessler, son of Isaac Kessler, who was found dead in the Joy Street jail."

McKenna's eyes widened. "You're kidding. Really?" He bent over to look at the body and pointed to the hypodermic needle. "Another drug fiend? What, did it run in the family? Lomasney's going to have another conniption. Can I help it if these Hebes keep dropping from the drugs?" He told a man to get an ambulance to remove the body. Mack told him he had to wait for the medical examiner. McKenna turned red and strutted over to stare in Mack's face when Dr. Magrath and Edwin pounded down the steps from above. Mack wasn't surprised at how quickly they'd arrived. They had an elaborate system to alert them even when they were out of the morgue. Magrath had learned the hard way not to trust the police in any questionable death. And Mack had a lot of questions about this death.

Magrath pushed his way through to the body. He said a few words to the doctor, who stood up and stepped away. "Get these people out of here," he told McKenna.

"Now, look, Magrath. This guy killed himself. He took too much of the happy juice. I'm not letting you make something out of it that it's not. We have to release all those people upstairs." He pointed up. "There's no need to keep them."

Magrath stood up. "McKenna, this body is mine. Get these people out of here and make sure you have all their names. McNally will talk to them up above while Edwin and I take a look at the scene to see how this happened.

You and your men, out. You're like a troop of elephants the way you tramp around the scene. Get out!"

Growling, McKenna told his men to take the actors and the doctor up the stairs. Before Mack followed them, he stood over the body as Jake Magrath and Edwin examined him.

"An overdose of something, for sure," Magrath said. He handed the hypodermic to Edwin, who put it in a bag, then in his case. Edwin assembled his camera and began taking pictures. He took pictures of the whole room, and Magrath held up Bernie Kessler's arms and head to show bruises. "The sooner we get him on the examination table, the better," Jake Magrath said. "He's not long dead."

The ambulance men came, and Mack went up to get information from the actors. The theater had mostly emptied, but he saw Holly, Milly, and Teddy standing with the director. He told them to leave; he'd talk later. He saw Teddy put his arms around both of the women's waists and lead them away.

Mack turned back to the task at hand. It would be a long night. When he couldn't find Ari Zellman among the gathered actors, he insisted on a search. They took him to the dressing room Zellman used. There, under the table, he found a leather bag. Inside were a hypodermic needle and vials.

Morphine? Edwin would be able to tell. The dressing room was used by other actors, not just Zellman, but Mack thought the West End House law student would have a lot of questions to answer. Had Zellman given Bernie Kessler an overdose of morphine?

Chapter Thirty-Nine

Mack questioned the actors. He discovered more of them, not just Zellman, had already gone home. Tatania, Bottom, and the fairies who'd been lowered to the under-stage area hadn't seen anything of use. They'd panicked when they saw Bernie Kessler's body. After he dismissed them, the luscious Tatania was ushered away by Bottom. They were old friends and trained actors, but they claimed they didn't know Bernie Kessler at all. They also had nothing to say about Zellman who they seemed to consider a minor cast member.

The stage manager was the most useful person. He showed Mack several ways that someone could reach the below-stage area. It was only too easy. In addition to the stairs down from the wings of the stage, there was a door that led to a corridor in the building's basement. As the stage manager led him out that way, Mack recognized a familiar figure mopping the floor.

"Mr. Johnson, you're here," Mack said.

"Yes, sir. I work here. Night janitor," he said. The stage manager confirmed that.

"Did you see anyone use this door?" Mack asked. "We found a man dead under the stage."

"I heard," Johnson said. "Didn't see no one. But I wasn't here earlier. I was upstairs at the pool. Clean that every night."

"Okay. If you remember anything, let me know," Mack said. He thought he could talk to his neighbor later and get some background on the settlement house.

Meanwhile, Mack dismissed the stage manager and went back to Milly

Greene's office on the ground floor. He found Milly, Teddy, and Holly waiting.

"Mr. Greene, you were one of the last people to see Bernard Kessler tonight. What happened after you left us?"

Teddy shook his head. "I can't believe Bernie is dead. He came to tell me there might be a problem with the money we all invested. That's all. He was all revved up. I told him to calm down." Teddy pulled a folded newspaper page from his pocket. "He saw this and he panicked."

Unfolding the thin sheet, Mack read an article about how a local investment broker named Charles Ponzi was being questioned regarding unrealistic returns he was promising to his customers. Mack didn't know about finance, but he pocketed the sheet to show Jake Magrath.

Teddy claimed he'd left Bernie Kessler in this office when he returned to the play. He said, yes, Bernie knew how to get to the under-stage. He'd participated in theater performances. Nearly everyone in the West End did at one time or another.

Milly asked, "Teddy, how much money did Bernie lose in those investments? How worried was he? Did you lose money, too?"

Teddy looked at his sister. His face lost color. Mack thought he might faint. Holly pushed him into a chair. "Bernie was worried. He was terrified. He said we lost everything." Teddy winced and avoided looking at his sister. Uh oh, Mack thought Teddy didn't want to tell his sister how much of their money he lost. Teddy had left Bernie in the office to hurry back to the play. Mack figured Teddy Greene was intent on courting Holly. Was his infatuation with Holly why he hadn't been as upset as Bernie about the failed investment scheme? It was only now, under his sister's angry glare, that Teddy realized what a mistake he'd made with their money. Mack didn't envy him the inevitable confrontation with an angry sister.

Teddy looked at the floor and gulped. "I think they put all their money in from the jewelry business. Bernie and Abrams. I think he said something about some diamonds being lost. You don't think he was so upset he purposely took too much..." He buried his face in his hands.

Milly looked grim. "You shouldn't have left him, Teddy. You should have stayed with him if he was that upset."

Mack saw a look of pain cross Holly's face. She realized Teddy's desire to get back to his seat beside her had caused him to leave Bernie to fend for himself. Mack remembered the exchange between Bernie Kessler and Leonard Abrams at the jewelry store. Had they invested so much, they were ruined? Did Leonard Abrams know?

"The last time you saw him, he was in the office," Mack said. "Miss Greene, you left the theater before the play began. Did you see Bernard Kessler?"

"No. I didn't go to the office. I went backstage. They were having trouble finding Mr. Zellman, and they couldn't begin the play without him. Finally, we found him near the street door."

"What was he doing there?" Mack asked. He'd already had questions for Zellman before the play. Now, he had more.

"I don't know." Milly hesitated. She glanced at Holly. "I think he might have met Miss Kessler. I think I saw her slipping away into the alley when I finally found Mr. Zellman."

"Rachel," Holly said.

Milly looked at her. "I don't know what they were talking about. She's engaged to Mr. Abrams now. Perhaps she wanted to explain that to Mr. Zellman. You'll have to ask him."

Mack wondered. He also wondered where Bernie had gotten the morphine that he used that night. Had he come to Zellman for it? Had he confronted Zellman about the death of Isaac Kessler? Had Bernie found out his father knew who had been selling him drugs? Or was the young man just so depressed about his father's death, his expulsion from Harvard, and now his loss of money that he killed himself?

Mack let them go, and Teddy insisted on walking Holly to her father's Beacon Hill home.

As Mack stood with Milly Greene, watching them leave, she said. "Perhaps at least now the police will release Peter."

Chapter Forty

At the morgue the next day, Jake confronted an angry McKenna. The man was buzzing with nervous energy as if he were plagued by a nest of hornets.

"What do you mean he didn't kill himself? He was a drug fiend. You showed me on his arms that he'd been taking drugs by hypodermic for a long time. You said he was probably kicked out of Harvard for it. You told me he lost money in this investment scam. Do you know how bad that can hit a man? Do you know how it feels to have every damn penny you've saved in your life to be gone in an instant? After it was doubling every three weeks, till it was more than you'd ever had, and you expected if you left it in just a little longer, you'd not only be set for life you could live like a king. Like a king."

Jake considered the angry man. Over his head, he saw Mack shrug his shoulders. He didn't know why the Chief Detective was blowing a gasket. Neither did Edwin when Jake looked over at his assistant.

"I take it you're talking about this fraud that's being investigated? The one run by a man named Ponzi?" The Post had broken a story the previous day. After headlines the day before about the unusually high returns, their reporters had looked more closely at the investment business and talked to bankers who could easily prove the dividends Ponzi claimed to pay out were impossible.

McKenna looked like a pot coming to a boil, too indignant to respond, but Mack looked like a lightbulb that was just lit. "Oh, a lot of the cops invested in that, didn't they?" Mack said.

"Most of the brass," McKenna wailed. "Who'd've thought you could go wrong following them? Now we find out it's probably all gone. Wait till I get my hands on that little wop…"

"Sorry to hear it, but let's talk about Mr. Bernard Kessler, if you will," Jake interrupted.

McKenna looked at him with hate, but he shut his mouth.

Jake beckoned to Edwin, who helped him raise Bernie's torso. "If you look at the back of his head and his shoulders, you'll see bruising. It's from a short time before his death." They lowered the body. Jake raised an arm. "There's another bruise on his forearm where he tried to fend off a blow. There's a large amount of morphine in his system and two new hypodermic marks here. I would say he may have taken a dose, but then he was hit, and while he was down, a second higher dose was injected. He didn't kill himself, Chief McKenna. He was murdered."

"Murdered the same way, by the same person who murdered his father," Mack said.

McKenna snorted.

"It's true," Mack said. "Bernie Kessler may have been an addict, but his father was not."

"There were no signs of previous drug injections on Isaac Kessler," Jake said.

"They were both killed by someone, whether to hide the source of the drugs of for another reason," Mack insisted.

McKenna waved his arms as if to push them away. "I suppose you'll want that Attwood boy released," he sneered. "His father's been making a pest of himself, calling the mayor and everyone else."

"Peter Attwood may have been negligent in assuming Isaac Kessler was drunk, rather than drugged," Jake said. "But he never beat up the man, and a beating was not the cause of his death. It was an overdose of morphine, just as the cause of death of his son was an overdose of morphine."

"To cover up who was selling it, you're saying," McKenna said.

Jake could see him release his fixation on Peter to look for someone else to blame. "That's one possible motive," he said. He despaired of the Chief

Detective ever looking for other explanations once he found one he could make fit. It was typical laziness on the part of the man. Nonetheless, Jake told Mack and Edwin to report what they'd found out.

Reluctant to give up the investigation to McKenna, Mack reported on suggestions that the drugs were distributed by Solomon, and rumors about West End House.

Edwin, who hadn't had a chance to tell them before, reported on his trip to the speakeasy where he'd been told the drugs were probably being distributed through settlement houses.

"Houses?" Jake asked.

"That's what they said. As if Solomon had people in all of them," Edwin said.

"But this West End House," McKenna jumped on the suggestion. "Who's there? Who's selling it? That's mostly Jews, isn't it?"

Jake looked at Mack, who shrugged but reluctantly answered. "It's possible. Some people suspect a man named Ari Zellman. He's a Harvard law student. He claims they help drug addicts like Bernie Kessler kick the habit." Mack hesitated a moment. "There're rumors he was romantically linked to Rachel Kessler, Bernie's sister. But now she's engaged to another man who was the older Kessler's employee in the jewelry business. Zellman was in the play last night, and he disappeared for a while. Maybe to see Rachel. But he left before I could interview him. I need to question him. I found morphine in the dressing room he used."

Jake could see it pained Mack to give up such damning evidence to McKenna. Mack wanted to question Zellman himself, but he'd have to let the obnoxious Chief of Detectives do it.

McKenna growled. "It's my case now. You stay out of it. Where's this Zellman? West End House?"

The morgue doorbell rang. Edwin went to answer it and came back with Rachel Kessler and Ari Zellman. He said she was there to formally identify her brother. She looked pale, and she leaned on the handsome young man. Jake hadn't seen Zellman before. He was good-looking and appeared to care for the young woman on his arm. He could barely take his eyes from her.

"This is Zellman?" McKenna demanded. "Where were you last night when this man was killed?"

Jake rolled his eyes. He might have known McKenna would jump the gun.

Zellman guided Rachel to a chair and stood up. "I'm Ari Zellman. I was in a play at the Peabody House theater last night. I never saw Bernard Kessler."

"Yes, but I hear you were missing part of the night." McKenna stepped across and put a hand on Zellman's shoulder. "You are coming with me, sir. I've got some questions for you down at the station. Come along."

Zellman was speechless. Jake thought he would speak up. As a law student, he must know McKenna was on shaky grounds, but Zellman glanced at Rachel and decided not to make a fuss. He looked across at Jake, identifying him as the man in charge. "Look after Miss Kessler, will you?"

Chapter Forty-One

Jake could see that Rachel Kessler was shivering. Shock. He took a blanket from a shelf and put it around her shoulders, then told Edwin to get her hot tea with a lot of sugar.

"Miss Kessler, please sit back and rest. This has been a shock to you." Jake was afraid she would faint she was so pale. After a while, the shivering stopped, and Edwin brought the mug of tea. She sipped some, then warmed her hands with the mug.

"We are so sorry for your loss, Miss Kessler. We can call a taxi to take you home and you can do the formal identification when you're feeling better," Jake said. "Should we call someone for you? You're engaged to Mr. Abrams, aren't you? Shall we call him for you?"

"No," she snapped. She shook herself and said, "I'm all right. What happened to Mr. Zellman? Why did that man take him away?"

Being in the same room with her brother's body, then hearing McKenna verbally attack the man who had brought her, Rachel obviously hadn't understood. Jake glanced at Mack, who looked worried. "Mr. Zellman was taken to the police station to answer some questions," Mack told her.

Jake knew there were rumors of a romantic attachment between Rachel and Zellman, but he'd been told that she was engaged to Leonard Abrams. He didn't know how the relations stood between all the characters, but he thought the young woman deserved to know the case against Zellman. If she thought herself in love with him, she needed to know that he might very well have killed her father and brother.

Jake bent over the young woman. "Miss Kessler, I'm sorry to tell you that the police believe that Mr. Zellman supplied your brother with morphine, that your father found out and confronted him, and that he killed your father with morphine and then when your brother threatened to expose him, he killed your brother. Did you know your brother was addicted to morphine?"

Her eyes filled with tears. "Yes," she whispered. "My father didn't know. I asked Mr. Zellman to help Bernie to stop. Ari would never hurt Bernie. He didn't hurt anyone." She brushed away tears. "Can I see my brother, please?"

Jake nodded to Edwin, who folded down the sheet so that Bernard Kessler's face was visible. Jake took Rachel's arm and led her across the room to the table where he lay.

"Oh, Bernie," she whispered. She stroked his cheek with a hand. "What have you done?" She leaned on the table to steady herself as she stared at the dead man's face. "Did he do this to himself?" She glanced up into Jake's face. "Tell me the truth."

Jake would have liked to reassure her, but she was demanding the truth, and he thought those dark eyes would see through him if he tried to soften the blow. "We believe he was killed. We believe he took a dose of morphine, but he was struck down, and a second, fatal dose was administered."

She looked down. "Oh, Bernie." She stepped back and folded her arms, as if to protect herself. "How did this happen? Who did this to him? You can't think it was Ari. Who found him?" She stumbled back to the chair, sat, and looked up at them, hungry for information.

Jake nodded at Mack. "This is Detective McNally. He was at the scene."

Mack told her how her brother was found below the stage at Peabody House during the play and how Zellman had been missing part of the time.

"He was with me," Rachel said. "I went to see Ari at the theater door. I had to tell him…"

"What? Did you see your brother?" Mack asked.

She looked at him as if she were seeing something else. "No. I went to Ari to tell him why I had to marry Leonard Abrams." She stiffened.

"When did you last see your brother?" Mack asked.

She looked at him. "That evening. Before I went to find Ari. Bernie argued with Leonard Abrams. Leonard came to our apartment to tell Bernie about the money." She blew out a shot of breath. "Money. That's all he cares about. They risked a lot of money on something, and they lost all of it. Leonard was furious. Bernie kept apologizing. Finally, he ran off." She looked across at her brother. "That's the last time I saw him. I was angry with Leonard. I sent him away. Then I went to see Ari. For the last time, I thought." She fell into a reverie. "Bernie would have gone looking for morphine to ease the pain and forget. He was weak. He was so weak and so ashamed of his weakness."

"The police believe he went to Mr. Zellman for drugs," Jake said. He was beginning to doubt the story himself.

"No."

"He was at Peabody House," Mack said. "I saw him. He came to talk to Teddy Greene about the money loss. But Greene had nothing to do with your brother's overdose. He was in the audience when Bernie was killed. He sat beside me. Who sold your brother the drugs?"

"I don't know. He'd been trying so hard to stop. He was ashamed after my father's death." Jake wondered if Rachel Kessler had ever even imagined that her lover, Zellman, could have been the one to sell drugs to her brother.

"Did your brother know who killed your father?" Jake asked. "Is that why he was ashamed?"

"No. He was ashamed because of this." She took a folded letter from a pocket and offered it to Jake as if it were something dirty that she wanted to get rid of. Jake read it.

Rachel said. "My father received that letter the day he died. He read it at his office, then he left in a rage. I believe he found my brother and confronted him." She glanced at the body. "Bernie admitted that to me. But I don't know where he went afterwards. Leonard Abrams read the letter." She sounded bitter. "He knew what a disgrace it was. He threatened to tell everyone, our friends, our family, even our synagogue. He said if I didn't agree to marry him, he'd make sure everyone knew. It would destroy Bernie. And Bernie was all I had left of my family. That's what I had to explain to Ari."

When Jake looked up from the letter, he saw Mack and Edwin were anxious to know what was in it. "It's from the Harvard dean. He informs Isaac Kessler why his son was expelled from Harvard."

Chapter Forty-Two

Peter lay on the hard bunk in the cell at Joy Street station. He should have been transferred to the Charles Street Jail, but he thought McKenna was keeping him here so that he'd be mortified in front of all of his former colleagues. And he was in the cell where Isaac Kessler had died. Traces of a word that the dead man had scribbled on the wall with pipe ash still remained. If only Peter had recognized the man was sick, instead of assuming he was drunk. Kessler might have been saved.

Too late for that. But Peter's biggest regret was what Milly must think of him. Meeting her again, visiting with her every night when he walked his route. It had changed his life. The calamity of being demoted down to patrol officer had turned into the best thing that ever happened to him. He'd known her as Holly's friend before Milly's father lost all his money and committed suicide. Talking to her about his troubles, he'd realized how lucky he was compared to her and her brother. Yet she'd turned misfortune around to help others at the settlement house and support her brother, too. He'd never known anyone as sympathetic and able to coax him out of his misery. Not since his mother had died. He wanted to be able to talk to her every night for the rest of his life and he'd concocted a dream where he could propose marriage and they could live and work together. But just when he was going to finally speak to her about his desires, he'd found Kessler's body and the nightmare had begun. What could he do now but despair?

"Come on, you're getting out," a uniformed officer jiggled the key in the cell lock and motioned for Peter to get up.

Amazed, he followed the officer out to the lobby where, glory of glories,

Milly Greene waited for him with a distinguished grey-haired man. Peter was awestruck.

"Peter, this is Mr. Lamont. Your father hired him to represent you. They've arrested someone else for the deaths of Mr. Kessler and his son. They're releasing you."

Milly waved off his questions until they'd left the station and said goodbye to the lawyer. Then she took his arm and told him to walk her back to Peabody House. He listened as she told him how Bernie Kessler had been found dead in the theater and Ari Zellman had been arrested. They said he sold the morphine to Bernie, and when Bernie's father threatened to expose him, Zellman poisoned him, and when Bernie realized what Zellman had done and was going to expose him, he'd gotten rid of the son. Milly knew all of this because she'd insisted on accompanying the lawyer as he talked to officials about Peter.

"That awful man, McKenna, finally admitted he couldn't accuse Zellman of Mr. Kessler's death and also hold you responsible, so he agreed to your release. Peter, you must know that your father paid for the lawyer. He also exerted all the influence he could on the police to get them to release you. I know you've had your differences, but he does love you as his son. You really have him to thank for them letting you go."

Peter knew it was Milly who was responsible. She must have begged his stubborn father. For her sake, he'd thank the man, much as he didn't want to be in his debt. He'd do it for Milly.

"Oh, Peter, I'm so glad you're safe now. So much has gone wrong." At Peter's urging, she explained. "Teddy has done something awful. He took advice from Bernie Kessler, and he invested our money in what turned out to be a scheme. He lost all the money, Peter. I don't care for me, I can live at Peabody House but that money was for Teddy's tuition at Harvard next fall. He won't have the money now. I know my father wanted him to graduate. It would mean so much for his future, and now it's all gone."

She dropped his arm and walked briskly as she told him this, but he could see her discreetly wipe away some tears. They continued in silence for two blocks; then he put a hand on her elbow to stop her.

"Milly, I don't want you to worry. I don't want you to shoulder all these troubles alone. I'm here now. You can depend on me." She stared at the ground, not able to look him in the eye. Peter felt a thrill down his spine. "Listen, I thought hard about things while I was in that cell. I can't go back to the police force, I know that. I was so naive to think I could do good there. I'm such a fool. But I can make up for that. I've wanted to…I…Milly, marry me. Please. Together, we can face anything. I'll help your brother go to Harvard. I'll go back myself. I don't want to be a banker, but my father or grandmother would help me become a lawyer. That's almost as good as far as my father's concerned. I promise I'll do whatever it takes to support you and your work at Peabody House."

Milly looked up with tears in her eyes. "Oh, Peter. Of course, I'll marry you."

Chapter Forty-Three

At the morgue, Mack watched as Jake urged Miss Kessler to allow them to take her home. She insisted she had to stay with her brother's body until men could come to take him away to prepare him for burial. Mack knew Jake and Edwin had done a speedy autopsy since the custom of the Kesslers' faith was immediate burial. But Rachel told them in a shaky voice that she needed the men from Vilna Shul to come. Zellman had come with her and would have been the one to go to summon men from the burial society, but he'd been taken away by the police.

Jake seemed to understand what Rachel was asking, more than Mack did, anyhow. Mack also didn't understand what the letter from Harvard had meant. That weasel Abrams had been threatening the Kessler brother and sister with whatever was in the letter. When Jake beckoned Edwin and Mack into his office, Mack followed and said, "That Abrams is scum. Let me get my hands on him."

"No," Jake said. "Edwin, you go find Leonard Abrams and have him contact the Vilna Shul men to come for the body."

"But I found out Abrams and his mother left the play early last night," Mack said. "He could have killed Bernard Kessler." At first, Mack had been inclined to believe Zellman was supplying the drugs and that he'd had the opportunity to take Kessler to the below-stage area and kill him. When he found the bag of morphine hidden in the dressing room, it seemed conclusive. But since hearing Rachel Kessler's story, Mack had doubts about Zellman. He was a rival to Abrams. What if Abrams had seen Rachel with Zellman? He could have killed Bernie Kessler, then put the bag in Zellman's dressing room to make him look guilty.

Jake shooed Edwin off. "Go. Get them to come." He turned to Mack. "One thing at a time. Bernard Kessler's body needs to be buried. I don't know what to do with Miss Kessler. She's alone now. I doubt she wants to go to Abrams and his mother."

"Miss Attwood. Why don't we get Miss Attwood to see to her?" Mack said. Mack himself was at a loss to deal with a grieving woman. He thought handing her off to Holly Attwood was the way to deal with the situation.

"And Mrs. Lee," Jake said. He must have had the same idea that they needed more females to deal with Rachel.

Chapter Forty-Four

At the Jewish cemetery in East Boston, it rained for Bernie Kessler's funeral. Fanny leaned on Jake's arm under his big black umbrella. He hadn't attended Isaac Kessler's burial, but she'd insisted he come to this one. When he called for help the previous evening, Holly and Fanny had come together. After Edwin arrived with men from Vilna Shul, they'd taken Rachel to Cornelia's Beacon Hill house, where she stayed in the unused bedroom that had been prepared for Fanny's daughter. Fanny knew her daughter was safe in New Hampshire, happily motoring around the state gathering antiques for their business. Her daughter was fine. But Rachel Kessler would never be fine until they found out the truth about the deaths of her father and brother. She needed to know if her lover, Ari Zellman, had done what he was accused of.

Rachel stood near the grave, surrounded by Holly Attwood, Milly Greene, and Milly's brother. Peter Attwood had shown up with Mack. He'd been released the night before and had stayed with Mack rather than return to his father's house. Fanny sensed a change in the relationship between Peter and Milly. She knew from Holly that Milly had pleaded Peter's case with their father. The looks exchanged between Peter and Milly told Fanny they had reached some kind of understanding. With all that was going on, it was not surprising if they weren't yet sharing any news.

Mack, on the other hand, was restless in the drizzle at the gravesite. At one point, she worried he might start an argument with Leonard Abrams, who had his mother on his arm. They tried to elbow their way to Rachel, but Holly and the Greenes staunchly refused to move aside for them. Fanny saw some other older men in the group who discreetly guided Abrams and his mother to the back of the crowd. She wondered how much the community knew of the story Rachel had told Jake and the others about Abrams's attempt to blackmail her into marriage. There was sympathy for the bereaved young woman, yet there was some cloud hanging over the congregation as if some horrible disgrace had happened. Was it the knowledge that there was a killer somewhere in their midst? Or was there something else about the dead Bernard Kessler that caused ripples in the community? She'd learned from Rachel that Ari Zellman was not a member of the Vilna Shul, but perhaps his arrest underlay the disturbance.

Fanny knew McKenna had arrested Zellman in front of Rachel at the morgue. But Rachel didn't believe he was guilty. She might have been broken under the weight of sorrow she'd experienced in such a short time, but she burned with indignation instead. Released from the obligation to marry Leonard Abrams in order to protect her brother, Rachel was furious about his death, the death of their father, and the arrest of Zellman.

As the funeral broke up, Holly came to tell her that she and Milly and Teddy would go to Rachel's home with her. She saw Mack glance at Teddy Greene with a spot of jealousy in his eye. Could the bluff Irishman be taken with Peter's sister? Fanny felt sorry for him if it was so. She could see that Holly was a good foil for Mack. She had no problem standing up to him and was impervious to any slights or insults he might blunder into making. But Holly was pure Brahmin. Mack could only face disappointment. It was unlikely he'd do anything about it in any case. Jake and Peter would forever be blissfully unaware of such a situation, even if it existed beyond Fanny's imagination. She shook herself. There had to be more they could do to find out if Zellman really was responsible for these deaths.

Chapter Forty-Five

After the funeral, Peter sat opposite the medical examiner in his crowded office. He'd stayed with Mack the previous night after he left Milly at Peabody House. Peter couldn't face his father yet, despite his promise to Milly to make peace with the banker. Mack had filled him in on the investigation and assumed he'd go to the morgue to get instructions from Jake. Peter hadn't told Mack he planned to quit the police. He wasn't sure he could weather the big man's disgust if he told him he was returning to Harvard.

"Do you think Zellman killed them?" Peter asked.

"I don't see sufficient evidence to confirm that," Jake said. "I'm glad that fool McKenna saw fit to release you, but I'm not at all sure he can prove Ari Zellman sold drugs for Solomon, or that he killed Isaac and Bernard Kessler with morphine."

"But we know Mack found morphine in his dressing room," Peter said.

"Yes, but I ask you, does Zellman strike you as a stupid man? Would anyone who wasn't profoundly stupid kill a man with morphine then leave a bag of it in his dressing room to be found?" Jake asked.

"I see what you mean. What about Abrams? He sounds like a villain," Peter said.

"Mack interviewed him and other people from the theater, actors and audience. He found out Abrams had an opportunity to do it. At least Mack asked questions. McKenna's men just followed him back to the station," Jake said.

He was clearly frustrated with the sloppy police work. Peter knew the medical examiner would be disappointed when Peter told him his decision to leave the police. Mrs. Lee would be even more upset. He knew she had some idea that she and the medical examiner could mold Peter into the perfect police detective. Peter felt he was more like a useless lump of clay. He dreaded his grandmother's reaction as well. She'd think he was giving up.

Jake continued to report, "Abrams and his mother left the play before the body was discovered. Of course, Mrs. Abrams backs up anything her son says, but Abrams could have snuck in and killed Bernie Kessler. There are so many entrances to that backstage it's like a sieve. And apparently, Abrams was blackmailing Rachel Kessler into marrying him."

"Perhaps her brother Bernie found out what Abrams was up to and planned to expose him?" Peter suggested. He couldn't imagine any man would allow his sister to be blackmailed into marrying a despicable person on his own account. Peter would want to kill the man.

He was getting pulled into the investigation again. Despite his promise to leave the police profession behind, he wanted to find out what had really happened. "What did he use to blackmail her? Did it have to do with Zellman?" He was thinking Abrams had evidence of an illicit liaison. For a woman with the Kesslers' strict orthodox background, such an accusation could condemn her in her community's mind.

"He was blackmailing her with this." Jake handed Peter a piece of paper with a Harvard University letterhead. "It's a letter to Kessler's father explaining why he was kicked out of Harvard."

Dear Mr. Kessler,

I am greatly distressed and embarrassed to have to tell you that your son, Bernard, has involved himself in difficulties so extraordinarily grave that the President has instructed me to advise your son to leave the University at once. I have communicated these instructions to your son, and he is leaving. He has promised to tell you all about the matter, and I hope he will tell you the whole truth. His offense has nothing to do with low scholarship; it is not gambling, or drink, or ordinary sexual intercourse. If he does not confess to something worse than these things, he will not have told you the whole story. In that case, I can, of course, tell you all about it, if you will come to Cambridge.

The investigation, which was precipitated by the suicide of another student involved in this matter, has been conducted with great care; the evidence is absolutely conclusive, and, in point of fact, your son has confessed his guilt. The matter is altogether the most distressing that has occurred since I have been in office.

Yours very truly, C. N. Greenough

Peter frowned. "Greenough is Dean of the College. Not drink, gambling, or sexual matters? What does he mean?

"Not ordinary sexual intercourse," Jake said.

"Oh, no," said Peter. "What's going on over there?"

"I don't know. But there was an article in *The Boston American* about two Harvard men dying. It suggests they committed suicide, and it hints at an 'inquisition' in a darkened room. Harvard denied it," Jake said.

Peter handed the letter back across the desk as if it were liable to burst into flames in his hand. "Do you think this had something to do with Bernard Kessler's death?"

"Or his father's. Isaac Kessler read this letter then left his office in a fury."

"Did he confront his son?" Peter asked.

"Yes, according to his daughter. But she insisted he left his son and went off that night."

Mack lumbered in. "Did Dr. Magrath get you up to date on the investigations?" he asked. "McKenna has arrested Zellman, but Rachel Kessler insists she was with him when her brother was killed. In any case, this Abrams fellow was holding something about her brother over her head to get her to marry him. What a dirty scumbag. That's the letter he used, is it?"

Jake and Peter exchanged a glance. Peter knew Mack didn't have any respect for Harvard and spurned what he thought were airs of graduates. But Jake and Peter still had a desire to protect what they thought of as their university.

Jake folded up the letter and put it in his vest pocket. "That's right. And I think Peter and I should go to Cambridge and find out exactly what was going on that got this letter sent. I'm not sure it's pertinent to the deaths, but I'd like to find out."

Mack looked expectant, like he wanted to be invited. Jake frowned.

"While we're doing that, you can help Mrs. Lee bring her miniatures over from the Shurcliff house," he told Mack. When he saw a scowl on the big Irishman's face, he added, "Miss Attwood has created the miniatures in Mrs. Shurcliff's workshop. No doubt you'll have to get her to help you."

Chapter Forty-Six

"Be careful with that," Holly demanded as Mack and the driver hauled a wooden box out of the back of the truck. It was Mack's idea to recruit an ambulance to move the wooden structures from the Shurcliff home on Mount Vernon Street to the garage of the morgue. They'd had to remove the stretchers and benches to fit the two miniatures that were packed in four-foot square wooden boxes. Holly had harried the men when they helped crate her models and carry them down from the workshop. She continued to urge caution when they reached the morgue.

"For the love of God, get out of the way, woman, will you?" Mack said. They put the boxes on the floor, used a crowbar to open them, and lifted each one onto a long table against the wall. Holly had swept away tools from the surface. Mack wished Edwin was present to scold her for touching his implements. Mack thanked the driver and promised to stand him a beer.

Holly was fussing around the two structures, which stood about three feet tall. Mack was impressed by the details. There were two scenes. The sidewalk where Peter found Isaac Kessler, and the jail cell in the Joy Street Station where he'd died.

"Mrs. Lee is bringing the dolls for the figure of Mr. Kessler, and a lot of other tiny things for the rooms," Holly said.

Mack recognized the buildings on the sidewalk where Kessler was found. On the right was Pat's pub, which was being turned back into a shoe store due to prohibition. Mrs. Lee had painted the top windows with "ALE" and "BEER" in separate panes. She'd also sewn a curtain that was hung across the middle, so you couldn't see inside, and at the bottom of the window, a line of tiny bottles was painted with labels that could be read. He wondered if the bottles had been replaced by shoes on display yet. In the middle of that window hung a sign with beautifully written "Harvard" in large, scrolled letters with smaller type on the bottom "has what it takes." For what, Mack wondered. He supposed it must be in support of a team. He wouldn't have thought the West End would be a big supporter of the Yankee institution, but then, he kept hearing about how important it was to young men to find a way to the university across the river in Cambridge.

On the left was the ice cream shop and candy store. The storefront had "Candy" and "Cigars" painted on the top windows. When Mrs. Lee arrived with Rachel Kessler, she began pulling tiny accessories out of her carpet bag. The young women helped her to add balls, bats, gloves, and roller skates to the window display. They were all so small.

Holly hung some magazines with minuscule headlines like "American Home" and "Air Power" on their covers. She attached them to a string, then Rachel carefully tied it to display covers above the toys. There was even a stack of comic books. Amazing.

"How did you make all of this so quickly," Mack asked.

Mrs. Lee looked gratified by his admiration. "I had help from Rachel and Holly. We spent the night recreating objects from my sketches."

Mack supposed Rachel Kessler might have been too restless to sleep. Holly and Mrs. Lee must have kept her company. He knew Mrs. Lee had experience producing tiny crime scenes, and she was scrupulously faithful to details, as if that would solve the mystery. For all he knew, it might. He'd never have had the patience to letter those tiny magazines. He was glad his role took him out to the life-size crime scenes where he might get a life-size beer, if he was lucky.

There was little to decorate the jail cell that stood with the barred door a half foot away from the sidewalk scene. It was grim compared to the storefronts.

While Mrs. Lee pulled out a couple of dolls and began dressing them, Mack took Holly by the elbow and drew her away. "What's Miss Kessler doing here?" he asked in a whisper. "I thought she would stay home for a week to mourn her brother. Isn't that what they did for the father?" It bothered Mack that Bernard Kessler had been put in the ground so quickly with so little ceremony.

Holly pulled away and frowned at him. "Come on," she said and stalked away to Dr. Magrath's office. When Mack dutifully followed, she closed the door.

"Rachel is terribly upset. Of course, she grieves for her brother, but she says she can't possibly mourn him while Mr. Zellman is in jail. She's furious that he's been arrested. She wants to know the truth of what happened to her father and brother. She thinks the police are just trying to pin the deaths on Mr. Zellman because they don't like his politics."

"She doesn't blame your brother, does she?" Mack asked.

"Of course not. She's not stupid. She knows it was morphine that killed her father and her brother. She says Ari Zellman is a labor activist, he's been involved in strikes, and he's a Zionist. She thinks the authorities want to accuse him of the murders to get rid of a thorn in their sides. She thinks they'll just convict him and never find the real killer. She *can't* mourn her brother until his murderer is found and Zellman is freed."

"She and Zellman are seeing each other?" Mack thought that might give Rachel a motive to get rid of her father and brother, but he didn't want to say that to Holly, who was on the warpath.

"Oh, stop it. Can't you see someone is trying to make Ari Zellman look guilty? Yes, Rachel is in love with him. She was going to run away with him, but that's not why she doesn't believe he's guilty. She knows someone else must have done it. So, please, don't go asking her questions, just find out who really killed her father and her brother," Holly said.

Mack was at a loss. Holly's face glowed with sympathy for Rachel. She wanted him to clear her friend's lover. He didn't want to question Rachel while Holly was present. He only hoped she was right about her friend and her friend's lover. He dreaded disappointing Holly.

Mack wondered what Dr. Magrath and Peter were finding out over in Harvard. Mack resented being left out of that part of the investigation. Rachel Kessler might want to protect her lover from accusations, but were the Harvard men also intent on protecting that institution? Mack would find the truth in the long run, no matter what people were trying to hide. He just hoped the truth wouldn't devastate Holly. He followed her back to the garage, where the women were arguing over the dolls that represented the dead Isaac Kessler.

Rachel, who looked skeletal with dark shadows around her eyes, shook her head. "This is not right. My father never wore such a cap, or such a coat. They're the clothes of a working man, not a businessman, like my father."

"These are the clothes he wore," Mrs. Lee said patiently. "I was careful to examine the actual clothes. Dr. Magrath brought them out for me before I began making the clothing for the dolls."

"Mack, do you know where Mr. Kessler's clothes are?" Holly asked. She turned to Rachel, putting an arm on her shoulders. "We'll look at what they took off of your father." Rachel buried her face in her hands.

At Holly's command, Mack returned to the autopsy room. Where was Edwin? Had he gone to Cambridge, too? He rummaged around until he found several bags with the clothing and other items labelled Isaac Kessler.

Back in the garage, Mack dumped the contents onto a separate table in a corner. The work on the miniature scenes had stopped due to the dispute. Rachel's eyes shone, and it looked like Mrs. Lee and Holly wanted to calm her down. They all stepped over to surround the table.

Rachel grabbed the plaid cap and the brown woolen jacket. "These are not my father's," she insisted. She tossed them aside and grabbed the shirt and pants. "These belong to my father. I know them. I've laundered them myself. These pants are part of a suit. There should be a suit jacket to go with it. Where is that?" She dug through the clothing, identifying the tie and underwear but not finding the jacket to match the pants.

"Could your father have put on the cap and jacket as a disguise?" Holly asked.

Mack thought of the speakeasy in the basement of the candy shop. It was a meeting place for working men. Perhaps Kessler had gone there, as Edwin had, looking for information on drugs.

"Why would he be disguised?" Rachel asked. "That is not the sort of thing my father would do. And what are these? They don't belong to him." She held up a pipe and a leather tobacco pouch. "He didn't smoke."

"What about the lunch box and the banana peel?" Mrs. Lee asked. "Could those have been from your father?"

"Again, the lunchbox would be used by a workman. My father went out to a restaurant for lunch. He was a businessman. I don't know why he'd have a banana peel. He wouldn't eat fruit on the street like that. These aren't my father's clothes. Where did they come from? And where are his suit jacket and his hat and yarmulke?"

"What?" Mack asked. He was beginning to have an idea about the plaid cap and wool jacket.

"Yarmulke," Rachel said loudly. "It's what a Jewish man uses to cover his head. He doesn't use a plaid cap. And my father had a fine gray fedora. Where is that?"

Mack saw Holly wave a hand to stop him from questioning anything Rachel said, but he ignored her. "And you say your father didn't smoke a pipe?" He picked up the pipe that looked old and well worn, and the leather pouch. He smelled the tobacco. It reminded him of something.

"No. My father didn't smoke at all. Certainly not a pipe," Rachel insisted.

"I see," Mack said. "I think I might know where these clothes came from. But I don't know why he had them."

"What do you mean?" Holly demanded. Rachel and Mrs. Lee waited for an explanation.

"I'll let you know if I'm right," Mack said. "I've got to check this out." Taking the pipe and tobacco with him, he headed for the door.

"Where are you going?" Holly yelled after him. But he ignored her.

Chapter Forty-Seven

Peter glanced through the mullioned window to Harvard Yard while he listened to the men talk. Somehow, the faux Gothic of the stone buildings was less impressive this day than when he'd first crossed the Yard as a freshman. Perhaps it was because he and Jake Magrath had already endured a half hour of obfuscations from the Dean of Students, Chester Greenough. There appeared to be something sham about the wall of obstruction that the dean was trying to put up.

Jake interrupted. "Dean Greenough, as an alumnus, I'm aware of the university's need to protect its reputation. But we're pursuing a murder inquiry. Both Isaac Kessler and his son Bernard were given morphine that killed them. This letter," he slapped it down on the broad desk that separated the two visitors from the dean, "instigated the actions that led to two deaths. As the medical examiner of Suffolk County, where these men died, I'm asking you to explain why you sent this letter and why you expelled Bernard Kessler. It is my responsibility to report the cause and manner of these deaths. Stop beating around the bush."

Peter was grateful for Jake's forceful personality. Without it, they might be sitting there until doomsday. Dean Greenough was a good-looking but bland fellow in his forties. He appeared somewhat boyish, and Peter wondered if that quality was due to the man's long-term residence behind the ivy walls of academia. It seemed that Jake had finally breached those walls. The dean's shoulders collapsed, and he sighed.

"President Lowell insists this deplorable affair be treated with the utmost discretion," the dean said.

"I am acquainted with Lowell," Jake told him. "And I'm sure he'll be sorely disappointed if I'm forced to go to the local press for answers. Tell us what happened. What was this 'inquisition' the Herald reported? I can see the story got suppressed, but it wouldn't take much to dig it up again."

"Dr. Magrath, you can't do that. There could be irreparable harm." Greenough was outraged.

"I assure you I can and will do so if I don't get answers. Now."

Shaking his head, Greenough blurted it out. "There was no inquisition. There was a disciplinary court and President Lowell appointed that court that consisted of four other deans and faculty members with me as head. It was convened as a secret court to stem the corruption among undergraduate students that was reported. We had to move swiftly and strongly to prevent further contamination."

Peter thought it sounded like he was describing a smallpox epidemic. Peter had believed free and open discussion was a tenet of the university. Since when was there a "secret court" at Harvard?

"You're talking about homosexual activities among the students, is that it?" Jake wouldn't put up with innuendo. His bushy eyebrows were lowered in a frown as he stared at Greenough.

"You must understand. The brother of a student who committed suicide came to me with letters from other students that revealed an outbreak of immoral relations among a group of men in one of the dormitories. He accused the university of allowing such activities to seduce his brother, who then killed himself to escape the shame of what he'd done."

"Clive Wilcox," Jake said.

Dean Greenough looked startled. "Yes. He was the student. His brother's angry accusations started all this. President Lowell was furious, especially when we received an anonymous letter from a student complaining of the same activities. He formed the secret court, and we investigated the charges and expelled those who were proven guilty. Bernard Kessler was one of them."

"You investigated? How did you go about that? What are these 'rumors' of an inquisition and interrogations held in a windowless room?" Jake demanded. Peter couldn't imagine an inquisition at the august Harvard. Surely not.

Greenough stumbled a bit. He wasn't happy about being called to describe the actions his secret court had taken, but he blustered on. He pulled open a desk drawer and withdrew a thick file.

"Correct procedures were followed and documented," he said. "We had the dormitory proctor watch the room where the get-togethers were happening. There were not only Harvard men but also boys from Boston, some of them dressed as women. We called in the men and asked them about their own actions and the names of others involved." He shuffled through the pages. "In all, we interviewed twenty students, and we expelled those who were proven guilty." He held up a sheaf of papers.

"Proven guilty?" Jake was skeptical. "Exactly how were they proven guilty?"

"They admitted guilt. Or they were named by others who were interviewed.," Greenough said.

"They gave this testimony in a darkened room?" Jake asked. Peter thought he was being sarcastic. Jake spent all his efforts obtaining evidence that could be reviewed in an open court. He'd never try to use secret testimony. Peter realized what Harvard had done went against everything Jake had been trying to ensure wouldn't happen in criminal cases. Was Harvard as bad as McKenna?

Greenough was exasperated. "You must understand that we wanted to impress on these young men the seriousness of the allegations. President Lowell charged us with secrecy in order to prevent further contagion. This was a small group of men who had been corrupted and were corrupting others. We were determined to root them out and stop the damage from spreading."

Peter knew that if he'd been summoned to a darkened room by the Dean of Students and interrogated by figures sitting in darkness beyond a single light shining on him, he'd have been terrified. At least he would have been before he left for the police and worked on the streets of Boston. Then, he'd have been intimidated. Now, he'd be defiant.

"Exactly what did you prove against Bernard Kessler?" Jake demanded.

Greenough consulted his list of students until he found Bernie's name. "He admitted to one occasion of immoral relations with a fellow student. He admitted attending the parties in the dormitory, passing phone messages from Boston boys to other accused men. He refused to give names of other students involved but was named by another interviewee as one of the guilty ones." He looked up, as if this was damning. Peter nearly gasped but held it back. Greenough thought that was evidence.

Jake scoffed at the accusations as well. "You don't see this is hearsay evidence?" he asked.

Greenough looked down at his papers, as if for reassurance. "He admitted to an immoral act. You can't expect us to condone that activity. We were tasked with removing any trace of abnormal relations to protect the other students under our care. Surely you can understand that. Did Mr. Kessler perchance commit suicide?"

"Why do you ask?" Jake snapped.

"It's just that, there was a dental student who was also expelled who poisoned himself. It's possible that, like him, Mr. Kessler felt so deeply guilty, he took his own life. Have you considered that?"

"Yes. Unlike you, we consider all possibilities. He did not kill himself. His father was murdered, and so was Bernard Kessler. Who named Kessler as one of the so-called guilty ones?"

Greenough consulted his sheets of paper, flipping through till he found the answer. "Theodore Greene. He was also housed in that dormitory where the parties were held."

Peter's mouth dropped open.

"Was Greene also expelled?" Jake asked.

Greenough looked down. "No. He was admonished but not found guilty."

Chapter Forty-Eight

Mack found Mr. Johnson lingering outside their tenement, as was his habit during the day. The thin man smoked a short pipe. Mack breathed in the smell of the pipe smoke. Yes, a sort of wood fire fragrance with a hint of spice. That was it. "Found your pipe yet?" he asked.

Johnson considered him for a moment, then blew a few rings out. "Nah. Got this new one cheap. Not the same. Take a long time to season it just right. Miss my old one."

Mack pulled the curved pipe with the deep bowl from his pocket. "This yours?"

Johnson took it and rolled it in his hand, putting it to his nose to smell it. "Sure is. Where'd you find it?"

Mack handed him the pouch of tobacco. "On the dead man, Isaac Kessler. Found in front of Pat's pub, across from Peabody House."

Johnson stared at him. "Heard about that. Didn't know the man, though." Mack saw a glint of fear in Johnson's eye.

"Didn't think you did. But he had a plaid cap and a brown wool jacket that didn't belong to him also. Those yours?" Mack asked.

Johnson's eyes opened wide. "Could be. I been missing that jacket and hat more'n a week now. Guess if they were on a dead guy, I'm going to have to give in and get new ones. Don't much care to be wearing a dead man's clothes." He held out the pipe. "You think he used this?"

"No, his daughter said he didn't smoke at all. Probably they were just in the pocket. Any idea where he could have got your clothes that night?"

"Well, I work Peabody House, like you saw me doing the other night. I leave the jacket and hat in the staff closet, first floor. Next to Miss Greene's office."

Miss Greene's office. Mack guessed Isaac Kessler must have forced his son to tell him who sold him drugs. Kessler didn't go to the speakeasy looking for who was selling drugs to his son. He went to Peabody House. Edwin had found out the drugs were sold from the settlement houses. Kessler had found out, too.

Mack looked at Johnson. "You ever see anybody sell drugs at Peabody House?"

"Oh, no. I don't look for trouble. I don't see trouble," Johnson said. He was filling the curved pipe with sweet-smelling tobacco now that he knew the dead man hadn't used it. When he went to stuff the tobacco pouch into a pocket, a banana peel fell out.

"You eat bananas often?" Mack asked.

"Most days," Johnson said. He was puzzled by the questions. "Why're you asking about Peabody House?"

Mack wasn't entirely sure himself. He thought Kessler went to Peabody House looking for whoever sold drugs to his son. But why would he put on Johnson's jacket and cap? Maybe someone at the settlement had sent him to the speakeasy after all, and he'd needed a disguise? It hardly made sense.

"Have you ever seen Ari Zellman from the West End House at the Peabody House?" he asked. "He was in the play the other night as Theseus."

"Everybody in the West End comes to Peabody House to do theater," Johnson told him. "No place else with a theater like that. Don't know the man, but wouldn't doubt he could be there for rehearsals and all."

The one thing that was obvious to Mack was that Isaac Kessler had been at Peabody House. He just didn't know who he was with, or why he left wearing Johnson's clothes.

"By the way," Johnson said, puffing on the pipe to get it to draw. "Somebody been around looking for you."

"Who?"

"Think he might be 'representing' Mr. Solomon." He blew smoke. "Here he comes now. You be careful, Mack. Real careful."

Chapter Forty-Nine

A tall, heavyset man in a flashy striped suit with well-oiled hair approached Mack, then swung out his hand as an invitation. A large blue Rolls Royce with its white canvas top down pulled up in front of them. Mack glanced at Johnson, who shrugged.

"Mr. Solomon would like a word." The big guy put out a hand to take Mack's elbow, but Mack glared at him until the hand dropped. Mack stepped to the curb. Charles Solomon sat in the back seat while a chauffeur sat in front. Solomon smiled and waved his lit cigar at the rear door.

Mack opened it and got in, settling down in the blue leather seat. What a ride. The other guy jumped into the passenger seat, and the driver pulled away. Mack had a slightly queasy feeling as they motored down Causeway, but he figured it was all too public for Solomon and his goons to do anything dangerous. Then they drove around one of the office buildings and stopped in a lot. The two in the front got out and strolled away for a smoke. Solomon puffed on his cigar and faced Mack. He looked him over like he was thinking of a purchase.

"You wanted something?" Mack said. He wasn't going to let a cheap gangster ruffle his feathers, no matter how expensive his automobile was.

"You're looking for who sold the morphine that killed the Kesslers, aren't you?"

Mack just stared back. Why should he tell Solomon anything?

"That dumb mick chief of detectives arrested Ari Zellman for it. I figure you and Magrath have got more brains than that knucklehead." Solomon smelled of a floral cologne. Mack could detect it even through the cigar smoke. Solomon knocked off some ash over the side of the convertible. "Somebody told you there's distribution going on through the settlement houses."

Mack remained wooden as a cigar store Indian, but he hoped Edwin hadn't been identified by the gangster as a spy. He got the impression Solomon wasn't gunning for Magrath's office, though he didn't know why.

"Don't worry, it's not that big a secret," Solomon said. "But I don't want you getting led down the wrong track. You see, Zellman, he's a fellow hebe. It occurred to me I might have given you the wrong impression last time we spoke." At the Club Garden, Solomon had pointed Mack to the West End House. Now, he'd changed his mind. "Maybe you can get a hit of something at West End House," Solomon said, "but not from Zellman."

As if anyone would believe King Solomon when he said someone wasn't working for him. "So," Mack said. "Why tell me? Tell McKenna." Even McKenna wouldn't be stupid enough to believe the gangster. Mack wondered what Solomon was getting at.

"That clown couldn't tie his shoes without help." He waved the cigar at his men, who hurried back and started the car up. "You know where," Solomon told them.

Again, Mack felt an icy finger at the top of his spine and down to his ass. But he wouldn't let the gangster see any concern. "Let me off, will you? I got work to do."

Solomon laughed. "Don't worry, we won't take you far." They drove by St. Joseph's, and Mack said a silent prayer. "Now, I'm not about to tell you who's selling morphine. Not that I'd know anyhow, being the legitimate businessman that I am."

Mack could see they were heading down Charles Street towards the river. They stopped in front of the candy store and bar-turned-shoe store where Kessler's body was found.

Solomon reached across Mack to open his door. "Kessler wasn't near the West End House settlement when he keeled over, was he? He was here." The gangster sat back, and with his cigar, he gestured across the street to Peabody House.

As soon as Mack was on the sidewalk, the Rolls Royce shot off.

Chapter Fifty

After Jake and Peter had gone to Harvard, and Mack suddenly departed to no one knew where Fanny was left with Holly and Rachel.

Holly described her visit to Café Dreyfus with the big Irishman. "Poor Mack didn't have a clue," she told them. Rachel told them about the contents of the letter from Harvard. None of the women were shocked to discover Bernie's "bohemian" lifestyle. Rachel believed it was a sense of guilt about those associations that had led to his drug addiction. Fanny could tell that Rachel had recognized her brother's inclinations and had actively helped him to hide them from their father. "Papa must have been devastated," she said.

Later, when Fanny had just completed putting in all the tiny accessories for the sidewalk miniature, the old Ford Model T that Jake Magrath used to run around the city rattled to a stop in the garage of the morgue. Jake and Peter had returned from Harvard looking grim. Whatever they'd discovered was not good news.

Fanny hesitated to ask about their trip, but the irrepressible Holly assaulted her brother with questions. "What did you find out? Bernard Kessler was expelled for being a homosexual. We know that. But how did that lead to the death of his father?"

Jake and Peter looked shocked to learn the women already knew about Bernard Kessler's secret life as a homosexual. Fanny knew they expected their own repugnance at the dead man's homosexuality to be even more disturbing to the females. As usual, they underestimated the women's intellect and understanding.

Face to face with his sister, Peter cringed. "Holly, please." He glanced at Rachel.

"Don't be silly. Of course, Rachel knew. She helped him hide it from their father. Harvard exposed Bernie with that letter. Then what happened? Mr. Kessler must have confronted Bernie. Then what? Did Bernie tell him the names of others who were expelled? Or did he tell him who sold him the drugs? What did the dean tell you?"

Peter frowned, and Fanny could see he was appalled that his sister was trumpeting such sensitive information. Holly was impatient, and Fanny understood that. Peter didn't seem to grasp that Bernard Kessler's big secret had already been breached by his sister and her friend.

"Shall we go to my office?" Jake came up behind Fanny and tapped her arm. She followed him through the door, and they bypassed the empty examination tables of the autopsy room to sit down in Jake's office. He shut the door behind them. "Where's Mack?"

Fanny thought they'd learned something at Harvard, and Jake had returned to the morgue to get Mack before acting on the information. Apparently, he didn't want Peter to accompany him on his next outing. Fanny wondered if Jake knew who the murderer was and planned to confront him. Why did he need Mack?

She explained that Mack had hurried away after Rachel insisted the clothes her father wore when he was found were not his. "He took the pipe. I don't know why or where he went. We haven't seen Edwin either."

"Edwin asked for some time off to arrange his affairs," Jake said dismissively. Fanny wondered what that meant.

"Can't Peter help you?" she asked.

Jake described their meeting with Dean Greenough.

"How awful," Fanny said. "They questioned the young men secretly and expelled them?"

"Greenough marked them 'Proven guilty' if they were accused by others or admitted to attendance at the soirees or passed messages from Boston boys who came to the parties in women's dresses."

"They were forced to tattle on each other, and then they were all thrown out?" Fanny asked.

"Not all. It seems some of them could save themselves by telling on others. It was Bernard Kessler's bad luck that he was intimidated into admitting the truth." Jake told her about the darkened room where students were interrogated and dismissed.

Fanny was shocked by the actions of the university authorities. "But did you tell the dean about the deaths of Bernard and his father? Didn't he feel any regret? Couldn't he see that his letter somehow led to Mr. Kessler's death?"

"He suggested that Bernie might have killed himself. Apparently, at least one of the students grilled by this secret court did so." Jake sounded disgusted.

"But you don't believe he killed himself, do you?" she asked.

"No. Both of the Kesslers were murdered. I think Isaac Kessler read the letter and then went to his son and forced a full confession. I think Mr. Kessler was enraged to find out Theodore Greene had testified against Bernie, then lied about his own activities and was rewarded by being allowed to return to Harvard. Kessler's son was expelled forever with no hope of reinstatement while Greene was scolded but allowed to enroll for next year."

"You think Isaac Kessler confronted Teddy Greene? Do you think Greene killed him? You want to confront Greene, that's why you're looking for Mack. But why not go with Peter?"

"Because Peter told me on the way back that he's engaged to Milly Greene. And he thinks Holly might be romantically involved with Milly's brother."

"He thinks Holly has affections for Teddy Greene?" Fanny doubted this. But Peter must believe it. Anyhow, it was enough that the brother of Peter's fiancée was suspected. That would be difficult to explain to Milly Greene. No wonder Jake didn't want Peter with him when he confronted Teddy Greene. She was relieved that Jake was taking action to find out the truth about the Kessler deaths. She could tell he was determined not to let McKenna barrel through a conviction of the wrong man. He couldn't and wouldn't watch that happen. She hoped he would see that if he retired now, such injustices would be the norm. She was more sure than ever that Jake needed to insist on the fair and unbiased collection of facts to explain questionable deaths like those of the Kesslers. As medical examiner, Jake had standing to influence investigations. Without his interest and backing, procedure in this type of investigation would never improve, and she knew how dear to his heart such improvements were.

"What will you do?" she asked.

"Go to Peabody House. I'll take Peter Attwood. He'll have to break it to Milly about her brother. If Mack returns, send him after us."

Chapter Fifty-One

At Peabody House, Mack found Milly Greene in her office. He was sure Solomon had a reason for leaving him on the doorstep of the settlement. Someone here was selling drugs for the gangster, who wouldn't give away a name, but wanted to clear Ari Zellman.

Tendrils of blonde curls escaped a kerchief on Milly's head. She held a dust cloth, and her dress was protected by an apron. Mack hated the idea he might have to break it to her that her brother might be involved with Solomon in the drug trade. First, he needed to follow up on the stolen clothing.

"Mr. Johnson is your night janitor, isn't he? Can you show me where he leaves his hat and jacket while he's at work?"

A puzzled look crossed her face. "Yes, we employ Mr. Johnson." She hesitated but decided not to question him. "Come with me. I'll show you the coat closet."

She led him out of her office and a few steps away, where a walk-in closet with hooks on the wall held a few light jackets. Mack jiggled the door handle. "You don't lock it?"

"No," she looked surprised. "We've never had any trouble. The boys and girls are in and out on their way to our activities, but we've never had anything stolen."

Mack faced her. "Mr. Johnson didn't tell you his hat and jacket disappeared?"

"Oh, that. A couple of weeks ago. He mentioned it, but we thought he might have left them somewhere on his way to work." She looked down.

"I don't like to get him in any trouble, but he has been known to stop for a drink on his way. I've smelt it on him in the past. When I mentioned that, he admitted he might have stopped and forgotten his things. He never asked about it again, so I assumed he'd found them." She bit her lip as if worried that she'd gotten the janitor into trouble.

"That's all right," Mack said. This shone a new light on Johnson. He'd never seen the man drink, but then he'd only ever talked to him when he was smoking outside their building. Mack couldn't quite believe Solomon would do business with the janitor, but then it was well known that heroin and morphine were to be found in some of the negro entertainment establishments in the South End. He'd have to have another discussion with Johnson.

Meanwhile, Mack asked to speak to Milly's brother. He'd originally thought of Teddy Greene as Solomon's contact before Solomon had pointed him at West End House. When Milly left to find her brother, Mack paced around her office. He struggled with his feelings about Teddy Greene. He'd never liked the man who seemed too smooth to Mack. And he remembered how Bernie Kessler had pulled him away to talk about investments the night of the play. He didn't like the way Teddy put an arm around Holly and how they seemed to know each other so well. He stopped at a picture on a bookcase. It was of four youngsters, about ten or twelve years old.

"That's Teddy and me with Holly and Peter," Milly said. She'd returned without her brother. She took the picture down and smiled at it. "We were so young. We had a house on Beacon Hill near the Attwoods, so we played together growing up." She put the picture back and looked up at him. "Can I tell you a secret? Peter and I are engaged. I'm so happy. We haven't told everyone because we wanted to break it to our families first. I'm not sure if Peter has told Holly yet, and we want to tell his father together. I hope it will help to bridge the gap between them. And his grandmother, she's been so helpful to them. I know Holly and Teddy will support us. But you'll keep this to yourself, won't you? And if Peter tells you, pretend to be surprised."

She looked giddy with happiness. Mack's stomach dropped a foot. What if he had to accuse her brother of selling drugs and murdering the Kesslers?

He shuddered to think of the blight that would throw over the would-be bride. Would it matter to Peter's father? Mack suspected it would. In any case, he disliked the sticky situation where he found himself and wished she hadn't confided in him.

A faint blush spread over Milly's cheeks. She must expect congratulations, but before he could think of something to say, she turned businesslike. "I couldn't find Teddy for you. They said he'd gone to do an errand. But I told them to send him up to my rooms when he returns. He usually comes for lunch about this time. Please come with me. I'm on the top floor. We've got an elevator. It's small but I've got a view, and we can even climb up to the roof for a breeze."

Feeling like a traitor, Mack followed her.

Chapter Fifty-Two

Jake and Peter found Teddy Greene in the men's locker room beside the big pool on the first floor of Peabody House. Peter had questioned several young people before a youth in swimming trunks pointed them to the locker room. Jake felt sticky from the humidity in the pool area by the time they found Teddy Greene.

He was seated on a wooden bench, pulling something out of the locker. He flinched when he saw them and quickly stuffed it into a canvas bag. He gave them a big smile. "Peter, congratulations. Milly told me." He stood up and embraced Peter. "I can't think of anyone I'd rather have as a brother-in-law. Have you told Holly? Milly's going to ask her to be maid of honor. Dr. Magrath, how nice to see you." He held out a hand that Jake took reluctantly. The bony hand felt slick with sweat and quickly slid away from Jake's. Despite the hearty welcome, Teddy Greene was nervous.

Faced by his future relative, Peter appeared tongue-tied. Jake was glad they were in the men's locker room. He dreaded Teddy's sister making an entrance. Peter would be hard put to explain.

"We've just been to visit Dean Greenough at Harvard," Jake said. "We learned that Bernard Kessler was expelled for homosexual activities."

Teddy glanced around to make sure no one else was within earshot. He gulped air and dropped the canvas bag. A leather pouch fell out. Peter ducked down and grabbed it before Teddy could hide it. Teddy squeezed his eyes closed as if to prevent him from seeing Peter's response. He'd been found out.

Peter put the leather case on the wooden seat beside Teddy to open it.

Inside were several hypodermic needles and a dozen ampules. Jake took one. "Morphine," he said. Peter looked at the ceiling as if pleading with heaven. Jake wasn't in a mood to care about Peter's feelings.

"There's more here than you could use yourself," Jake said. "You distribute the drugs for the gangster Solomon, don't you? Did you sell morphine to Bernie Kessler?"

Teddy slumped forward, hanging his head. "I was just trying to help him," he said. "You don't know the pressure he was under. He needed it."

Jake grabbed Teddy's arm and pulled it out. "Bernie wasn't the only one. You've been using drugs, haven't you?"

Teddy pulled his arm back and hugged it to his stomach. "You don't understand. We were both under such pressure. We couldn't get away from it."

"You got paid by Solomon," Peter said. "You used it to buy luxuries you couldn't afford. You used it for Harvard tuition. I wondered how you handled that after the bankruptcy."

"You wouldn't know," Teddy twisted toward Peter and sneered. "You've still got your wealthy father, and if he won't come through, your grandmother. You wouldn't know what it's like to have everything taken away from you. Everything. We're just trying to get by. Milly insisted I had to keep up the tradition and go to Harvard. She made me. She'd have thrown me out on the street, her own brother, if I didn't do it."

Peter was indignant. "How can you blame your sister for this? How dare you?"

"Harvard," Jake spit out the word. "You were so intent on staying at Harvard you betrayed your friend Bernie Kessler to Dean Greenough and his secret court. Didn't you?" He was disgusted by the drug-addled young man and angry about the consequences of his actions.

Peter was about to light into Teddy again, but Jake held up a hand to stop him. "Bernie's father found out, didn't he? He found out not only were you supplying his son with morphine, but you told Harvard authorities about Bernie's homosexual activities and lied about yourself. Didn't you?"

Teddy shivered. "Bernie told him. Bernie told his father I got to stay at Harvard while he was expelled." He grasped his knees with his hands and looked up at Jake. "You don't understand. I couldn't be expelled from Harvard. If Bernie had just kept his mouth shut, none of this would have happened."

Peter was outraged. "If Bernie'd kept his mouth shut. You're the one who tattled on Bernie and others to Dean Greenough."

"I had to. I had to. I had to," Teddy murmured.

Again, Jake motioned to Peter to be quiet. "What happened that night? Isaac Kessler received the letter from Harvard and rushed away from his work. Did he come looking for you here?"

"First he found Bernie and forced him to admit he'd been expelled with the others and that I'd managed to keep my place."

"He told him about the drugs, too?" Jake asked.

"Yes. Bernie knew I had to do that to get the money for tuition. His father had the money for him, but Milly and I have nothing. I had to sell for Solomon to get the money."

"Stop making excuses," Peter said.

"Bernie was just as bad," Teddy squealed. "I told his father. Bernie and Leonard Abrams tried to steal from his jewelry company. Bernie needed the money to buy the morphine. He was desperate. Abrams needed money to get engaged to Bernie's sister. They tried to steal from his own father. But they messed it up."

Peter looked like he was going to burst, but Jake wanted to hear exactly what had happened to the dead men. "When you couldn't keep Isaac Kessler quiet, you stuck him with a needle and left him across the street on the ground. You poured whiskey on him, so he'd seem to be drunk."

"No. It wasn't me."

"You liar," Peter said. "Who did it if not you?"

Glassy-eyed, Teddy turned to Peter. "It was my sister. She was with you in her office, but she saw Kessler come in, and she left you to find out what was happening. She heard us argue. She came up to him and stuck the needle in. She did it."

"No," Peter yelled. Jake put out an arm to keep him from attacking Teddy.

"It was her idea. She told me to get the workmen's jacket and cap and the lunchbox from the closet. Kessler was groggy. Milly went back to you, and she told me to get him across the street in front of the speakeasy. She gave me the whiskey to pour on him. Then she went back to make sure you didn't leave until it was done. It was Milly. She said we had to do it."

Chapter Fifty-Three

After Jake and Peter left for Peabody House, Fanny returned to the garage where Holly and Rachel were fiddling with the miniatures to avoid discussion of what Peter had said to them. They both had a lot to think about. Fanny's return opened the floodgates for them.

"I always knew Bernie was different," Rachel said. "My mother knew. He wasn't fit to run a jewelry business like my father. My mother was the one to suggest papa hire Leonard Abrams and that Bernie go to Harvard. She knew my father would be proud of him. Papa didn't have a university degree himself. He was disappointed in Bernie for so many things. He hated the art classes and the refusal to do sports. Bernie wasn't enthusiastic about synagogue either. Orthodox Jews don't accept homosexuals any more than other religions. If they'd known, he'd have been scorned."

Fanny watched as Rachel picked up the doll from the miniature's sidewalk. The girl sighed as she straightened the jacket and cap. "It was all right until my mother died of the flu. My father became more demanding, and Bernie drew further away. I think that's when he started using morphine. Ari tried to help. He's not orthodox, and his reform congregation are more open to men who are different. Like Bernie. He introduced Bernie to other Jewish men like him. He got him enrolled in the art class, and he tried to wean him off the morphine."

"Getting thrown out of Harvard must have been a catastrophe for Bernie," Holly said. "Why did they do that?"

Peter hadn't told them. Fanny sat down in an armchair she used when working on the miniatures and told them about the secret court at Harvard.

"What hypocrites," Holly said. "Everyone knows there have always been some bohemian types at Harvard. It's hardly a secret. Yale has a song making fun of Harvard for it."

"A young man killed himself, and his brother lodged a very noisy complaint about immoral activities and outrageous parties in the dormitory where Bernie and Teddy Greene lived." Fanny reminded her.

"So, Harvard authorities pretend to be shocked and hold these secret interrogations. Just to placate the manly views of a very loud and angry relative, they attack and abuse their own students," Holly said. "If the dead man's angry brother caused such vicious actions against those young men, no wonder his brother killed himself."

"How many were expelled, like Bernie?" Rachel asked.

"There were about twenty accused, but some of them got away with reporting on the others and were not expelled." Fanny wanted to tell them how Teddy Greene had betrayed Rachel's brother, but she wasn't sure how attached Holly was to her childhood playmate.

"They made them turn on their friends to save themselves?" Holly asked. "That's despicable."

"I suppose the traitors were as scared of expulsion as Bernie," Rachel said. "If only he'd told me, I'd have helped him to tell my father. But finding out from a letter like that must have infuriated my father. I knew he had a screaming argument with Bernie. But Bernie didn't kill him."

"Dr. Magrath believes your brother told your father how he'd been betrayed by a friend who had kept his own place at Harvard by turning on Bernie and others," Fanny said.

"Teddy Greene," Rachel guessed.

"No," Holly moaned.

"I'm afraid so," Fanny said. She wondered if Holly realized that by testifying about others, Teddy had been suspected himself of homosexual activities. Did Holly harbor feelings for her childhood playmate? Would it shock her that he had such inclinations?

"Poor Teddy," Holly said, oblivious to Fanny's concerns about her. "He's always been a bit of a fairy. I never said it to Milly because she'd be appalled, she's so intent on making him a Harvard man. It's what her father wanted."

Fanny felt a surge of surprise. Rachel also seemed unshocked by the exposure of Teddy Greene.

"I never liked Teddy Greene as a friend of my brother. I thought he was a bad influence. Ari never trusted him, either. I think he suspected Teddy was the source of Bernie's morphine, but he had nothing to prove it.

Mention of Ari Zellman reminded them that he was currently being held for the murders of Rachel's father and brother. Fanny could see that Rachel was anxious for her lover. She put the doll back on the fake sidewalk and bent forward to stare into the tiny jail cell where the second doll lay on the ground.

"Dr. Magrath and Peter have gone to question Teddy about this, haven't they?" Holly asked. "They think he could have met an angry Mr. Kessler and killed him to shut him up? What about Bernie? Did Bernie find out Teddy had killed his father?"

"He would have said something," Rachel said. "The night he died, he went to tell Teddy how much money they lost in the Ponzi scam. Lennie Abrams was furious. They'd used diamonds from the firm as collateral, and they lost everything," Rachel said.

Fanny thought she sensed some satisfaction in Rachel's attitude. She must have thought Abrams deserved to lose the money.

"Lennie was forcing Bernie to work at the firm, as he was forcing me to marry him. He had the letter. He used it to threaten us. If he'd told everyone, Bernie would have been shunned by our synagogue and all the orthodox Jews. My father would have been so disgraced. No one would do business with us. I should have known Lennie couldn't expose Bernie without ruining the business, but I was so stupid. It was only when Bernie was dead that I took the letter from Lennie and told him I'd never marry him."

Holly moved over to pat her friend on the shoulder. Rachel grimaced. Fanny felt sorry for the young woman who was so alone in the world. Rachel bent closer to the miniature jail cell.

"What is that on the wall?" Rachel asked.

"We don't know. We can't make it out," Fanny told her. "We looked at the photographs Edwin took as well, but we can't make it out." When Rachel continued to squint, Fanny went to her carpet bag and pulled out her sketchbook. She turned to the page where she had tried to copy the scribblings on the wall:

דרדלים

It seemed likely Rachel's father had made the marks with ash from the pipe in his pocket. Perhaps Rachel knew what they meant.

She held the pad up to the light and gasped. "It's Hebrew," she said. "for Mildred."

Chapter Fifty-Four

Mack was uncomfortable. The elevator that took Milly and him to the top floor of Peabody House was too small for him. He felt drops of sweat slide down his back under his shirt. Peter was going to marry this happy, petite woman. Mack resented being entrusted with the couple's secret. He was annoyed. How did Peter Attwood expect to support a wife on a patrolman's salary? In any case, why would he propose in the middle of a murder investigation? Peter Attwood was a fool, and it was too late for Mack to escape a tête-à-tête with Peter's fiancée.

The doors slid open, and Mack obediently trotted after Milly Greene to a set of rooms at the end of a corridor. She lived in the building. If she were a man, Mack would put his foot down and demand to see her brother. Instead, he cursed himself for following her like a sheep.

The room they entered was overcrowded with furniture. A huge portrait with a gilded frame hung across from the door. A stern-looking man glared down at Mack. Must be some revered ancestor. These Beacon Hill types always had to show you and tell you how their families had staked a claim on New England a hundred years before the modern immigrants. It was a form of ancestor worship Mack couldn't understand. He'd been brought up to take a trip to the cemetery and lay down some flowers if you wanted to remember your dead relatives. Brahmins practically embalmed theirs in these heavy oil paintings.

"Please come in. I'll just get some lunch set up. Take a seat at the table," Milly told him.

This was awkward, visiting the woman's rooms without a chaperone.

Where was that dope Peter when you needed him? Because the woman was Peter's chosen companion, Mack had to treat her with kid gloves. He sat down in a substantial mahogany dining chair at a matching table that was much too big for the cramped quarters. The sitting and dining room looked like a storage area where all the furniture from the Greene's Beacon Hill townhouse had been dumped. Fussy lace doilies were hung on the backs and arms of some stuffed chairs and a sofa. The rug under them was threadbare along one side. The room could have had a stunning view across the Charles River to Cambridge, but the windows were hung with heavy velvet drapes, leaving only a sliver of light to get through.

"Do take off your jacket," Milly said.

Mack stood as she carried in a tray with bread, cheese, and pickles. She insisted she help him remove his suit coat and hang it from the back of his chair. She returned with a pot of tea for herself and a mug of beer for Mack. Resigning himself to a chat with Peter's fiancée, he took a sip. "It's cold," he said. Nothing was cold in the heat of this late spring day, so the temperature of the beer was a surprise.

Milly smiled as she sat down. "Teddy brings some up every day, and he sets it in a pail of ice. We've got a tiny icebox that's no bigger than a breadbox, but it keeps things cool in this weather." She poured herself a dainty cup of tea as Mack took another welcome gulp. "Have some bread and cheese," she said, cutting pieces and serving them to him on a plate. "I'm sorry there's not more, but the pickles help and the bread is hearty."

Mack bit into a slice of bread with a hefty chunk of cheddar cheese. At least, with his mouth full, he could avoid talking to the woman.

"Teddy should be here any minute," she said. "What do you want to ask him? Perhaps I can help."

Mack felt tired. He swallowed a mouthful, then dropped the rest of the bread onto the plate. Anticipation of the coming conversation with Milly's brother killed his appetite. What was happening to him? He wasn't going to allow Peter Attwood's love affairs to keep him from finding the truth. "I'm sorry," he said and noticed he slurred his words a bit. "I'm sorry, but we have reason to believe your brother is working for Charles Solomon, selling drugs for him."

"Mmm," Milly said. She watched him intently.

Mack shook his big head to clear away the cobwebs. Now was no time for a nap. "Morphine," he said. "The Kessler's were killed with morphine." Mack worked his jaw, but all he came up with was a big yawn.

Milly got up. "I heard it was morphine. Mr. Zellman was the source for the drugs, wasn't he? Solomon is a Jew like Zellman, isn't he? The police have arrested Mr. Zellman for the deaths, haven't they?" She returned to the table with a cloth bag. Mack wondered if she was going to start knitting.

He struggled to keep his eyes open. That was some strong beer Greene drank. Had he drunk more of it than he realized? He needed to think straight. "Zellman has an alibi. Kessler was here. Peabody House. That's where he got Johnson's hat and jacket and his pipe. Johnson really missed his pipe. But Zellman wasn't here. Teddy Greene was here."

She frowned, one hand rummaging in her knitting bag. "Zellman could have been here. There were rehearsals for the play."

"Not Zellman," Mack said. "Solomon told me. Teddy had a deal with Solomon. Not Zellman." His head felt heavy, and he really wanted to let it drop onto his chest, but he resisted the urge. If he were in a bar, he'd think the bartender had slipped him something…

Milly pursed her lips as she pulled a cloth-covered box from the bag. "Teddy made a deal with King Solomon?" She scoffed. "Teddy couldn't make a deal with a street peddler. I talked to Mr. Solomon. We needed money. Teddy suggested it. I agreed, but only after I came to terms with Mr. Solomon myself."

Bleary-eyed, Mack had a picture in his mind of proper little Milly Greene beside Charles Solomon in his fancy blue Rolls Royce. What a sight that must have been. No. he was hallucinating. It was the heat. Mack wanted to wipe sweat from his brow, but he couldn't move his hand. "What's that?" Milly had hypodermic needles in her little cloth-covered box. Was she playing at being a nurse? Mack's vision was dark around the edges, as if he were looking down a darkened tunnel to the light at the end. He took a breath and tried to sit up, but the pinpoint of light got smaller and smaller till it was gone.

Chapter Fifty-Five

At the morgue garage, Holly felt like she had a stone in her stomach. She wanted to sit down, but her nerves were on fire. "Why would your father write Milly's name on his jail cell?" she asked. "There must be some mistake. Are you sure that's what it says?"

"That's what it says," Rachel insisted. "He wanted to tell us it was Mildred who killed him. I know she's your childhood friend, Holly. But I don't trust her. She's never wanted to stand on her own feet. She's always on the lookout for someone to lean on. Ari went to her once to propose a joint project with West End House to help souls addicted to drugs like Bernie. She smiled and smiled politely, but she refused. She said working with already corrupted souls would risk spreading the corruption to the youths they served at the settlement."

Holly thought Rachel was biased toward her lover. Milly might have felt she needed to protect the reputation of Peabody House. Holly could understand that even if Rachel couldn't. She didn't want to contradict Rachel as she sensed a deep animosity toward Milly Greene. They were both Holly's friends, but she'd known Milly since childhood. Rachel was her partner in woodworking, someone she'd befriended as an adult. They shared the struggle against the expectations of their families and their need to follow their own ambitions as independent women. "Mrs. Lee, you don't think Milly Greene could have been responsible for Mr. Kessler's death, do you?" Holly asked. The older woman stood to face her. Holly had a lot of confidence in Mrs. Lee's point of view. She was friend to Holly's grandmother, but she was also a woman who bucked tradition to work with

Dr. Magrath.

"Holly, did you know Milly and your brother are engaged?" Mrs. Lee asked. "Peter told Dr. Magrath about that on their way back from Cambridge. That's why Dr. Magrath wanted Detective McNally to go with him to interview Teddy Greene. He didn't want Peter to have to accuse his fiancée's brother of murder."

"Peter? Peter proposed? I should have seen it coming," Holly said.

"Hah," Rachel scoffed. "When she marries your brother, Milly will get to return to Beacon Hill."

"That's not fair," Holly said. "They've been friends forever. She's always helping people. That's why she's at Peabody House. That's why she's helping Peter reconcile with our father." Listening to herself, Holly thought she was protesting too much. Milly had always found ways to get what she wanted, even as a child. She was never one for blunt confrontations. She knew how to gain sympathy for a sprained ankle that kept her from a test at school, or a timely snag to a worn dress that forced her to buy something new. Holly had to admit Milly'd always been more successful at getting her way through subterfuge while Holly suffered from blurting the truth. But she couldn't believe Milly could be the cold-blooded killer of Rachel's father and brother. It wasn't possible.

"We need to ask her if she saw your father that night," Holly said. "She can't have done anything to your brother. She was sitting in the same row as me at the play that night." She remembered that Milly had been late to her seat, but that was only because she was looking for Zellman. Holly also remembered Teddy Greene was beside her during the play. He couldn't have killed Bernie, either.

"Dr. Magrath and your brother have already gone to Peabody House to confront Teddy Greene," Mrs. Lee said. "I think you should find Dr. Magrath and tell him we've puzzled out the word on the jail cell. He'll want to know." She looked between Rachel and Holly. She seemed like she wanted to make peace between them. "I don't think we should jump to conclusions about the role of Milly Greene until we know more."

Leaving Mrs. Lee to look out for Dr. Magrath in case he returned, Holly and Rachel walked to Peabody House. In the busy lobby, they got conflicting information about where to find Dr. Magrath, Teddy, and Milly Greene. From one helpful young girl, it sounded like Milly might be with Mack. "A big fellow, an Irishman, I think. They were at the elevator," she said.

A young man with wet hair and a towel around his neck claimed that Teddy was talking to some men in the locker room.

Rachel was anxious to tell Dr. Magrath about the writing on the wall. Holly knew Rachel thought the medical examiner would be more open to believing Milly had something to do with her father's death. Rachel was strung out on nervous energy after the deaths in her family and the arrest of her lover. Holly trusted Dr. Magrath could deal with the grieving Rachel better than she could.

Holly said she'd go after Milly. She'd been to Milly's rooms on the top floor. She promised to bring Milly back down to her office on the first floor, where she'd meet Rachel and the others. They'd figure this out.

Rachel rushed away. Holly knew she'd have no scruples about plunging into the men's locker room to find Dr. Magrath. As Holly stood before the elevators, she wondered why Mack was with Milly. The last they'd seen him, he'd rushed away, saying he knew whose clothes Isaac Kessler had been wearing. Had they come from Peabody House? Was Milly helping him to find out? She pictured the big Irishman towering over the petite Brahmin and felt a twinge of anxiety.

Chapter Fifty-Six

Mack felt the bee sting on his forearm. Ouch. He struggled up from a deadening layer of darkness. With a big effort, he raised his head and opened his eyes. Where was he? Milly Greene sat opposite him, shuffling her knitting back into her workbag. That was it. He was waiting for Teddy Greene. Workmen's clothes, the curved pipe, Johnson outside the tenement. Images flitted through his mind and slipped away again.

"You wanted to talk to Teddy," Milly told him. She didn't seem to mind that he'd fallen asleep at her table. She patted his hand. "You were tired. Teddy's here. He took chairs up to the roof. It's cooler up there. Come along. You need some air. You can talk to him there."

Mack felt an urge to close his eyes again, but he resisted it. He needed air badly. Meanwhile, a comfortable surge of warmth flooded his body. Milly looked quite pretty. He remembered Peter was going to marry her. Lucky guy. Too bad Mack couldn't have that. But not Milly. She was too small for a big guy like him. As she took his arm to help him up, he worried he'd fall on her and crush her. What would Peter say then? But getting out into some air was a good idea. He really needed something to wake him up.

The chair scratched across the wood floor as Milly pulled it away from him. He braced a big paw on the mahogany table to straighten up. He'd had too much of Teddy Greene's cold beer. Felt more like he'd downed a quart of whiskey. But he felt a glow of happiness anyhow. It would be all right. Everything would be all right. If only he could get to the roof.

Milly insisted on drawing his arm across her shoulder to help him out the door and down the hall to the stairs to the roof. When they got there, he grabbed the railing and pulled himself up the stairway, longing for a breath of fresh air.

Standing at the top, he swayed a bit as he looked around. There was a spectacular view of the skyline. He got dizzy, looking across rooftops to the golden dome of the statehouse, then the spire of the Old North Church, and across the Charles River to Cambridge. Oops. He grabbed the door frame. Steady on.

That reminded him. What happened to Dr. Magrath? And that dope Attwood? Why hadn't they taken him with them to Cambridge? Mack remembered he was offended. Didn't matter, though. He'd got the goods. Where was that Teddy Greene? He had a lot to account for.

"Oh, Teddy must have gone downstairs. He wanted to show you why we know Ari Zellman attacked Mr. Kessler. I think he was going to the speakeasy where Mr. Kessler was found. It's over at this corner." She let go of Mack, who swayed involuntarily, to walk to the corner. She pointed down. "There he is. Come look."

Mack tried to orient himself. It was hard to do in such a cloud of warm air like cotton balls that surrounded him. With an effort, he could see the building fronted Charles Street and the banks of the Charles River. Where Milly stood must look down on Pat's pub and the candy shop where Kessler was found. He felt like his feet were encased in mud when he tried to follow Milly Greene to the edge. *Get a grip*, he told himself. *Get on with it.*

Chapter Fifty-Seven

In the locker room, Jake shook his head in disgust as he looked down on Teddy Greene. The spineless worm held his face in his hands as if to ward off blows that weren't coming.

"Bernie recognized the suit jacket," Teddy whimpered.

Jake had enough. Peter stood glowering a few feet away. "Stand up, Greene," Jake said. "Tell us what you're talking about. Leave the drugs there for the police detectives."

Teddy reluctantly let go of the bag and stood up. "Before the play. Bernie came to complain about how all the money was lost in the Ponzi scam. I wanted to shut him up so Milly wouldn't know what I'd done."

"What had you done?" Jake asked.

"I put all our money there. It was a sure investment. I thought if I could double or triple what we already had, I could stop working for Solomon. If Milly would let me."

Peter stiffened, his hands in fists by his side. "Are you going to listen to the lies from this coward?" he demanded.

Jake waved him off. "Be quiet."

"Bernie recognized the jacket. It was good quality, so I kept it after we put Johnson's jacket and cap on Kessler. Milly told me to get rid of it, so I took it away. But I wore it to the play. Who would ever know? But Bernie knew. He wasn't supposed to be there. He wasn't going to the play." Teddy was plaintive. "I took him to Milly's office, but he began to work it out, that his father came looking for me after fighting with his son. Bernie told him I'd given the dean his name and saved myself from expulsion. Bernie figured it out. I tried to calm him down with a shot of morphine. He always wanted morphine. I thought it would knock him out, and we could deal with him after the play. But he didn't go down. I sent one of the kids to get Milly."

"She was furious." As Teddy stumbled on with his tale, Peter was fuming and muttering to himself. Jake frowned at him, and he stopped. Peter would just have to come to terms with the fact that his lady love was, at the very least, responsible for covering up for her brother, even if she wasn't the mastermind Teddy was making her out to be. Jake's instinct was that the woman was a lot more intelligent with more spine than her weakling brother. But could she really be responsible for Kessler's death?

"What happened to Bernard Kessler after that?" Jake asked.

"I didn't do it. I wasn't there. I was in the audience. Milly must have taken him under the stage. He'd had a hit of the stuff, so he'd be easy to lead. She must have given him more and left him down there."

"No," Peter said. "He's only trying to put the blame on Milly to save himself."

A breathless Rachel Kessler burst into the men's locker room. "It was Mildred," she said. "The word my father wrote on the jail cell wall was Hebrew for Mildred."

Chapter Fifty-Eight

Holly found the door to Milly's rooms open. She knocked and called out, but no one answered. She pushed the door open and entered to find the table littered with the remains of lunch. Where was Milly?

Holly saw the jacket hanging on the back of one of the chairs. She stepped over and rubbed her hand on the fabric. It was Mack's. Her scalp prickled with an electrical charge, what was going on? "Mack," she yelled. "Mack, where are you? Are you here?"

When no one answered, Holly searched the table for a clue. When she saw Milly's knitting bag she grabbed it. What had she done to Mack? Or had he done something to her? Had he taken her away already? It was ludicrous to think the big Irishman would be in danger from the little petite Milly. She couldn't stab him with a knitting needle or something, could she?

Desperate, Holly rummaged in the cloth bag and drew out the fabric-covered box. Inside, she found two hypodermic needles and glass ampoules, some empty. No. It couldn't be. Was Milly addicted to morphine? Never. She was much too controlled for that. Always in control, Milly. Always able to organize any activity. A born administrator, Milly.

Holly called out again and when she got no answer, she ran to the door. Where could they be? In the back of her mind, she remembered how certain Rachel was that Milly was responsible for her father's death. Why had Kessler written 'Mildred'? Holly thought she knew Milly well enough to deny she could be involved. But Rachel knew her father well enough to guess his motive for accusing Milly.

What did Mack know? He didn't know about the translation of the Hebrew word. She thought he suspected Teddy Greene, but he'd never think little Milly knew anything about drugs or the Harvard crusade against homosexuals. Mack was so naive. A pretty girl like Milly could pull the wool over his eyes in a minute. Oh, Mack. Holly felt her heart beat fast. It echoed in her ears. Think, she told herself. Where could they be?

She spotted the shadows in the stairway at the end of the hall. The roof. Teddy had taken her up there one time for a view of the city. Could they have gone there?

She ran up the stairs. At the top, the bright sunlight made her blink. She squinted around and saw Mack swaying like a birch tree in a breeze at the edge of the roof. Milly stooped toward him. "NO!" Hearing her voice, Mack twisted toward her, then swayed back. Holly ran and jumped in time to clutch Mack around his chest. She kicked at Milly, who clung to Mack's legs. When they swayed, and she had a glimpse of the sidewalk below, blood flowed to her head, making her dizzy. "Mack," she screamed.

She felt the big man suddenly change direction, and he crashed down on top of her. She banged her head. Her hips and shoulder blades cried out with pain, but she clutched Mack to her in an unbreakable embrace until she let go when he started to roll off of her. He lay beside her, shaking his big head as if trying to clear away smoke.

Milly started to rise from the roof where she'd fallen. "Thank God you got here, Holly. He almost fell. I was trying to stop him."

Holly shook as she sat up. "Mildred Greene, you're a bare-faced liar."

Chapter Fifty-Nine

Jake hurried through the lobby of Peabody House. Rachel led the way, shouting that Holly had gone to Milly's rooms on the top floor. She projected waves of hate and anger as she punched the button to call the elevator car. Peter dragged Teddy Greene along by the collar. Jake told a staff member to call Chief of Detectives McKenna to come with police officers.

At the top floor, they found Milly's rooms empty. Peter slapped Teddy, who winced and pointed to the stairway. "The roof," he said.

Jake was last up the steps, dreading what they would find. It was quite a scene. Milly Greene was bent over, panting at a corner of the roof. On the ground before her lay Mack and Holly. Holly was on her knees beside the big Irishman, trying to wake him up. "Mack, Mack, wake up. What has she done to you? Wake up." Holly slapped him across the face.

Milly took a step towards them, but Holly raised an arm. Milly turned towards the newcomers. "He nearly fell. He was going to jump. Holly got the wrong idea. I was trying to stop him."

"Liar!" Holly looked up at Jake. "Help, she gave him morphine. She's trying to kill him."

As Jake hurried to look at Mack, he could hear Peter behind him. "Holly, what are you saying?"

Jake lifted Mack's eyelids. He was drugged. How much he'd taken or been given might decide if he lived or died. Jake called to the others. "Come over here, Peter, and help me get him up. Miss Kessler, go down and call for an ambulance. Morphine poisoning."

"It's true," Milly said, on the verge of tears. "He took it. He arrived here in the gangster Solomon's Rolls Royce. I'm sorry, Holly, you don't want to hear it, but Mr. McNally has been working for Solomon all along. When he saw he would be found out, he came up here to kill himself. He couldn't stand for all of you to know."

"You killed him. I saw the morphine in your bag. You killed him," Holly yelled. When she jumped at Milly, Peter dropped Mack's arm to stop her.

"Holly, stop it. What are you doing?" Peter said as he grabbed his sister by the shoulders.

Mack's body weighed down Jake till he had to let him slide down. He was worried about the Irishman. His one hope was that the big body would be able to digest the morphine dose. "Peter, get over here and help me." Peter ignored him, but Holly knelt by Mack's side. Between them, they kept Mack sitting up. His head lolled, but he was making an effort to open his eyes. Holly watched anxiously. Jake hoped the medics would arrive soon.

Peter stood between the siblings. Looking back and forth at them as they argued.

"Milly, I'm sorry," Teddy was tearful. He also looked afraid. "I told them."

"Told them what?" Milly asked coldly. "You told them how you took the drugs you were selling? Told them how you went to parties with faggoty boys and nearly got thrown out of Harvard? Told them how you gave up Bernie Kessler's name to save your skin?" She sneered. Jake could see Peter's eyes widen as he got a new view of his fiancée. With her curls blown around by a breeze and her stony expression, Jake thought she looked like a Medusa. If Jake were younger, he might have looked away from the startling metamorphosis of the petite young woman. Both Peter and Teddy blinked and turned away as if from blinding sunlight. But Jake was disappointed more than surprised. It was harder to be surprised as he aged.

Holly glared at Milly while she supported Mack's shoulder and rubbed his back. "Mr. Kessler came to accuse Teddy of betraying his son to save himself. You couldn't let him tell people, so you gave him morphine. What did you do, put something into his drink, then use a needle with the drugs?"

Peter's mouth was open. He turned on Milly. "Teddy said you made him dress Kessler in Johnson's clothes and take him across the street to leave him in front of the speakeasy. How could you do that, Milly?" He was on the brink of tears, but he swallowed to keep back a sob.

Milly looked at her brother. "You said that? You coward." Teddy cringed. She faced Peter, but she backed away to the corner of the roof. "You believe him? You're supposed to love me. You're supposed to be on my side. What do you care about these outsiders? They're invaders, people like the Kesslers. And that Ari Zellman. Going to Harvard, going to law school. You're a fool, Peter. You'd let the Kesslers and the Zellmans of this world move into your position on Beacon Hill. Your father understands, but you and Holly are naïve. You're stupid."

Milly swung towards her brother. "You ruined everything. You spineless worm." She turned back to the rest of them. Jake saw her suddenly awaken to the audience. "You can't prove anything." She pointed at Mack. "He did it. He works for Solomon! Are you going to believe a drunken Irishman like him?"

Jake felt Mack's big shoulders move. He must be fighting the morphine. The big head swayed back and forth, and with an effort, he struggled to his feet. Holly tried to hold him down, but Mack swayed to his full height. Jake was sure he'd fall down again as soon as he took a step, but too late, he saw that Milly Greene stared at him with open-mouthed horror. Jake yelled, "Stop her."

Too late. With a face twisted with anger and bile, Milly Greene stepped off the corner of the roof.

Chapter Sixty

A week later, Mack was at his desk in the morgue, arranging pencils in neat lines, when Holly Attwood rang the bell. With Edwin still out, Mack let her in, and she swept past him, then let him lead her into the autopsy room and his own corner desk.

"Dr. Magrath will be in later," he said. Holly was looking cool in a flimsy dress that was white with pale flowers. She wore a funny little hat with a couple of feathers. He thought women had it easier in the warm weather. His suitcoat felt scratchy, and he longed to remove it. But he thought he needed it to preserve his solemn authority. He felt that Holly was always rushing in, upending the order in the office. He almost wished Dr. Magrath was present. He felt the older man could handle the women who seemed to dash through the morgue better than he did. They didn't belong in such a place, but what could you do?

"I wanted to talk to you," Holly said, alarming him. "Did you get one of these?' she held out a thick piece of card stock with writing in a beautiful curly calligraphy.

"Edwin's wedding. Sure, I got one." It turned out Edwin had been missing so often because he was finalizing the details of his wedding to the widow he'd been seeing for over a year. Mack thought it was about time he'd popped the question. He was happy for the ex-infantryman who'd been scarred by burns in the war. He figured if an ugly puss like that could attract a good woman, there was hope for all of them.

"This is Peter's," Holly said. "It was nice of Mr. O'Connell to invite him, but Peter's saying he won't go."

"Ah, too soon?" Mack could see that the invitation might pain Peter Attwood. It was only a week since Peter's fiancée had turned out to be a murderer who jumped from the roof of Peabody House. Mack thought it was the best possible ending for the doomed affair. What was Peter to do if she lived? Defend a woman who had callously murdered two people and tried to not only murder but to slander Mack. Best all round that she'd removed herself. But he could see how an invite to Edwin's nuptials would be a dreary reminder. Just think how bad it would have been if Peter had married that awful woman before they exposed her as the murderer.

"I'm sure Edwin will understand if Peter doesn't come," he said. "At least he's back on the job." Mack was pleasantly surprised when the powers that be finally recognized that McKenna was a crooked cop. He'd had to release Ari Zellman and arrest Teddy Greene. Complaints from Magrath as medical examiner and Lomasney as the local politician in charge had finally led to McKenna's ouster and Peter Attwood's reinstatement as a police detective. Mack had heard McKenna's role in promoting the bad investments of Charles Ponzi had influenced the decision to get rid of the nasty chief of detectives. He knew the change had been partly responsible for Dr. Magrath withdrawing his own resignation. Mack also knew that Mrs. Lee was greatly relieved she could continue to work with the medical examiner to train investigators. He had to admit the police force needed help to recover from incompetents like McKenna.

Meanwhile, Holly was determined to argue about Peter attending the wedding. "It would be good for him," she was saying. "He's awfully gloomy. He should be glad he escaped from Milly's claws, but he doesn't see it that way. Going to the wedding would take him out of the dumps."

"He moved home with your father?" Mack was a bit curious about that. He knew the elder Attwood didn't encourage Peter's police career.

"Hah! That was good. My father finally had to back off when he found out how awful Milly Greene was. She had him in the palm of her hand, agreeing with him all the time and telling him she'd get Peter to go back to Harvard and banking. She just wanted the family money, is what it is, and he had to admit it. He can't really object to Peter being a detective anymore. In fact, he had supported getting Peter released from jail when McKenna arrested him. Milly convinced him to do that. He could hardly turn his back on Peter when he was cleared and reinstated. He has to swallow his pride and keep his objections to himself now. It's good."

"Greene's not going to trial, though," Mack said. It was the one aspect that disappointed him. Teddy Greene had agreed to plead guilty to the murders of Isaac and Bernard Kessler. Influential men had managed to keep details of the case, including the morphine sales and the Harvard secret court, out of the papers. It was all deeply buried. The attempt on Mack's life was all due to Milly. There was no charging her with anything since she'd been quietly buried beside her parents, an apparent suicide. Mack was glad to see the last of them.

Holly held up the wedding invitation again. "So, it says you can bring a guest, right? I'm thinking I can fix it so Peter goes with one of my girlfriends." Mack bit back a comment about Holly's girlfriends. The horrible Milly had been one, but he decided not to mention that. "Who are you bringing?" Holly asked.

Uh oh. Danger. Was she going to try to hang one of her girlfriends on him? Mack was alarmed. Not that he wasn't grateful to Holly for giving him that big hug on that rooftop that made him swing away from the edge, but he wasn't about to trust her guidance when it came to her women friends. Besides Milly, the thought of whom made him want to shiver, Rachel Kessler had also been an eye-opener. When Zellman was released, they married in a civil ceremony, and she moved in with him. Finally, she was able to mourn her brother and father. Mack was impressed by how she'd stood by Zellman and refused to give up on proving his innocence, but he found her somewhat alarming.

"Who?" Holly demanded.

"No one in particular. I don't have to bring someone," he said. He had been running over the names of women he knew in East Boston, but most of them had gotten married, including his brother's wife, who had been Mack's girl before the police strike. Mack still resented that, but he'd stood up for his brother as best man the previous winter. Mack was leery of asking his sister to recommend someone as he knew she'd get all het up and have him married to the woman before spring.

"That's all right then. I'll go with you, and I can get my friend Inga to go with Pete. It'll be just a friendly affair. Nice and easy."

Mack frowned. Was she serious? "It's a Catholic wedding, you know. At St. Joseph's. There's a mass. It's all in Latin." Mack couldn't imagine what Holly and Peter would make of it all. There was a full-blown high mass followed by a little reception in the church basement. Mack knew there would be a small band playing Irish music. Edwin and his betrothed were both Boston Irish. There'd be some singing and dancing and drinking of beer and whiskey (from a closet off the big room, and for an Irish wedding at St. Joseph's, you'd be sure there'd be no police raids involved). But what the Brahmins from Beacon Hill would think of it, he had no idea.

"That's fine. We'll learn something." Holly saw that he doubted her. "Dr. Magrath and Mrs. Lee will be there. They're not Catholic." She waved a hand at him. "It's all arranged then. I'll make Peter come. It'll be a big help in cheering him up. I'll ask Mrs. Lee what to get for a present." With that, she skipped out to the door.

It seemed to Mack that there was an empty space in the air of the room after she left. He didn't quite know what to make of her. But one thing he'd learned, when these bossy women wanted something, it was politic to go along with it. You didn't want to rouse their wrath. He thought he could survive Edwin's wedding just fine. Better than Peter, probably.

Epilogue

September 1946

Private dining room at the Ritz Carlton Hotel, Boston

Frances Glessner Lee, Captain of the New Hampshire State Police, watched as staff of the Ritz Carlton Hotel put the finishing touches on the long table in the private dining room. She circled the table, switching a couple of name cards after consulting her seating chart. She liked to make sure police officers from different parts of the country got to know each other. Meeting and consulting with colleagues was a critical aspect of the twice a year Seminars in Homicide Investigation. They were hosted by the Harvard Department of Legal Medicine, but Fanny ran them.

She was especially pleased that in only the second year of the seminars, men from the first year had formed the Harvard Associates in Police Science. It was an alumni association for seminar graduates. They planned to offer an annual refresher course as well as provide an ongoing connection for graduates.

How much she wished her old friend Jake Magrath were here. She missed him. He'd taught her so much, not the least of which was that a middle-aged woman with no degrees could make a major contribution to the science of detection. As the room began to fill up with men, she knew their company helped to fill the void left by Jake's death almost a decade ago. The seminars were the fruit of all their work together.

She noticed a detective from New Jersey who stood alone, preoccupied by his thoughts. She joined him. "You did a fine job in your report on The Saloon and Jail. You know, that's the only Nutshell Study that consists of two scenes." A man was found sprawled on a sidewalk. The next day, he was dead in the jail cell. Both places were represented in the miniature crime scenes. As part of the seminar, detectives were assigned Nutshell Studies to review before reporting out to the group. When Fanny heard detectives talk about this particular Nutshell, she'd noticed they'd all seemed regretful.

The New Jersey detective was startled by her words. He hadn't noticed her approach. "Oh, yes, Captain Lee. I think most of us know of a similar case, one where false assumptions may have contributed to a death." His name was Levin, and he was a big bear of a man who reminded Fanny of Jake's first investigator, Mack. Levin continued. "You can't help wondering if they hadn't assumed he was drunk, could they have saved him."

"An important lesson," Fanny said. "You need to examine the facts in an unbiased manner. A hunch, or gut reaction, or easy assumption can be the bane of the investigator. It was clever of you to list underlying health issues, like heart problems, or even poison, as possible causes of the death," she told Levin. "Most men assume the dead man fell and hit his head, and that was the cause."

"Because of the banana peel, probably," he said.

"Yes, I had to include that. Unbelievable as it may seem, there was a case where a banana peel was present at the scene." Fanny remembered sitting in front of Peabody House sketching Peter Attwood's body and the banana peel as he played dead. She shook herself.

"As I told the group at the beginning, the Nutshell Studies are not there as crimes to be solved. They're designed as exercises in observing and evaluating indirect evidence, especially when it might be medically significant."

"As it was in this case," Levin said. "The fact that he didn't die until the next morning is not easily explained. It would be natural to suspect police malfeasance, when he died in custody."

She looked at his face and saw regret. "Have you experienced that kind of suspicion?" she asked.

He nodded. "I hate to remember it. A man died in our precinct. We knew he was never mistreated, but the local press and politicians were so fierce in their criticism of our captain.... Well, he died cleaning his weapon."

"How unfortunate," Fanny said. The man had committed suicide over the incident

"He had other worries, but I've always regretted that we never discovered the cause of death for the man who died in our custody."

Fanny felt her scalp itch. Jake would have been angry at such a lapse. It was the kind of incompetent examination of a death that left it unexplained forever. She remembered clearly how the death of Isaac Kessler had very nearly driven Jake out of his medical examiner position. Exasperation with political influence and sloppy police work had almost led Jake to give up and resign. She remembered clearly how worried she'd been. In the aftermath of the case, she'd gone into Jake's office in the North Grove Street morgue. Under a pile of papers, she found the envelope with his resignation and took it away. Jake never mentioned it again, and she never regretted her actions. She still had that envelope in a cubbyhole of her desk up in New Hampshire. If Jake Magrath resigned, then, as he threatened, these seminars would never have happened.

"It's terrible to be left with doubt and suspicion when someone dies. That's precisely what we can avoid by improving investigation techniques," she told Levin. "The detective has a twofold responsibility—to clear the innocent as well as expose the guilty. He must seek the facts and all the facts. They alone provide truth in a nutshell."

"You're right," he said. He waved at the room. "We all know it. That's why your work is valued by all of us."

Fanny felt a rush of warmth. It was why she insisted on these seminars and why she always wanted to celebrate the conclusion with a banquet. She knew Jake would tease her about liking to be surrounded by adoring young men, but it was more than that. Recognition of the need to strictly determine facts at a crime scene resulted in fewer unexplained deaths. It was what Jake had strived for, and she was beginning to see a change in police procedures as men from the seminars spread across the nation like seeds spread by the wind. There was much more work to be done. She planned to rally support to replace politically influenced coroners with scientific medical examiners in many more communities. Wherever he was, Jake must be glad they'd persevered. Together.

"Come, Detective Levin, I like to begin these dinners with a toast to my old friend and comrade, Dr. Magrath."

Afterword

This book is fiction, but I do research into Boston history for each of the books, and I know readers wonder what's real in the story. I wanted to set this third Nutshell Murder Mystery in the West End of Boston for several reasons. I rent in a condominium building in the area and when I first moved here, I remember saying I lived in the West End and someone saying, "oh, I thought that was gone." Boston's West End is a famous example of how not to implement urban renewal.

In the 1950's the West End included the north slope of Beacon Hill and the expanse of mainly tenement dwellings that spread to the banks of the Charles River and to the edge of the North End. The North End and South End were also run down at that point but they both resisted mass destruction. The West End became the target for well-meaning reformers who pushed the plan to tear down the tenements they labelled "slums." Eventually homeowners and renters were forced out and "luxury" apartments took the place of lower income housing.

But the people elbowed out by this renewal did not go quietly. It turned out that the West End was a robust community that was more diverse than most other neighborhoods. It was home to influxes of immigrants beginning with Irish, later Jewish and East Europeans, Italians and there were always some African Americans. The north slope of Beacon Hill had been populated by African Americans since before the Civil War.

Destruction of the area led to lawsuits by people displaced by the development. This actually resulted in formation of the West End Museum https://thewestendmuseum.org/ which collects, preserves and shares history of the West End. A lot of the information I used came from the wonderful articles on the museum site and also the many YouTube videos made by former inhabitants of the area. I've attended various programs and tours presented by the museum, and I highly recommend them.

Settlement houses are important in the story. The institutions were real, but the characters I have attached to them are all fictional. Articles on Peabody House and West End House from the West End Museum website were especially helpful. Information on Fanny Goldstein, a historical person who was librarian at the West End branch of the Boston Public Library, and on speakeasies in the West End, like Club Garden, came from various sources but the articles on the West End Museum site were especially helpful.

Martin Lomasney's life is covered in *Boston Mahatma* by Leslie G. Ainley, and also one of the West End Museum YouTube videos where a former resident describes how his father was a member of Lomasney's Hendricks Club. It is a fact that Lomasney began as a ward boss with a following of Irish immigrants, but he continued on to represent Jewish and Italian immigrants when they moved into his ward.

Margaret Shurcliff, woodworking mentor to the fictional Holly and Rachel, was a real person. Third of the Nichols sisters, you can read about her interesting life at https://www.nicholshousemuseum.org/margaret/ Her older sister Rose appeared in *Molasses Murder in a Nutshell.* I volunteered at Nichols House Museum on Beacon Hill where I learned about those women who were active during the time of my stories, so I had to include them. *At Home On Beacon Hill: Rose Standish Nichols and Her Family* (2011) is a source as well as the website for Nichols House. Thanks to Linda Marshall and the staff there for hosting some book presentations for my series. I'm thinking Margaret Shurcliff may appear in the next book, as well as this one.

Charles Solomon, "King" Solomon, really was a prominent gangster of the time. The Wikipedia article on him mentions characters in recent TV series *Boardwalk Empire* and *Peaky Blinders* who were based on the real Solomon. Since his part of town was the West End, it seemed right to have him appear.

For much of the information about the Jewish residents of the West End, I used *Jews of Boston* (2005). Vilna Shul https://vilnashul.org/ is a restored synagogue that is now a cultural center on Phillips Street. They offer useful programs and tours. I had the Kessler family live on that street and attend that shul which was built and opened in 1919.

The story of the harsh judgement on a group of gay men at Harvard in 1920 is covered in the book *Harvard's Secret Court: the Savage 1920 Purge of Campus Homosexuals* by William Wright (2005). I used a couple of the real men involved and the real Café Dreyfus. However, my characters Bernard Kessler and Theodore Greene are entirely fictional, as are the other Kesslers, Milly Greene and Ari Zellman.

Of course, Frances Glessner Lee and George (Jake) Meredith Magrath were historical people. Mrs. Lee worked with Magrath and learned from him and continued to work with the Harvard Department of Legal Medicine after Magrath's death. The series is based on fictional events in the 1920's that provided the background for the creation of the Nutshell Studies of Unexplained Death in the 1940's. Those miniature crime scenes continue to be used in training police detectives. They reside at the Office of the Medical Examiner in Maryland. They are photographed and cataloged in *The Nutshell Studies of Unexplained Death* by Corinne May Botz (2004) and they are described in *18 Tiny Deaths: The Untold Story of Frances Glessner Lee and the Invention of Modern Forensics* by Bruce Goldfarb (2020).

The Nutshells appear in many places on the Internet and many people have written about them. One of the most interesting examples is on the Smithsonian website https://americanart.si.edu/exhibitions/nutshells

After work was done by the Smithsonian to repair the Nutshells, they were displayed at the Renwick Gallery of the Smithsonian October 20, 2017 to January 28, 2018. Sorry to say I missed that one public showing of the dioramas. The website includes a short video and some 3D presentations of some of the Nutshells.

Glessner House Museum in Chicago https://www.glessnerhouse.org/ celebrates Frances Glessner Lee's birthday on March 25 each year. I've been happy to participate the past couple of years. The website also had a wealth of fascinating information about Mrs. Lee's family, including their New Hampshire home the Rocks.

Since there are eighteen Nutshells, I hope to continue these stories with more volumes in the Nutshell Murder Mystery series. No telling where the next tiny crime scenes will take us.

Acknowledgements

Thanks to the staff of the West End Museum, Nichols House Museum, and my writing group, which includes Leslie Wheeler, Katherine Fast, Cheryl Marceau, and Mark Ammons. Also, thank you to Verena Rose and the staff at Level Best Books.

About the Author

Frances McNamara is the author of the *Nutshell Murder Mystery series* featuring "Mother of Forensic Science" Frances Glessner Lee. The first in the series *Molasses Murder in a Nutshell* was released in 2023. Book 2 *Three-Decker Murder in a Nutshell* was released in 2024. Book 3 *Joy Street Jail Murder in a Nutshell* will be released in 2025.

She is also author of *The Emily Cabot Mysteries* about a social activist in Chicago in the late 19th and early 20th centuries, Frances is a member of Sisters in Crime New England and active in MWA New England. *Death in a Time of Spanish Flu,* book 9 of the series, was released in 2022. Frances grew up in Boston, where her father served as Police Commissioner for ten years. She has degrees from Mount Holyoke and Simmons Colleges, and is retired from the University of Chicago. She now divides her time between Boston and Cape Cod.

AUTHOR WEBSITE:
https://francesmcnamara.com

SOCIAL MEDIA HANDLES:
https://www.facebook.com/fdmcnama
@francesmcnamaraauthor Instagram

Also by Frances McNamara

Nutshell Murder Mysteries
Molasses Murder in a Nutshell
Three-Decker Murder in a Nutshell

Emily Cabot Mysteries
Death at the Fair
Death at Hull House
Death at Pullman
Death at Woods Hole
Death at Chinatown
Death at the Paris Exposition
Death at Selig Studios
Death at the Homefront
Death in a Time of Spanish Flu